THE REALMGATE WARS

BLADESTORM

THE REALMGATE WARS

BLADESTORM

MATT WESTBROOK

BLACK LIBRARY

A BLACK LIBRARY PUBLICATION

First published in Great Britain in 2016 by
Black Library
Games Workshop Ltd
Willow Road
Nottingham NG7 2WS UK

10 9 8 7 6 5 4 3 2 1

Produced by Games Workshop in Nottingham

A CIP record for this book is available from the British Library.

Numbered edition ISBN 13: 978 1 78496 107 7
Standard edition ISBN 13: 978 1 78496 106 0

Numbered edition product code: 60040281053
Standard edition product code: 60040281052

See Black Library on the internet at

blacklibrary.com

Find out more about Games Workshop
and the world of Warhammer at

games-workshop.com

Printed and bound by CPI Group (UK) Ltd, Croydon, CR0 4YY

From the maelstrom of a sundered world, the
Eight Realms were born. The formless and the divine
exploded into life.

Strange, new worlds appeared in the firmament, each one gilded
with spirits, gods and men. Noblest of the gods was Sigmar. For
years beyond reckoning he illuminated the realms, wreathed in light
and majesty as he carved out his reign. His strength was the power
of thunder. His wisdom was infinite. Mortal and immortal alike
kneeled before his lofty throne. Great empires rose and, for a while,
treachery was banished. Sigmar claimed the land and sky as his own
and ruled over a glorious age of myth.

But cruelty is tenacious. As had been foreseen, the great alliance
of gods and men tore itself apart. Myth and legend crumbled into
Chaos. Darkness flooded the realms. Torture, slavery and fear
replaced the glory that came before. Sigmar turned his back on the
mortal kingdoms, disgusted by their fate. He fixed his gaze instead
on the remains of the world he had lost long ago, brooding over its
charred core, searching endlessly for a sign of hope. And then, in the
dark heat of his rage, he caught a glimpse of something magnificent.
He pictured a weapon born of the heavens. A beacon powerful
enough to pierce the endless night. An army hewn from everything
he had lost.

Sigmar set his artisans to work and for long ages they toiled, striving
to harness the power of the stars. As Sigmar's great work neared
completion, he turned back to the realms and saw that the dominion
of Chaos was almost complete. The hour for vengeance had come.
Finally, with lightning blazing across his brow, he stepped forth to
unleash his creation.

The Age of Sigmar had begun.

CHAPTER ONE

Vengeance Eternal

They gathered in their hundreds to hear the words of their God-King. Azyrheim was a changed place since the blessed hammer Ghal Maraz, symbol of Sigmar's might, had been returned. It had always been a city of wonders, of soaring archways and winding crystalline stairs, of boundless treasures that echoed an age when the light of humanity had shone in every corner of the realms, but now its glory appeared greater. When the first realm-gate had been opened by the heroism of Vandus Hammerhand, there had been relief and joy, and then a frisson of nervous excitement as the Stormhosts poured forth into the Mortal Realms, taking the war to the great enemy with the indefatigable fervour of the righteous.

But it was symbolic victories that incited a people at war like little else, and nothing could be more emblematic of the changing times than witnessing the God-King take up his fabled weapon once more.

The hammer had been reclaimed, and with that triumph the halls of Sigmaron rang with renewed purpose. Mortal servants and workers rushed here and there, filling serene halls and quiet chambers with a flurry of excited whispers. Stormhosts were despatched in ever greater numbers, marching to war with thunderous fanfare, roaring their hymns of faith in a tumult so loud it could be heard all across the great city. And then there was the rhythmic ringing of the forges, which truly never ceased; Azyr's armouries were the miracle that kept the gears of re-conquest moving at their relentless pace.

The Bladestorm, a Warrior Chamber of the Celestial Vindicators, had barely rested since their return from the Eldritch Fortress. They had forged countless new legends in their pursuit of Ghal Maraz there, and now they were summoned to Sigmar's throne room. From there, the God-King himself would send them forth once more. Mortal warriors might have balked at being thrown back into the war so quickly, but these demigods were no mortals; they were giants, forged for war and destined for battle.

The Stormcasts' boots beat a perfect rhythm on the gleaming floor of Sigmar's throne room, a vaulted wonder filled with flawlessly carved sculptures and artisanal iconography celebrating the countless legends of the God-King. All this splendour was nothing compared to the vision of Sigmar himself. He sat upon his throne, watching proudly as his loyal warriors assembled, an avatar of righteousness and strength, radiant armour glittering, eyes burning with resolve.

Lord-Castellant Eldroc's heart rose to see his master's glory. It felt like an age since they had last returned to Azyr, and he drank in every wondrous sight anew, from the breathtaking statuary to the masterful paintings and tapestries that draped the walls. This was what they were fighting for, he reminded himself: to return the light of civilisation to every corner of the Mortal Realms, to bring about a world where smiths and artisans could create such works, and where simple, honest folk could bask in their glory. They would earn that future, he swore, as he took his place in the front rank of warriors. Armour creaking under the weight of relic-bones and holy parchments, the Lord-Relictor Tharros Soulwarden came to a halt by his side.

'I cannot help but wonder at this place, no matter how many times I see it,' Eldroc whispered.

'It has a certain grandeur to it,' the Lord-Relictor said, briefly regarding the vaulted ceiling above, which was immaculately painted with images of great heroes, captured in the moment of their triumph.

'You have no art in your soul, my friend,' said Eldroc, grinning. 'You would be just as happy if we gathered in some dusty old crypt to hear Sigmar's words.'

'In my experience there is often a great deal to be learned from dusty old crypts.'

They ceased their conversation as Lord-Celestant Thostos Bladestorm strode past and his cold blue gaze briefly washed over them. Their liege made his way to the foot of the stairway leading to the throne, and took his place at the head of his Warrior Chamber. There he stood, still as one of the statues lining the great hall, and waited for the word of the God-King.

'How is he?' Tharros asked.

Eldroc felt a pang of sadness and frustration seize him. It would be a better, easier world if he knew the answer to that question.

'He is… still not himself,' he said. That was understating things to a laughable degree, but Eldroc had not the words to describe what he felt when he looked upon his lost friend.

'No,' Tharros said. 'And he never will be. To be reforged…'

Tharros paused a moment, then turned his skull-faced visage to Eldroc.

'There is always a price for cheating death, brother. We will all pay it, before the end. Too many of us forget that. They think this is a game we play.' He shook his head. 'No. We fight a war beyond mortal comprehension. There is always a price.'

There was a creaking yawn as the grand double doors to the throne room opened. Again, the floor rumbled with the steps of hundreds of warriors. Marching into position alongside their brothers came a second Warrior Chamber of the Celestial Vindicators. These warriors wore the same turquoise armour as the Bladestorms, trimmed with golden sigmarite and deep red leather, but where Thostos' officers wore purple helmet crests and plumes signifying their rank, the newcomers wore a rich, royal blue. Their leader was tall even for a Stormcast, and carried a grandblade across his back, the huge weapon almost reaching to the floor.

'Lord-Celestant Argellon and his Argellonites,' Eldroc murmured. 'His star rises, it is said.'

'His head swells, you mean,' Tharros said.

Mykos Argellon took his place at the head of his chamber, before the throne. His mien could not have been more different to that of Thostos. Where the Bladestorm stood stock still, his fellow Lord-Celestant burned with pride and righteousness, his hands clenching and unclenching, his body fairly trembling with fervour.

'By all accounts he has performed admirably thus far,' said the Lord-Castellant. 'Perhaps we should give him a chance.'

'Perhaps,' Tharros replied.

The God-King rose from his throne, ending the conversation. He was as magnificent a figure as ever, but now emanated an even greater power with Ghal Maraz held in one mighty fist. His radiance was so bright that it almost hurt to look upon him, but not one of the Stormcast Eternals averted their eyes.

And Sigmar spoke.

'The realms shake beneath our righteous justice!' he roared, and the throne room erupted in an echoing chorus of shouts and cheers. Sigmar smiled fiercely as he looked upon his warriors, and he let the cheers fill the room for many moments before resuming. 'On all fronts your valiant brothers purge the taint of Chaos with the hammer and the storm, and thanks to the legends you yourselves forged in pursuit of Ghal Maraz, we can now prepare for the next stage of the great war.'

There was a breathless silence as the Celestial Vindicators waited to hear where they would bring the light of Sigmar.

'You will travel to Ghur, the Realm of Beasts, to a wild region known as the Roaring Plains,' the God-King proclaimed. 'There lies a foul bastion of Chaos known as the Manticore Dreadhold. This fortress guards a realmgate that is critical to our next offensive. Destroy the dreadhold and secure this gate. Put its cursed defenders to the sword, and send their wretched souls screaming to their dark masters. This I task to you.'

Another cacophony of cheers resonated throughout the hall. Sigmar held up a hand for silence.

'There will be many dangers,' the God-King said. 'The Roaring Plains is an untamed wilderness, and its dangers have already sent many of my loyal warriors back to the forge.'

His eyes bored into Thostos, whose own blazing blue orbs stared back implacably. Eldroc felt that Sigmar's iron gaze softened for just a moment as he as he studied his champion.

'Look to your brothers,' Sigmar said, eyes full of pride as he surveyed his conquering heroes. 'Trust in the gifts I have given you, and remember your oaths. Remember what it is that we fight for.'

He raised Ghal Maraz, and the light caught the intricate craftsmanship of the legendary hammer, reflecting back off the gleaming turquoise ranks of the Celestial Vindicators. There was no darkness, no cruelty or malice that could stand in the face of that holy brilliance.

'Vengeance for the lost,' bellowed the Celestial Vindicators. 'Glory to Sigmar's chosen!'

Lord-Celestant Mykos Argellon parried a rat-thing's wild swing and slammed his fist into the creature's eye socket. It yelped and toppled backwards, and he thrust his grandblade, named Mercutia, into its panting chest. Its scream cut off abruptly, and Mykos slipped his blade out and swept it to the side to draw a red line across another creature's throat. Alongside him, his warriors hacked their way through the last of the skaven stragglers.

Liberators battered the creatures to the ground with their heavy shields, then ran them through with swords, or crushed them with hammers. Retributors cared not for such precision; they barrelled in with heavy hammers, breaking through the ratmen's weak guard, and shattering bones with every swing. There was no gap in the Stormcast line, no weakness for the skaven to exploit. In every direction the creatures turned they were met with sharpened steel and an impassable wall of storm-forged metal. The Lord-Celestant felt a surge of pride as he watched his men make perfect war.

Mykos looked around the cavern. No sign of Thostos and his chamber, though judging by the shattered and broken bodies that were already lying in heaps before the Argellonites had entered, they had certainly passed through this way. Mykos frowned, not for the first time concerned about his fellow Lord-Celestant's incautious approach.

'Sigmar casts us in blessed sigmarite, hurls us out into the realms, and there we find our true calling,' roared Knight-Heraldor Axilon, shaking his broadsword free of gore. 'We are gilded tavern cats, tasked with hunting mice!'

The warriors laughed, and Mykos couldn't help but smile. 'Pray, do not speak again, brother Axilon,' he pleaded with mock sincerity. 'Else you'll bring these walls down upon us.'

The Knight-Heraldor covered his mouth with one gauntlet and nodded fervently. That earned another chuckle from the others. Axilon was the implacable herald of the Argellonites, his voice a roar of thunder that could be heard across a battlefield, extolling his brothers to ever-greater acts of valour. It was joked amongst the warriors that Axilon need not bother with his battle-horn – the radiant instrument that all Knights-Heraldor carried – for his voice alone would suffice.

'Not good terrain, this,' said Axilon, approaching Mykos and gesturing at the rough stone walls and winding, gnawed-out tunnels. 'It favours the stinking rats. We cannot see ahead, and we cannot guard our flanks. I cannot even give them a taste of the God-King's thunder, lest it brings this cursed labyrinth down on our heads.'

'Brother,' said Mykos, shaking his head and pointing one finger down at the floor. 'The ground is below us, and the ceiling above. Consider our last venture, and thank Sigmar we are not battling through the warped geometry of the Tower of Lost Souls, pursued once more by the mutant scions of the Broken Prince.'

'A fair point, my Lord,' Axilon smiled, but his mirth did not last long. He lowered his voice as he came closer. 'Lord-Celestant Thostos has pushed too far ahead without us. He's going to get himself surrounded.'

'I am certain that the Lord-Celestant's tactical situation shifted,' said Mykos, a note of warning in his voice, 'and he was forced to adjust our battle plan.' It would not do for the rest of the chamber to start voicing their own concerns about Thostos' behaviour.

'As you say, lord,' said Axilon.

The Knight-Heraldor kicked one of the dead ratmen disdainfully, turning it over with the tip of his boot. The creature was ridden with boils and rashes, and wrapped in black leather marked with obscene symbols that Mykos did not care to look upon.

'So soon we see battle,' Axilon said. 'We barely made it out of the realmgate before we came upon these foul creatures.'

'Who had taken up position throughout the only pass that leads down to the Roaring Plains,' Mykos nodded gravely. 'It has not escaped my notice, my friend. It feels uncomfortably like these creatures were sent here to bleed us.'

That was not a pleasant thought. They had been counting on the element of surprise, but if the enemy was already aware they were coming... He shook his head. It was no use second-guessing their mission now. They could do nothing but push on and try to find a way out of these warrens, which meant his force had to link back up with Thostos as soon as possible.

'We will push forwards, into the central passage,' Mykos said, pointing a gauntleted finger at the largest of the three tunnels that split off from the cramped nexus that they currently occupied.

Prosecutor-Prime Evios Goldfeather stepped to the tunnel entrance.

'Battle has been joined, my Lord-Celestant,' he said, in his clipped, distinguished voice. Goldfeather was so named for the fabulous golden quill he kept tucked into his war-helm. When asked about it, or even when none had asked, the airborne warrior would loudly proclaim that it was a gift from the 'Father of Griffons', in return for his slaying of a rampaging manticore, and proceed to tell that tale in punishing length and detail. Mykos considered this a small price to pay in exchange for the man's keen senses.

'They have encountered heavy resistance,' he continued gravely. 'It's not just swarm rats – I can hear the vermin's heavier weapons in the field. Foul, sorcerous siege pieces.'

Mykos approached, and even without the Prosecutor's superior senses, he could hear it too. The spatter-whine of the skaven's filthy magic, and the barking crack of their bizarre weapon-pieces. Undercutting those alien sounds, faint but unmistakable, were the battle-hymns of his Vindicator brothers, the tramp of booted feet, and the cleansing celestial thunder of Sigmar's storm.

'We must move quickly,' Mykos muttered, and raised his runeblade high. 'To me, Argellonites. Forwards to glory!'

Thostos Bladestorm swept his runeblade back and forth in great arcs, hewing his way through dozens of the shrieking vermin. Heads flew. Limbs shattered. The warren stank of fear, the sour terror of the ratfolk and the foul reek of their diseased blood. One of the degenerates, bolder than its fellows, jabbed at Thostos with a crude shortspear. The blow skipped off his blessed sigmarite, barely denting the god-forged metal. The Bladestorm replied with a backhand sweep of his sword that bisected the unfortunate creature, sending its torso spinning away over the heads of its fellows. Hot blood splashed across Thostos' battle-mask, and he roared in exultation.

Exultation? No, that implied that pleasure was found in the act. Fury? That came closer, but what he felt lacked the cleansing, satisfying heat of true rage. He settled for whatever it was he did feel, because he felt something, and that was enough.

In truth, the filthy skaven were poor subjects for his anger. They fell before him in their dozens, hacked and hewed apart. Those nearest to him barely even attempted to block his attacks. Instead they scampered as far away as they could in the cramped confines of the warren, scratching and pulling at their fellows, dragging others into the path of blows aimed at them. He was dimly aware of his brothers following in his wake, launching themselves at the skaven in a sea-green blur.

In the face of Thostos' onslaught, the pack broke. Dropping weapons, abandoning all pretence of organised retreat, they swarmed from the cavern in a ragged tide of brown-and-grey fur. Something buried deep within Thostos called for caution; the skaven were unpredictable and treacherous foes, and these tunnels were suited to their deviant, backstabbing form of warfare. That caution met the desperate battle-lust that filled him, and evaporated in an instant.

'Vengeance,' he roared, his voice thick with hatred, 'Vengeance in the name of Sigmar!'

The Lord-Celestant charged after the fleeing vermin. Bellowing battle-hymns of praise to the God-King, the Bladestorm Warrior Chamber followed him to war.

* * *

The Celestial Vindicators followed the skaven through a rough-hewn corridor no taller than a mortal man, losing pace with their quarry as they bent to force their way through the cramped confines. The Stormcasts had many reasons to be thankful for their blessed armour, but here, in the skaven's favoured terrain, it slowed them and made movement cumbersome.

Thostos simply smashed his way through the dry earth, his momentum hardly slowed by the ramshackle, makeshift nature of the skaven excavations. He broke free of the tunnel in a rain of debris, sword and hammer raised.

He had entered a central chamber of the warren, some thirty feet high and maybe four times that across. In the centre was a raised mound of dirt, flecked with rat spoor and other filth, around which the fleeing ratmen swarmed in their hundreds. Upon the raised earth stood several larger beasts. Near three times the height of their multifarious kin, these skaven rippled with muscles. Bizarre, arcane devices were bolted to their flesh, strange, cylindrical tubes of metal capped with several small nozzles. As Thostos burst into the chamber, the creatures screeched as one, and as one their strange weapons blared with a vile eldritch light, and let loose a repeating blast that echoed like thunder.

Retributor Arodus was the first Stormcast to follow his Lord-Celestant into the central chamber, and was rewarded with a hail of bullets that blasted him backwards into his fellows, blood pouring from countless holes punched through his armour. Retributor Wulkus leapt forwards in fury at his brother's death, crushing a one-eyed skaven foot soldier into the dirt with a wild overhead swing of his hammer. As he brought the weapon back up there was a loud crack, and a hole appeared in the centre of his faceplate, releasing a faint pink mist. He collapsed, and both Stormcast bodies disappeared in a blast of pale light. As the main force of Celestial Vindicators poured out to meet the skaven infantry, a whickering storm of fire met them.

The cavern was strobed with violent green light as the strange contraptions continued to fire. Those skaven unfortunate enough to be nearest to the Stormcasts exploded in torrents of gore, and others went down howling as ricochets found thighs, ankles and fingers.

Even the devastating hail of bullets could not hold back the fury of the Celestial Vindicators, who broke into the main chamber and launched themselves at the enemy. Thostos ignored the chattel that snapped at his heels, barrelling further into the press of bodies, straining to reach the escarpment. Daggers were thrust at him as he ground his way into the skaven ranks, tapping out a staccato rhythm as they scraped against his war-plate. He butted a taller, wire-furred rat-thing, splattering its nose, then slammed his hammer into its gut and trampled over its mewling, bleeding form. On to the next, a pot-bellied fiend encased in pockmarked iron. That one died quickly as his sword bit into its skull, blessed sigmarite tearing through bone and tissue as if it were parchment. To the next, a runt of a thing wearing robes, which tasted the blunt face of his hammer and burst apart in a spray of viscera.

And on to the next…

Lord-Castellant Eldroc realised, with a horrible clarity, that they had been baited neatly into the skaven's trap. Caught up in their fury, they had pushed forwards too far from their brothers, and now the enemy hurled fresh troops at them from every angle. Eldroc's loyal gryph-hound Redbeak snarled and spat at his side, his trusty senses overwhelmed by the stench of the enveloping skaven mass. Ratmen dropped from hidden holes in the roof of the cavern, clawed their way free from cunningly disguised apertures in the walls, and leapt upon the Bladestorm's exposed flanks. Suddenly the Stormcasts were an island of turquoise in a sea of wretched grey fur.

Cursing their foolhardiness, and cursing himself for allowing the joy of righteous battle to overrule his caution, Eldroc scanned the packed ranks of the Celestial Vindicators for a glimpse of his Lord-Celestant. He found him, of course, at the very forefront of the battle.

Vermin assailed him from every side, but they could not slow his furious advance. Eldroc knew well how mighty Thostos was in battle, but even he was shocked at the raw-edged brutality his commander displayed. The Bladestorm had always tempered fury with caution; that was why he was chosen to lead, because he could channel the rage and lust for vengeance of the Celestial Vindicators – ever the most aggressive of Sigmar's sons, ever the first to leap into battle – to its true potential.

Now, he barely seemed to acknowledge his brothers. He never looked back, merely ploughing forwards into the packed ranks of the enemy like a tormented hound let loose.

In such numbers, even the primitive weapons of the skaven clanrats began to take their toll. Stormcasts were dragged down by dozens of the creatures, which stabbed and cut at them in a frenzied orgy of carnage. Daggers found eye sockets, the gaps between gorgets, and vulnerable spots where the barrage of bullets had weakened even the mighty sigmarite battle-plate. It was honourless murder, of the sort at which the ratmen excelled. Eldroc rushed to one fallen Stormcast, stuck with half a dozen blades and weakly pawing at a band of wretches who cackled as they clambered over him, dissecting him with wicked glee. Redbeak hurled himself onto one of the creatures, ripping with his sharp beak and raking with four powerful talons, but another skaven quickly scrabbled up to replace it.

Eldroc raised his warding lantern and intoned the name of blessed Sigmar as he unleashed its celestial energies. Warm, cleansing light washed over the stricken Stormcast, wrapping his form in a halo of flickering luminescence. The skaven skittered back from the power of the holy light, screeching as it burned at their cruel, beady eyes. The fallen warrior's back arched, and as the glow washed over his body, the sigmarite melted and flowed like wax, refashioning the rents in his armour so that his hallowed war-plate glistened as if it had been freshly forged. Up came the Stormcast, blade in hand, howling his hatred at the enemy with renewed vigour.

Yet Eldroc could not reach all his brothers. Bursts of lightning rippled across the cavern walls as loyal warriors were called back to Azyr, strobing the unfolding carnage with blue light. Even these few losses were too many; they had barely begun their holy purpose, and already they were weakened.

Thostos had reached the central mound now, and was hewing his way through the Stormfiends that had opened fire on them. He thrust his sword into the neck of one creature, then swept his hammer across, low, to snap the vermin's legs. It screeched in agony and toppled to the floor. As Eldroc watched, Thostos let gravity drag the broken thing from his blade, then caved in its chest with another mighty blow from his hammer. Ahead, cowering behind its taller bodyguards, was a wiry, grey-mottled creature whose yelps and screeches echoed over even the general clatter and chaos of battle. Its bronzed armour carried a shoulder-rack upon which were mounted several strange icons, ragged banners and shrivelled heads. The skaven commander, Eldroc surmised.

Thostos was killing his way towards the warlord, bleeding now from a dozen wounds. More Stormcasts hauled themselves up onto the mound, but still the skaven guns blazed, now joined by an enfilade from the right flank. The skaven had brought forth a heavy wooden shield, from behind which several long-barrelled rifles laid down a vicious crossfire. Another Liberator went down, crimson spurting from his ruined gorget, spasming as he fell. Eldroc felt a dull thud on his thigh, and growled as it was followed by searing, white-hot agony. Not the sharp, honest pain of a flesh wound, but something more sinister, a rapidly spreading toxic ache that burned across his leg. He lowered his warding lantern and let the blessed light bathe his smoking limb.

They had pushed too hard and too fast, and they had fallen for the enemy's trap.

Then, the blaring of a war-horn shook the cavern.

The battle was over as soon as the Argellonites crashed into the flank of the skaven horde. At the tip of the spear, Knight-Heraldor Axilon and his retinue, hardy Retributors wielding mighty two-handed hammers, smashed apart the skaven's vile weapon platforms, slaughtering the operators and ending their savage crossfire. More Celestial Vindicators followed in their wake, shields together in a line of blessed sigmarite that crashed into the enemy's softened ranks, battering broken ratmen to the floor where they were either ground underneath the boots of onrushing Stormcasts, or despatched with swift blows.

As the first wave pushed left to clear the flank of the besieged Bladestorm, Mykos Argellon led the rest of his warriors straight through to the mound and Thostos. The Argellonites' Lord-Celestant was the very image of the God-King's glory in his ornate plate, luminescent even in the darkness of the cavern as he cut a bloody swathe through the enemy horde.

'Forward, Argellonites!' he shouted, voice rising even above the chaotic din of battle. 'Show them the fury of the Celestial Vindicators.'

He wielded Mercutia in a blur, thrusting, slashing and battering with the heavy pommel in a whirlwind rush so fast it seemed impossible that he could retain any measure of control. Yet not a single strike was misplaced, and the Lord-Celestant left great piles of broken and torn skaven behind him as he went.

'Take the Stormfiends,' shouted Prosecutor-Prime Goldfeather to his men, finally given space to stretch his wings in the vaults of the cavern.

His retinue swept above the fray, calling lightning-wreathed javelins into their hands to hurl at the towering beasts. One went down under a hail of missiles, still firing its bizarre weapon as it toppled from the central mound. Another turned and fired at the Prosecutors, projectiles stitching across the roof of the cavern and cutting down two heralds in clouds of bloody smoke.

Emboldened by the arrival of their allies, the Bladestorms renewed their own vicious assault. Now the skaven's superior numbers became their downfall; pressed against two unyielding walls of steel, there was no room to scrabble free, and barely space to gasp a desperate lungful of air. Dead skaven were packed so tight in the melee that they were held upright by their fellows, who scratched and tore in panic but could find no escape. Those vermin fortunate enough to be on the outskirts of the battle wavered, their fear-musk foul and pungent.

Blessed with that uniquely skaven insight of when to cut your losses and scamper away, Warlord Zirix cursed, spat and turned to flee, content in the knowledge that his filthy kin would keep these metal warriors busy long enough for him to disappear into the darkness.

As he turned, he met a pair of blazing blue eyes.

Terror escaped him in a sharp, sour odour as the giant before him snapped out a gauntlet to wrap around his neck. He tried to scrabble for his blade, a rusted, green-tinged shard of metal whose toxic coating had eaten away the flesh of many man-creatures in his short and wretched life. The blade was slapped free from his paw and skittered away.

Zirix screeched and gasped as he was lifted slowly into the air. The giant was so strong. He scratched and clawed at its arm, but to no avail. His eyes bulged and his vision swam with crimson as blood vessels burst under the pressure of the vice-like grip. The giant brought him closer.

'Vengeance,' it growled, its voice the pitiless inevitability of an avalanche. 'Ever vengeance.'

The creature stopped struggling, and Thostos placed one gauntlet behind its neck, wrenched its head around with a sickening crunch and hurled the dead thing into the sea of ratmen that surged around the foot of the raised knoll, where it was swept up like a leaf in a rushing river.

The warlord's death marked the end of any semblance of skaven resistance. Away the ratmen scurried, hurtling down hidden passages and burrows, scrambling over each in terrified desperation. The Celestial Vindicators culled those too slow to run, and Mykos' warriors flowed around the Bladestorm formation, forming a wall of steel at every entrance to the cavern in case of counter-attack.

The Lord-Celestant of the Argellonites surveyed the carnage. The Bladestorm had wreaked a horrific toll on the skaven. The cavern was a charnel-pit of dead vermin, their stinking blood marking every surface, spattering the armour of the Celestial Vindicators from helm to boot. The nature of the Stormcasts' god-given immortality meant that it was hard to judge losses, but there were more than a few stricken warriors lying amongst the wreckage of corpses. They were being tended to by Lord-Relictor Tharros Soulwarden, who went from man to man, salving their wounds with the power of his healing storm.

Alone at the heart of the wreckage stood Thostos himself, surrounded by the broken and hewn corpses of the skaven Stormfiends, weapons hanging limply by his side. He stared at the dead creatures, barely moving. Mykos approached him and as the Lord-Celestant turned, he felt a shiver run down his spine as those pitiless eyes bored into him.

'Their leader is dead,' Thostos said. 'The vermin will not trouble us further as we progress through these warrens.'

Mykos cleared his throat. 'You slew many of these foul beasts today, brother,' he said, cautiously. 'You and your men fought a valiant battle.'

He paused, on the verge of saying more. There was a silence that dragged on too long, broken only by the groans of the wounded and the low, droning chant of the Lord-Relictor at work. The Bladestorm had a way of leaving him tongue-tied.

'You wish to chastise me for my rashness,' said Thostos. 'For not regrouping with your Argellonites before making a push into the core chamber.'

'I...' Mykos blinked in surprise.

'The movement of the enemy force suggested coordination, which meant there had to be a leader directing the vermin. The largest concentration was coming from a single direction, where I judged that the leader was likely to be. There was no time to inform you of my decision, so I trusted that the sound of battle would lead you to us.'

Mykos smiled behind his mask and shook his head.

'You disagree with my actions?'

'No, not entirely. I would prefer that our communication was more open, but I understand the value of risk in war. That is the Celestial Vindicators' way.' The Lord-Celestant shrugged. 'It's simply that this is the most words we've exchanged since we first joined our forces for this mission.'

If he was hoping that some comradely small talk would thaw the Bladestorm's icy mood, Mykos found himself disappointed. His fellow warrior simply stared at him, saying nothing. Mykos heard the approaching steps of Lord-Castellant Eldroc with something approaching relief.

'The men are ready to move out,' he said, limping slightly on one leg as he approached. Redbeak was at his side, blood staining his noble features, proud eyes narrowed. 'We lost twenty-six warriors, Liberator-Prime Lucos among them.'

Thostos nodded without any sign of regret. 'The air is fresher this way,' he said, pointing at the northern end of the cavern, the opposite side to which they had entered. 'It may lead to a way out of these warrens. You can feel the wind. Move the men out.'

'You are wounded, sire,' Eldroc said, his voice rising in concern. Mykos saw that the Lord-Castellant was right. Thostos' arm was bleeding heavily, and he could see several small holes dotted across the Lord-Celestant's plate where bullets had penetrated.

'I… had not noticed,' said Thostos quietly, staring at the blood.

Eldroc went to his Lord-Celestant's side and bathed Thostos in the renewing glow of his warding lantern. The Bladestorm bowed his head, and the blue flame behind his eyes flickered and dimmed. Mykos thought, with no small amount of surprise, that he could hear an exhausted sigh – but the Bladestorm seemed beyond such mortal displays of fatigue. As he watched, the Lord-Celestant's wounds closed, and sigmarite flowed across the ruptured areas of his plate armour.

Thostos nodded to his Lord-Castellant and rotated his shoulder, testing the joint and stretching his arm.

'Move the men out,' he said again, and the emptiness was back. He gave Mykos one last look, the briefest nod of his head, and then strode away.

The Stormcasts emerged from the stinking warrens onto a wide shelf of rock overlooking the Roaring Plains. Pale yellow grass stretched to the horizon, shifting so violently in the restless wind that it almost seemed to ripple like fire. Clouds rushed across the sky, swirling and reforming in an endless, roiling tempest. It was a foul-tempered wind. At this height, a mortal man would be at risk of being blown clean off of the mountaintop – only the Stormcasts' weight and strength kept them rooted. A single, steep stair was cut into the edge of the platform, winding away towards the foothills below, which reached out to the grasslands in raised veins of blackened rock, ridged and twisted, almost skeletal.

'The Roaring Plains,' Eldroc said, stepping up to the brink of the ledge and peering down at the vista that spread below. He raised his voice as a lash of thunder broke, rolling across the sky so loudly that the mountain itself seemed to shake beneath them. 'Seems a pleasant enough place,' he said, with no little sarcasm.

'Across this plain lies the Manticore Dreadhold,' said Thostos, his voice a granite rumble. 'We must make haste. The next stage of Sigmar's plan cannot proceed until we secure it and hold it.'

Mykos watched the Lord-Celestant. Thostos showed no interest in the grand spectacle of the plains, nor did he make any attempt to bolster his warriors' spirits after their struggle through the warrens. His hands were clenched at his sides, and he stared listlessly at the distant horizon as the Celestial Vindicators formed up behind him. The fervour and the anger were long gone, and in their place was stillness, but not calm. His armour and battle-mask obscured any expression, but Mykos could feel the tension in him even at this distance. He was coiled like a spring, ready to snap at the slightest opportunity.

'Goldfeather,' Mykos shouted, dragging his mind back to more immediate matters. The Prosecutor-Prime dropped neatly off the rock where he had been perching, and glided down to where the Argellonites were still ranking up.

'My Lord?' he asked.

'Take your swiftest men and survey the foothills and the immediate area. I want no more surprises. Anything suspicious, anything at all, and you report back to me. This land has already sent many broken brothers back to Azyr, and I do not intend to take its dangers lightly. Go.'

The Prosecutor-Prime nodded and went to gather his fellow heralds. The rest of the Argellonites and the Bladestorm had begun to filter down the winding stair, though it was so narrow that only two could walk side by side. It would take several hours to reach the foothills and redress once more into proper fighting ranks. That worried Mykos. Of the Stormcasts' manifold virtues, stealth was not one; they were exposed here, and the skaven had amply proven the potential of a swift surprise attack.

As the Argellonites began to file down the twisting steps, Eldroc came to Mykos' side. His armour was freshly repaired, and the hint of a limp that had marked him in the warrens had disappeared. Once again he was an image of strength and implacable fortitude. Of all the Bladestorm's warriors, Eldroc had been the most forthcoming, and Mykos was grateful for it. He liked the man's simple honesty and level-headedness.

'You seem troubled, my friend,' Eldroc said.

'It is nothing, Lord-Castellan. Merely concern that we found battle so soon. I had hoped to arrive at our destination without issue.'

'How fine that would be,' Eldroc chuckled. 'In these times that would be a rare blessing, in any corner of the realms.'

He rested his halberd on his shoulder and leaned upon the haft. They were silent a moment, listening to the tramp of boots and the howling of the wind as it whipped its way through the mountain pass.

'He can be difficult, I know,' the Lord-Castellan said, quietly.

Mykos said nothing. It was clear that Eldroc was choosing his words carefully, and he gave the man time to gather his thoughts. It was no easy thing for a Stormcast to question a fellow warrior, let alone his leader. Absolute loyalty and brotherhood was as much a part of them as their armour, as their weapons and their fearlessness.

'I have spoken to many of our reforged brothers,' Eldroc sighed, 'and the change is more marked in Thostos than in any of them. He used to be such a thoughtful man. I think that was why he was chosen to lead. We are a wrathful host, and we need such men to temper us.'

Eldroc turned to Mykos. There was a pleading edge to his voice,

26

and Mykos realised that the Lord-Castellant had likely never spoken to another soul regarding his concerns.

'Give him time, my lord,' Eldroc said.

Prosecutor-Prime Evios Goldfeather enjoyed the spiteful power of the winds of the Roaring Plains as they buffeted him mercilessly. It was pleasant enough to glide in the tranquil air of the Singing Gardens, or even over the celestial valleys of Erianos, but if there was one thing Goldfeather valued, it was a challenge. The wind here had no sense to it; a zephyr would drift west, allowing him to glide on its gentle arc, then a wall of force would slam him back the other direction, blasting him so hard that he dropped several yards, and spinning him so fast that he could barely control his descent.

At first it was unsettling, but he quickly found himself relishing the unforgiving nature of the place. There was a pattern to be found in the midst of the madness. He caught a rising gust and let it lift him, felt it sway and weaken, and sought a westerly gale that filled his radiant wings with air, letting it take him on a wide arc over the churning grass of the Roaring Plains. His fellow Prosecutors followed in his wake, though he noted with no surprise, and no small amount of satisfaction, that they were finding the turbulent winds far trickier to deal with. Galeth and Harion had already been blown off course, despite the power of their Azyrite wings. He would have to speak to them later; he demanded a certain level of excellence from his men, after all.

He returned his gaze to the plains. It was an astonishing sight, the Prosecutor-Prime had to concede. The great grass seas stretched for miles in every direction, punctuated by jagged, twisting spears of rock and wind-scoured mesa clusters that broke through the earth's surface, clutching at the sky. In all that space one might expect a measure of stillness, but that was not the case; everywhere Goldfeather looked, there was motion. Around the base of the rocky protrusions the grass grew longer, grasping at the escaping formations, wrapping around them in choking vine clusters. The wind shifted and pulled at these vines, tightening them like a hangman's noose. As the shifting clouds passed overhead and darkened the plain for a moment, Goldfeather thought he saw one great claw of rock lurch, dragged down towards the earth by a thick belt of thorns that encircled it. Then sunlight speared though the clouds once more and it was still. Just a trick of the light, he supposed.

He was distracted by a low, rumbling noise that built into a roar. In the distance, the earth itself split. Dirt was kicked up as a great gouge tore across the plain, as if something monstrous was attempting to wrench itself free. No sooner had the earth ceased its writhing movement than a second rent appeared, following the path of the first. There was a tremor, signified by a series of great cracks that rippled across the ground, and then an uneasy quiet.

Soaring higher, Goldfeather saw more terrible wonders. A carpet of flesh roiled across the plain far to the Stormcasts' left, a shifting mass of stampeding beasts so thickly packed together that he could not see the ground beneath them. They were flat-headed, quadruped grazing beasts, with mighty horns that wrapped backwards around their skulls. There were thousands… hundreds of thousands of them.

The Prosecutor-Prime dropped closer and saw another flock of creatures, scaled and lizard-like, but with brightly coloured feathers across their wings and hindquarters. Each was bigger than a man, almost the same size as a Stormcast, and as Evios watched they rolled and dived into the stampede, nipping at the flanks of the beasts and trying to drive them into one another. As he watched, one of the larger avians succeeded in tripping an unfortunate creature; there was a horrific avalanche of hooves and screaming flesh, and a great chunk of the onrushing tide collapsed in on itself. Nothing could survive such carnage and Evios

watched, impressed despite himself at the winged creatures' ingenuity, as a mountain of crushed beasts piled up, ground to pieces
under the sheer weight of the onrushing mass. They would eat
well once the stampede had passed on.

One of the avian creatures noticed his presence and began to
shriek, and Goldfeather decided it was time to move on. He signalled his retinue, and as one they peeled away from the massacre.

He dropped again and found another gust of wind, and let it
sweep him back to the south, towards the Stormcast position. The
Prosecutor-Prime had almost satisfied himself that he had a clear
reading on the region when he caught something out of the corner of his eye. Heading in a lateral direction towards the foothills
that the Stormcasts were heading to, he saw a number of specks.
He signalled his men to follow and soared towards the movement.

As he swept closer, he saw that a large mob of creatures was
pursuing a smaller, scattered band across the plain. The pursuers
numbered a couple of hundred, perhaps, and their size, lumbering
gait and bulky, crudely grafted armour marked them out as orruks.

Prosecutor Omeris finally caught up with him. 'They head
towards our brothers,' he said, straining to be heard above the howl
of the wind. 'We should head back to inform the Lord-Celestants.'

'Orruks,' spat Goldfeather. 'Low-minded filth, the lot of them.'

'They almost have their prey,' said Omeris.

'Hardly surprising,' Goldfeather replied. 'The cursed brutes can
run for hours when their blood is up.'

His gaze fell upon the fleeing band. They were scrawny and
battered, and they wore ragged scraps of leather not much more
refined than that of the primitive savages chasing them, but there
was no mistaking it.

They were human.

The Stormcasts wound their way through the bluffs, alert at every
howl, every creak of earth. Eldroc marched at the head of the

column, a few paces behind Thostos. He watched his lord stride onwards, heedless of the noises around them. Eldroc, and all of his brothers in the Celestial Vindicators, had seen their families and friends slaughtered by the vile hordes of Chaos. As the blades finally came for them too, they had bellowed their defiance to the skies, and prayed to mighty Sigmar for the chance to wreak their vengeance upon the hated minions of the Dark Gods. This oath had been offered willingly, and any price had been a price worth paying.

And yet, looking at what had become of his Lord-Celestant, Eldroc was filled with doubt. The man was hollow, an unfeeling shell filled with nothing but an insatiable need to exact his vengeance. Gone was the thoughtful, righteous man that Eldroc had battled and trained with for so many years leading up to the great venture into the realms. They had talked together once, sharing dreams of a new era of hope and glory for the scions of Sigmar, both knowing that they would never get to experience that peace for themselves. They had accepted that truth gladly, but it was one thing to welcome an inevitable, honourable death, and another to die eternally, each fresh Reforging bringing a symphony of agonies, further draining and weakening the soul.

And what else did the Stormcasts risk, every time they went to war for the God-King? The truth only Sigmar knew. Each warrior came back altered in his own way. There was a Liberator in the Bladestorm who returned unable to remember any of his former friends, but able, with perfect clarity, to recall hundreds of ancient sonnets in some archaic language that could barely be deciphered. Others remembered only fragments of their former lives, as though they were seeing them through the eyes of another person.

Eldroc himself had felt the agony of Reforging. Yet somehow he had emerged without the traumas that his friends and brothers had suffered. His memories had faded, yes, like a rich tapestry left in the blazing sun, but deep down he knew himself; he remembered the man he had been and what he fought for.

There was guilt, too, when he looked upon the haunted visage of his Lord-Celestant, the broken shell that Thostos had become. Why had he not suffered as brutally as his friend? This terrified him more than any malady or sickness of the mind. A gnawing thought echoed inside Eldroc's head: he had not yet discovered just what he had sacrificed – when he did, would it make what Thostos had gone through seem minor?

Absolute loyalty and devotion to his God-King ran through Eldroc like a rich vein through unyielding stone, but still he could not set aside his misgivings. Nor could he sleep at night.

The beating of wings stirred him from his dark thoughts. The Argellonites' Prosecutor-Prime had returned, arriving some way ahead of his fellow scouts. He dropped nimbly from the sky, landing before Lord-Celestant Argellon with ease.

'My lord,' he said, his voice tight and urgent. 'A mob of orruks is heading towards us, pursuing a band of mortals.'

Mykos visibly tensed. 'Have they fallen? Do they bear the mark of the Dark Gods?'

The Prosecutor-Prime considered this a moment, and shrugged. 'They are savage-looking, wrapped in animal skins like primitive brutes,' he replied, and Eldroc could hear the disdain in his words, 'but I saw none of the wretched symbols or marks of Chaos. I cannot say for certain, though I do know they will not make it much further before they tire and the orruks run them down.'

'How many orruks?' said Thostos, and Goldfeather gave a start at the Lord-Celestant's sudden presence.

'Roughly two hundred,' he replied.

Mykos exchanged a look with Thostos. 'We do not need a fight with the orruks,' he said. 'Our mission will be difficult enough already without their interference. Yet these mortals may be able to provide us with valuable information regarding this region. We should show our strength.'

The Bladestorm stared at Mykos for a long time, then gave an almost imperceptible nod and turned to survey their current position. They were coming to the mouth of the foothills, and the terrain was sloping down to meet the plains. It was still rough ground, jagged, heat-baked and dry, but it formed a natural defensive position against an infantry assault. The embankments that channelled them were roughly the height of two Stormcasts, and the ground between was narrow enough for two-score warriors to hold the line without threat of being outflanked. Some thousand yards or so ahead, the rocky earth sloped down one final time, and beyond that Thostos could see a glimpse of open ground.

'Retributor-Prime Hyphon,' he shouted, 'summon your warriors. Lord-Celestant Argellon, we will take a hundred men and make haste for the ridge ahead of our main force.'

Liberators dashed to the summit of the ridge, forming into lines and smashing their colossal shields down into the dirt to form an impenetrable ring of steel. Behind them the Judicators judged their range and held their bows taut and ready as the orruks rumbled closer. It was easy to hear them now, hooting and hollering their bestial war cries as they drove themselves ever harder, desperate to catch the fleeing mortals.

Staggering with the half-drunk sway of exhausted prey, the beleaguered humans spotted the formation of Stormcasts and stopped still. Several dropped to their knees, exhausted.

'Move your idle backsides,' roared Goldfeather, hovering above the ragged band. He scanned the group to indentify the leader and settled on a wiry female who was down on one knee, a curved blade in her hand. She seemed to be the one the others looked to.

He swooped down to meet her. 'Get your people behind those shields, or we'll leave you to the greenskins,' he said.

The mortals' nervous eyes flicked towards the woman, who stared up at the Prosecutor-Prime with a familiarity and lack of fear that made him feel surprisingly uncomfortable. He was used to little more than servile deference from mortals. Finally, she nodded, put two calloused fingers between her lips and gave a sharp whistle, clearly deciding that a slim chance of survival was better than the certainty of death. Summoning up one last reserve of energy, the mortals dragged themselves forwards, scrambling up the shallow incline towards the Stormcasts' shield wall, which opened to let them through. As they passed, the Celestial Vindicators slid back into position expertly.

'They're a ragged lot,' said Knight-Heraldor Axilon as the humans passed. Mykos could hardly disagree.

They were wiry and weathered, with a leanness to their frame that suggested many nights had gone by without a decent meal. Ritual scars and red-ink tattoos covered their sun-browned skin; they wore little armour besides thin hide shirts and breeches, and leather wrappings on their feet and hands. The tall, raven-haired warrior who led them in had her hair bound up on one side with leather scraps and shaved clean on the other. As her party staggered past, her eyes locked with those of the Lord-Celestant. They were cold, grey and hard – a hunter's eyes, a wolf's eyes. She showed no fear, and no surprise or awe that he could discern. These are killers, Mykos thought. He signalled Liberator-Prime Julon, who nodded and began to secure the mortals, stripping any weapons they carried and examining them for any overt signs of corruption.

The orruks howled, denied of their prey, and thundered forwards into a wide, loose semicircle some twenty yards ahead of the Stormcasts. They grunted and snarled, spat and snorted, but for now they seemed curious enough not to hurl themselves into the Stormcast line. Shoving his fellows out of his way, a hulking specimen stomped forward, lazily scratching his thick neck, a wicked-looking greataxe held loosely at his side. Several burly warriors followed him, each bearing a smeared, red claw mark upon their black-iron breastplates.

'What now?' asked Goldfeather, gently dropping to the ground beside his Lord-Celestant, a stormcall javelin held at the ready in one gauntleted fist.

'Now we parlay,' said Mykos grimly, looking to his fellow Lord-Celestant, who was gazing at the orruks dispassionately. Thostos said nothing, though his weapons were drawn and held in steady hands. 'Humanity has known a common purpose with the orruks before. Perhaps we can avoid a skirmish that will gain us nothing.'

He signalled to Axilon, and the Knight-Heraldor nodded and selected five broad-shouldered and eager Retributors. If this did come to blows, he wanted the orruks down and dying as soon as possible. Together, the retinue stepped out from the shield wall.

Mykos held Mercutia, and the wondrous grandblade caught the sun, sending a ripple of light over his armour. He motioned his men to halt and strode forwards, sword raised high. The orruks watched, their ape-like brows furrowed. With elaborate slowness, the Lord-Celestant made a show of lowering the weapon, sliding it securely into the scabbard at his thigh.

The orruks looked to their leader, inching forwards slowly. He held out a meaty palm to stop them, and raised his own weapon. Tongue protruding in mock concentration, he lifted the greataxe and slotted its haft through an imaginary scabbard. His warriors guffawed idiotically. He smirked, and barked something indecipherable at his warriors. Eight came forward, while the others loomed menacingly in the background.

'That, I think, is as close as we're likely to get to a formal truce,' said Eldroc from the shield wall.

'Follow me,' said Mykos. 'And keep your hand near your blade.'

* * *

Mykos and Eldroc led the way, armour gleaming bright turquoise in the midday sun, in stark contrast to the dull, crude metal scraps and chains that the orruks had wrapped around themselves. Thostos walked behind them, his eyes locked on the warband's leader. The orruks snickered and hollered amongst themselves in their crude tongue, and one began a mock drumbeat upon its chest plate. Its fellows roared with laughter at this lack-witted attempt at humour.

Behind his battle-mask, Mykos couldn't help but sneer. Orruks. It never failed to amaze him how such a savage, dull, self-destructive race could be so resilient. They possessed no honour, no discipline or ambition beyond finding their next brawl, and yet the foul creatures propagated in every corner of the realms. One of the first tasks of the Stormcast Eternals, after their forging in the halls of Azyr, had been to clear the wilds of the Celestial Realm free of orruks. They had torn down the creatures' crude icons and the totems erected to their bestial gods, and put the beasts to the sword. The greenskins had fought savagely – orruks always did – but against the plated fist of Sigmar's avenging warriors, their only fate was death. Mykos remembered those battles with little fondness. It had been a grim task, valourless butchery that was necessary before the Stormcasts took their war to the true enemy.

Despite his disdain, Mykos could not help but note the difference between these hulking creatures and the wretched, feral scraps that they had ground underboot in Azyr. Their armour, for one. These orruks had bound themselves in thick plates of black iron, with wicked armour spikes upon the joints. Whereas the sigmarite armour of the Stormhosts was sculpted to artisanal perfection, the orruks' plate was worn, scratched and dented, and daubed haphazardly with slashes of red paint, forming fangs and jaws on greaves and vambraces. The quality was crude, and the effect should have been ludicrous, but on the heavily muscled, scarred forms of the orruks, it instead spoke of blunt efficiency, of the race's atavistic, uncultured love of war.

They were bigger, too, broader and more heavily muscled, and marked from head to toe with scars, burns and all the other trophies that battle bestowed upon a warrior's skin. Most wore pot helms decorated with horns or more wicked spikes, though others went bareheaded. The leader, an anvil-jawed monster with a wicked scar that cut an angry red line across his porcine right eye as it travelled down to his jaw, was as tall as the Stormcasts. He leered at the Celestial Vindicators and swaggered forwards to meet them. His warriors spread out in a semicircle around him, hands resting on jagged axes and spiked mauls. Mykos felt his hand drift down to Mercutia, who yearned to break free of her scabbard. There was a pregnant silence, broken only by the howling wind, and then the orruk leader spoke.

'Ain't seen yore kind before,' he rumbled in a crude tongue that the Stormcasts could understand, licking his lips like a starving man presented with a bountiful feast. 'Very shiny, ain't ya?'

His warband rumbled with amusement, their leader gave a broken-toothed grin, and Mykos resisted a strong urge to slice his head off. Eldroc stepped forward.

'We are the Celestial Vindicators, the blessed swords of Sigmar,' he said in his deep, resonant voice. 'We have no quarrel with you or your kind, but these humans are now under our guard.'

''Sat right?' the orruk growled, scratching one filthy ear with a yellow-taloned finger. 'Here,' he turned to his warriors, cocking his great head, 'who 'sis land belong to, boyz?'

'Ironjawz!' they roared as one.

'An' who says what goes around 'ere?'

'Drekka! Drekka! Drekka!'

The orruk leaned in conspiratorially. 'There's that then,' he chuckled. 'Reckon I won't take no orders from some tinpot git dropped outta the sky. We'll be taking those humies, and they'll go right t–'

A sword whipped through the air and buried itself between the orruk leader's eyes.

The momentum of the throw hurled the creature back into the orruk standing behind him, knocking both to the ground with a clatter. Mykos turned and saw Thostos drawing his warhammer, an empty scabbard at his side.

Silence. A sharp peal of astonished laughter came from Goldfeather. Then the orruks charged.

Roaring more with eager battle-lust than any feelings of betrayal at their leader's death, the orruks poured forwards. The Retributors met them, hammers drawn and swinging. The close quarters robbed the majority of the momentum from the charge, but Mykos saw Stormcasts go down under the greenskins' boots and blades, trampled and broken. As a bellowing orruk wielding two axes charged him down, he drew his sword, spun to the side and let his momentum add power to a lateral swing. Mercutia sliced straight through the creature's torso, opening its belly horizontally, spilling its innards to gush over Mykos' boots. The dying orruk attempted a wild swing at the Lord-Celestant, but he avoided it easily and put his boot in its chest, sending it crashing backwards to land in a crumpled heap.

By now the front ranks of the larger orruk mob had reached the fray, though Mykos could also hear the stomping of heavy boots and the battle-hymns of the faithful as the Liberator shield wall abandoned its defensive position and rushed forwards to protect its leaders.

Eldroc had set his halberd, and Mykos saw him skewer an orruk though the shoulder blades, twist his weapon and send the creature spinning to the floor. Another charged him from the side, and the Lord-Castellant retracted the halberd and thrust again, driving its heavy spike deep into the beast's gut. It squealed in fury and hurled its axe in a last desperate act of spite. It sailed past Eldroc, staving in the chest armour of an unfortunate Stormcast, who collapsed immobile on the ground. Redbeak snarled and hurled himself at the dying orruk, tearing out its throat and ending its defiance.

The ridge ran red with blood, orruk and Stormcast, but the impact of the orruk leader's death had swayed the momentum in favour of the Celestial Vindicators. Without his bellows and beatings, whatever strange, mob mentality bound the orruk band together in battle was shattered by the rage of the Stormcast Eternals. They were simply too strong and too skilled for the artless form of warfare that the orruks favoured. Liberator shields intercepted axe blows, then were shifted to one side for a killing thrust of a sword, or the crushing blow of a warhammer. Retributors swept their heavy hammers from side to side, breaking bones and smashing skulls to pieces.

Thostos was a blur of turquoise fury at the heart of the melee. He had replaced his thrown sword with a gladius, holding the short blade in a reverse grip and using it to stab and drag the nearest greenskins towards him, where he bludgeoned them to the ground with his warhammer.

It quickly became a slaughtering field. Not a single orruk left the ridge alive.

The runeblade was still lodged in the foul creature's idiotic smirk. Thostos put his foot on the dead orruk's forehead and wrenched his weapon loose. It came free with a spurt of gore, yellowed teeth splinters and torn flesh.

He heard boots thumping towards him on the hard earth. Two pairs, one fast and angry, one slower, more tentative.

'What in the name of Sigmar was that, Bladestorm?' barked Mykos Argellon, loud enough to draw the stares of several

Stormcasts who had been dispensing Sigmar's mercy to any injured orruks. 'We were at parlay. They did not threaten us.'

'They have killed children of Sigmar,' Thostos said. 'That is reason enough for them to die.'

'They are cruel, unthinking savages, but they are not our enemy here. Sigmar gave us this righteous purpose, and you would risk it all to sate your bloodlust,' Mykos spat. 'We could have avoided all of this. Men have died for nothing.'

Thostos rolled the orruk over with his boot. 'Look at this one,' he said, his voice betraying not a hint of tension. 'He decorates his flesh with trophies. Human bones, hands, ears. He keeps a tally upon his armour, see?'

It was true. The dead orruk's chain hauberk was heavy with knucklebones, stolen jewels and other trinkets, all recognisably of human origin. Thostos reached down to snatch a trophy from the brute's belt. It was a gauntlet of spiked black iron, and upon the palm there was the eight-pointed star of the eternal enemy. Eldroc cursed, and Thostos threw the gauntlet for Mykos to catch.

'Have you ever known orruks so bold?' he asked. 'Look at their armour, their weapons. Hardly the sticks and stones that the greenskin rabble brought to bear on us in the Amaris Foothills. These are stronger, more vital. They are blooded and battle-hardened. They have met the forces of the Dark Gods in battle and triumphed.'

'They did not attack us,' insisted Mykos, 'not until you gave them reason to. This is not the first time your reckless fury has cost us lives.'

'Their curiosity was all that stayed their blades, and that would have lasted scant moments longer. Your indecision would have endangered us, and so I acted in your stead.'

Mykos started forward, but Eldroc placed himself between the two Lord-Celestants and slammed his halberd down into the earth.

'Enough,' Eldroc hissed. 'The men are watching. Remember yourselves.'

Mykos glanced back. Thostos' men stood there, staring impassively. His own warriors were looking at each other in uneasy confusion. He could not see his warriors' faces beneath their battle-masks, but he could sense their tension, and he cursed himself for losing control.

Thostos sheathed his weapons.

'You are right, brother,' he said, staring at the hewn corpse of the orruk leader. 'They are not our enemy here.'

He turned back to look at Mykos, who returned his blue-flame gaze without flinching, no matter that he felt that familiar ache of discomfort.

'But they are never allies,' Thostos growled. 'Sigmar's light has been gone from this place for too long, and these savages have grown bold in its absence. We will meet them in battle again, do not doubt.' He stalked away.

Mykos Argellon had never felt true anger at a fellow Stormcast before. He tried to calm his breathing and centre his humours, but all he could feel was a white-hot fury and an aching sense of betrayal. How could he command this expedition alongside a man who trusted only in his lust for battle? Thostos could not be reasoned with, and his recklessness had already cost them lives that they could ill afford with such a lengthy, dangerous quest ahead of them. His anger was so keenly focussed that he barely noticed Lord-Castellant Eldroc was still standing beside him, until he sensed that the man was about to speak.

'Say nothing, brother,' Mykos warned. 'I do not wish to hear it. Do not tell me that he needs time, or tell me of how he has suffered. Tell it to the Stormcasts who fell here, when they make their own return from the forge.'

He turned to Eldroc, daring him to say a word in his lord's defence. To his credit the warrior did not avoid the Lord-Celestant's wrathful gaze. Neither did he speak. Instead, he simply gave a sad nod and strode off after the Bladestorm, leaving the lord of the Argellonites standing on his own on the blood-soaked ridge, amongst the dead.

CHAPTER TWO

Righteous Blood

'You put your trust in witchcraft?' spat the masked warrior. Bloody phlegm dribbled over his gore-encrusted chestplate, trickling down past obscene runes of devotion and damnation.

'I put my trust in this,' said Varash Sunken-Eye, raising his wicked blade, a hand-and-a-half of cruel obsidian. 'It has never failed me.'

His opponent circled, as did the warrior's two accomplices. A rabid pack, pink-eyed and drooling with hunger. Not hunger for sustenance, but for carnage, for spilt blood and shattered skulls.

Though to any true warrior of the Blood God, such things were as vital as water and bread.

Varash kept in step with his assailants, a wide grin splitting his ravaged face. It had been a while since anyone had challenged him – no surprise after what he had done to the Eyegouger and his men. Varash had kept his killers largely in check while the sorcerer did the necessary work, but a Bloodbound warband needed… pruning every now and then. If you wanted to lead, you killed your rivals so brutally, so painfully, that nobody dared to step across your path. Then you repeated that process any time they showed signs of forgetting who was in charge. It was a pattern that he had repeated a hundred times over the decades he had spent slaughtering in the name of the Blood God.

'The sorcerer works a ritual at my command,' Varash said. 'No weakling magic, but an offering that will tear down the veil between worlds and free our blades to make murder once again.'

He said this for the audience's benefit, of course. Hakkos and the two fools he'd brought along in this failed bid for power were dead already, they were just too foolish to realise it. They had staged their ill-considered ambush in the main courtyard of the dreadhold, under the great shadow of the Everchosen's statue. The colossal monument had been repaired and enlarged since the orruks' last attempt to tear it down, and now towered over even the mighty fortress. Sword raised, imposing horned helm proclaiming his dominance of not only the dreadhold but of this entire realm, the statue captured just a sliver of the real Archaon's astonishing presence.

The dreadhold itself was a wedge of black metal built into the mountain, its walls lined with bronzed skulls and jagged spikes of obsidian. Daemonic faces glowered from beneath the battlements, eyes burning like hot coals, and banners of stitched skin marked with vile runes flew from the three watchtowers equidistant along the wall. Hooting, snarling, scarred killers formed a circle around the duelling warriors, or peered down from the skull-adorned ramparts.

Hakkos dashed forward, axe raised. At the same time, his two lackeys came in from each side, one swinging low, one aiming at Varash's back. Perhaps they hoped that the ruined left side of his face wouldn't catch the flanking attack.

Fools.

The Chaos lord was unthinkably fast. His bastard sword snapped out low, deflecting the attack from the left and hooking underneath the axe blade. He dragged the blade to his right, and sent the unfortunate warrior stumbling into the path of Hakkos. The traitor's swinging axe struck him in the side of the neck, and a spurt of crimson arced out, splashing across Varash's armour.

He didn't waste a moment to savour the taste, but instead untangled his blade, and somehow got it raised in time to meet the axeman on his right. He stepped in close and smashed the pommel of the sword into the man's face, pushing him back into an awkward stumble, then turned again and kicked the dying warrior on the floor into Hakkos. The traitor went down under the dead weight. Varash swept his blade in a figure-eight pattern, and roared in laughter.

The crowd roared with him.

'It's a great shame, Deathbringer,' he said, smiling broadly as Hakkos scrambled to his feet. 'The carnage. The mountains of skulls that we will tear from the orruks once Xos'Phet completes his ritual. The oceans of blood we'll bathe in, Hakkos. You'll miss it all.'

'Your time is done, cripple,' snarled Hakkos. 'I'll put out your other eye when I'm done here. I'll flay you alive and hang you from the ramparts.'

He charged again, his accomplice in tow. Varash quickstepped back, dodging and blocking, letting Hakkos' mad swipes rush past him. The man was devilishly strong, but faced with a competent opponent he had no answer but clumsy rage.

Varash ducked a wild swing and cut a gouge into the remaining accomplice's leg. The man dropped with a howl, and the Chaos lord turned with the momentum of his strike, spinning and bringing the blade across in a backhand slice that swept the fool's head from his shoulders.

'Blood for the Blood God!' he screamed. 'Skulls for the Skull Throne!'

Hakkos bellowed in return and leaped at him, axe leading.

Varash sidestepped and sliced the traitor's leg off at the knee, sending him skidding and bleeding across the floor. There was a roar from the crowd, and the lord of the dreadhold raised his blade in salute to his warriors, drinking in the applause.

He approached the stricken Hakkos, grabbed the warrior around the neck, and hauled him upright to stare into his ruined face.

'You betray me?' he growled. 'You think to cut me down? You? I am here by Archaon's command, you pitiful worm.'

He smashed a fist into Hakkos' face, and hurled the broken man to the floor.

'Witness this, you filth,' he roared, and he felt blood trickle from his shattered eye socket. It had never healed, but he welcomed the agony, drank it all in. 'Follow me and I'll lead you to a slaughter that the Blood Lord himself won't be able to tear his gaze from. Challenge me and I'll tear the skin from your bones. I'll drink your blood, you witless vermin.'

He drew his flensing knife from his belt, a short, wicked blade with a pronounced curve. He kneeled down beside Hakkos, felt ropes of bloody saliva drape across his chin.

'Flay me alive, will you?' he laughed, grabbing a fistful of the man's lank hair. 'Put out my eye?'

He leaned in close, and the smell of gore, sweat and fear was exquisite.

'We can do better than that,' he hissed, and brought the knife down.

Hakkos' scream was a pitiful, high-pitched thing, drowned amongst the blood-crazed cheers of the men of the dreadhold.

Sun broke across the Roaring Plains, drenching the land in soft crimson light. The sky was a blood-red promise of agony and slaughter. Lord Varash Sunken-Eye savoured it like a fine wine.

The warrior stood at the very top of the great Manticore Tower, looking out across the jagged, broken earth towards the west.

From here he could see the mouth of Splitskull Pass, beyond which were camped the numberless orruk hordes, mere miles from his position. He glanced down and smiled as he looked upon the flayed, ruined corpse of Hakkos, impaled on the spikes of the fortress wall. A satisfying kill, but little more than a momentary distraction from the real enemy.

The Blood God's favoured and the endless hordes of the orruks were well acquainted. They had slaughtered each other across the Roaring Plains for centuries beyond counting, and no fortress there had seen more bloodshed than the Manticore Dreadhold. It had almost become a ritual by now; the green-skinned beasts would sally forth, hollering and screeching their war cries as they poured towards the dreadhold, drawn by the promise of death and slaughter. Warriors of Chaos would meet them just as eagerly, keen axes swinging. Khorne himself would smile to see such carnage. But this was the orruks' land, and their numbers were beyond counting. They would take the dreadhold, they would deface its ruinous icons and the grand statue of Archaon and then, idiot brains sated by battle for a short while, they would retreat back to their stinking hovels. Archaon would rage at the creatures' impertinence, and order fresh defences and reinforcements. And the cycle would begin again.

Save that Varash Sunken-Eye was in charge now, and he had no intention of letting it happen again.

'The wretches have been quiet lately,' came the voice of the Slaughterpriest Slaadh, Varash's second in command. The towering warrior loped towards the Chaos lord, and Varash caught the sound of weight dragging across stone. Slaadh still favoured his left leg, the result of a wicked strike from an orruk flail that had torn most of the flesh from his right.

'We hurt them last time,' said Varash. 'The orruks are reckless, but their leader is no fool. He bides his time, replenishes his ranks. This is a place of strength for them.'

'So it is for us. The blood we have spilled here...' Slaadh ran a dry, torn tongue across his razor-filed teeth, and blood stained his lips scarlet. 'Our master does not forget our sanguine offering. The orruks will come again soon and we will make a mountain of their skulls.'

'Do not underestimate them,' said Varash. 'The creatures have routed this place twice already. I saw Archaon's fury when they defaced his great statue. I was one of the few to survive it.'

Slaadh grinned. 'That is why we are here,' he said. 'The Everchosen sends his favoured killers. He gives us a flesh offering that will drown these plains in blood.'

Varash nodded and wiped away a trail of blood from his eye. He had earned his name thanks to the tender administrations of an orruk war-chief. The beast's club had smashed into the Chaos lord's eye, shattering the socket and pulping the orb within. Such a wound would cripple a mortal warrior's ability to fight, but these days Varash was some way away from being mortal.

A fresh lance of agony stabbed through his skull, and Varash growled, grinding a mailed fist into the ruined socket. Every moment during which the Sunken-Eye was not spilling blood he was plagued with nausea and sharp, unforgiving headaches. Only in battle, only when he was claiming skulls and souls in the name of his dark master, was Varash free of this constant discomfort.

Screams echoed up the winding stairs of the tower. The gore-priests had begun carving their runes.

'No more waiting,' growled Varash. His ruined eye was drooling blood again, and it stained his vision crimson. 'No more *defending*.' The word left an acrid taste in his mouth. 'We will carve open the sky and birth an army that will rip and tear its way across the Roaring Plains.'

'The witchkin is already weaving his magic,' said Slaadh, not bothering to mask his disdain and revulsion. Followers of the Blood God put no stock in weakling magic-users. Only fear of

Varash had prevented his pet sorcerer from being torn limb from limb the moment he set foot in the Manticore Dreadhold. If his men did not shed blood soon, they would become even more restless. The Chaos lord cared nothing for the sorcerer's life, of course. Once he had finished what needed to be done, Varash had half a mind to tear the snivelling wretch's heart out himself.

No. Patience. Varash relished the flow of spilt blood as much as any warrior of Khorne, but he was no gore-crazed, reckless fool. That was why he was so high in the favour of the Everchosen, and why he had been trusted to defend the dreadhold.

'Gather a raiding party,' he said to the Slaughterpriest. 'Send them out through the pass. Have them bring back more bodies for Xos'Phet's ritual.'

'And some meat for the cooking fires,' said Slaadh, wistfully. 'We haven't eaten well in a good long time.'

'We were foolish,' said the scarred woman, and Lord-Celestant Mykos Argellon could hear the anger and shame in her words.

'We were hunting, and seeking water,' she continued. 'It has been a hard season, and our supplies are low. We rode hard, day and night, and when we came upon the spring I let my warriors drink deeply. We let our guard down for a moment, and they were on us.'

She spat. 'Foolish. They hacked our mounts to pieces, killed Jevir and a dozen others. The rest of us ran.'

'And you survived,' said Thostos Bladestorm.

The woman looked up and stared right at the Lord-Celestant. Her wolf-grey eyes met his own unnerving gaze and did not falter for a moment.

'They could have slaughtered us all, but instead they welcomed the chase. We made good sport.'

'What do they call you?' asked Mykos.

'I am Alzheer Nahazim,' the woman said. 'And this is what is left of my hunt.'

As she gestured, one of the prisoners let out a low groan and doubled over. Alzheer rushed to his side. Thick leaves of grass were bound around the man's waist, stained a dark red. Alzheer gently removed them, and Mykos caught a glimpse of angry purple. Blood poured from the man's midriff, and his pale face contorted in agony. A gut wound. If it was as bad as it looked, it was fairly remarkable that the man had made it this far. The Celestial Vindicators could do little to help. They carried no medical supplies, and the healing touch of Lord-Castellant Eldroc's warding lantern only soothed the wounds of the storm-forged scions of Azyr.

'How many of your people live?' asked Mykos.

She shrugged. 'We number a few thousand. Perhaps less, now. As I say, it has been a hard season. The orruks grow restless, and several of our hunting parties have disappeared without trace. Without food and water...'

Thostos turned to Mykos, and signalled him and the Lord-Castellant Eldroc over. The trio moved away from the prisoners, and were joined by Prosecutor-Prime Evios Goldfeather and Axilon, the Knight-Heraldor.

'What do we do with them?' asked Eldroc. 'They may look savage, but they do not bear the marks of Chaos.'

'Lord-Castellant,' said Evios, 'I do not think we can discount the possibility that these mortals may have been corrupted by the dark powers. We shouldn't blindly trust them simply because they aren't covered in flayed skulls and severed extremities.'

Mykos frowned. 'Neither should we judge them simply because they aren't well-dressed enough for your liking, Prosecutor-Prime. Look around you. This is a harsh place, and it breeds hard people.'

Goldfeather's helm twitched slightly, and for a moment it seemed like the Prosecutor was about to argue the point. Instead he nodded abruptly, and fell silent.

'We leave them,' said Thostos.

'They will die here,' said Mykos. 'They have no mounts and they're deep in hostile territory. They're exhausted and malnourished. Why did we save their lives, if we are simply to abandon them now?'

'We cannot spare the men to guard them, and we do not have time to wait for mortals to keep up with us,' said Thostos. 'They will obstruct our mission.'

'Our duty is to protect the sons and daughters of Sigmar,' said Mykos.

'You are wrong. Our duty, our only duty, is to defeat the forces of Chaos. If we fail to take the Manticore Dreadhold, the life of every mortal in this region is forfeit. Do not let emotion blind you to the importance of our task.'

'We do not know the Roaring Plains,' insisted Mykos. 'These people do. They have survived here against all the odds. Their resilience and bravery is not in doubt, and their advice may be invaluable.'

Thostos looked out across the plain. Carrion birds were already circling above the piles of dead orruks. The wind was picking up again, whistling as it whipped through the clusters of long grass.

'If they fail to keep the pace, we will not stop for them,' he said. 'Keep them under watch at all times.'

By the time the column was moving once more, the field of dead orruks was almost entirely carpeted by scavengers. Rat-mawed canine beasts ripped and tore, snapping at each other as often as they did the flesh of the corpses. Wiry, vicious-looking avian creatures tore strips of skin free and gobbled them down, while the ground itself began to crumble away as something unseen opened up great sinkholes to claim its own meal. Mykos Argellon watched the carnage with a kind of horrified fascination. Before the Stormcasts had passed out of sight of the battlefield, almost every scrap of matter had already been dragged away or consumed, even the orruks' thick iron armour.

'So much for the orruks stumbling across our little encounter,' said Knight-Heraldor Axilon. 'Almost makes one feel a little hungry, doesn't it?'

'Your appetite concerns me,' replied Mykos.

They advanced out onto the open plain, the Celestial Vindicators setting a fierce pace that quickly saw the craggy foothills shrink into the distance behind them. The prisoners marched along behind the Stormcast column, guarded closely by the Liberators, who formed a rough circle around the group. Despite the harsh pace, the mortals showed no signs of exhaustion, save the wounded man, who was being supported by two of his fellows. His skin was pallid, and sweat poured down his face. It was astonishing that he was still standing, let alone keeping up with the others. Whether that would last, Mykos was uncertain. The Lord-Celestant felt the mortal leader's eyes on his back. He turned, and she met his gaze unbowed.

'What do you seek here, sky warrior?' she said. Her voice had a soft, sing-song quality, at odds with her barbarous appearance.

'Silence,' said Liberator Phalryn, but Mykos held up a hand.

'I cannot tell you,' he said. 'We do not know if you are trustworthy yet, and I will not risk my brothers' lives on a hunch.'

She nodded. 'Wise. But you have no need to mistrust us. You are sons of the Sky God, and you are our salvation. It is written.'

'This Sky God you worship,' asked Mykos. 'Tell me more of him.'

'Zi'Mar, the Rage upon the Storm. It is he who guides our arrows. He who welcomes brave warriors home when they fall in battle. He who blesses the hunt. He is far from us, but his strength guides us still. I am his daughter, and his priestess.'

'You're not exactly what I expect from a priestess, my lady,' said Mykos.

She smiled, pulling aside the leather armour at her neck to reveal a lightning tattoo that reached from beneath her jaw to just above her collarbone. A symbol of a god of the sky, of battle and of lightning. It had been observed before amongst mortals who had survived the age of darkness without succumbing to the wiles of Chaos. Faith in a being as mighty as Sigmar did not die easily, even if the finer details of worship had been altered during the long years of his absence.

'He sent you, didn't he?' she went on. 'He sent you to kill the orruks and help us reclaim our lands.'

Mykos marched beside her in silence for a while.

'No,' he said, finally. The truth was best, always. 'The God-King Sigmar created us, forged us in celestial fire. Our task is to take back the Eight Realms from Chaos and restore the law of order. But we are not here for you. Not today.'

She fell silent for a while.

'Chaos?' she said at last. 'You mean the orruks?'

'No,' Mykos replied. 'Warped human warriors. Minions of the Dark Gods.'

'The Bloodstarved,' she said. 'The men of the fortress.'

'You know of them?'

She nodded. 'Yes. They have held that place for many years. Once their raiding parties were common. Now that the orruks have them holed up in the mountains, they rarely bother us.'

'You don't seem to bear them much ill will,' said Mykos.

'On the plain, everything but your fellow tribesman wants you dead,' she said, and shrugged. 'The Bloodstarved are cruel, and despised amongst my people, but they are one of many foes. For us, it is good that they hold the dark fortress. It keeps the greenskins' eyes fixed on them.'

They walked in silence for a while, Mykos mulling over this latest revelation. The presence of the orruks complicated things, especially since they appeared to be far stronger than the Celestial Vindicators had anticipated, but the fact that the Chaos filth were holed up in the dreadhold could only help their plans.

'We can help you,' Alzheer said at last. 'Whatever you are

looking for here, we can help you find it. The Sky Seekers know every hand-width of this land. It is our home.'

'I believe we can trust you,' Mykos replied, 'but you must understand that this is no simple thing for us to risk. We cannot know for sure that you are not tainted by the touch of Chaos yourselves.'

'Come with us,' said Alzheer. 'Come to the camp of the Sky Seekers, and you will know the truth of my people. We can help you.'

'Enough,' came a growl from ahead, and Mykos saw the blue eyes of Thostos gazing back at them. 'We know our business, and we need no help completing it. There are many miles left to march. Keep up or we will leave you behind.'

Constant, furious motion defined the Roaring Plains. The grass whipped and churned in the howling wind, giving the impression that the Stormcasts were wading through knee-deep water. The flocks of carrion-birds and flying lizards that had feasted on the dead orruks now followed the war party, as if they sensed the strangers' impending doom and were simply waiting for their opportunity to swoop down for the feast. The clouds boiled and surged overhead, and in the distance the striated forks of a lightning storm heralded a rumble of thunder loud enough to shake the earth. The Stormcast Eternals watched as a distant spear of rock was struck by an arc of lightning and exploded into a cloud of shattered stone and displaced dust.

'I do not like how exposed we are out here,' grumbled Axilon. 'It feels like I'm marching out onto a frozen lake with a weight tied around me.'

'Lord-Celestant Thostos!' shouted a Bladestorm warrior at the head of the formation. 'Movement.'

Immediately the Stormcasts moved into position, readying their blades on all sides in case of an ambush. Mykos, Thostos and Lord-Relictor Tharros ran forwards and glanced out across the plain. In the distance, the earth shifted. At first, Mykos thought it was some sort of herd animal that drifted across the plain towards them, but as he came closer he saw the truth of it.

They were plants. Vaguely spherical, enclosed entirely in bands of thorns that protruded like knives from the centre. Each spike was tipped red, as if it had already been doused in the blood of its prey. They roared along on the wind, picking up impressive speed as they bounded and rolled across the plains. They were heading just past the Stormcasts, their path taking them ahead of the front ranks of Liberators by a few dozen meters.

Liberator Iodus strayed too close. One of the razor-spheres veered tightly to the right, lurching so quickly that it seemed more like a hunting creature than a plant. It hurtled through the air, striking Iodus in the chest and wrapping itself around his body with a shriek of scored metal. He gasped in pain, and Mykos was astonished to see the armour that encased the Liberator warp and crack under the pressure.

'Help him!' roared Eldroc, as Stormcasts ran to the prone warrior.

They tugged and hacked at the vines, but could not dislodge them without striking hard enough to damage the stricken warrior. Iodus gasped in agony as his armour began to crumple under the extreme pressure. He was being crushed to death.

'Halt!' shouted Liberator Galven, and Mykos turned to see what had happened.

Alzheer had slipped from the circle of guards, and she rolled right past a Judicator who tried to grab her. As she came up, her hands went to her neck and yanked at the necklace she wore around her throat. It came loose, and Mykos saw her grasp the wicked tooth that sat in the centre in one hand.

He moved to block her, thinking that she was trying to escape them.

Alzheer grabbed her wounded warrior and drove the makeshift blade into his neck. The man's eyes bulged and he gasped in shock.

A mist of blood sprayed across the woman's face, but she did not look away. One calloused hand wrapped the dying warrior's face, and she whispered something in his ear. Her other hand drove the knife in again, and the man's eyes glazed over.

Not wasting a second, Alzheer hauled the body upright, staggered over to where the stricken Stormcast lay, and dropped it to the floor. Blood poured from the dead man's ruined throat, staining the earth a dull brown.

'To the sky, my friend,' said the priestess.

The razor-vine that had wrapped itself around Liberator Iodus went suddenly slack, gently slipping from the Stormcast like an unspooling rope. It whipped across the ground and looped around the bloody corpse. The wicked thorns tore into the dead man's flesh, and the vines pulsed hideously as they began to exsanguinate their fresh prize.

'Back!' shouted Alzheer.

Mykos grabbed her arm and spun her around to face him.

'Drake's blood, woman!' he shouted. 'What have you done?'

She wrenched her arm free.

'He was dying,' she said. 'His death saved your man's life. Blood for blood.'

'Did I not say these people were tainted?' said Goldfeather, who had a javelin readied in one hand. 'Murderous savages.'

'Hold!' shouted Thostos Bladestorm. He was looking back at Liberator Iodus, who was staggering to his feet, aided by several of his fellow warriors. Lord-Castellant Eldroc approached, drawing his celestial lantern. Radiant light washed over the Stormcast's ruptured armour, and the rents in the sigmarite began to heal over. Thostos turned to Alzheer, and blue eyes met unflinching grey.

'You saved me a dead soldier,' said the Lord-Celestant, giving Alzheer the briefest nod. 'You have my gratitude.'

'My lord,' spluttered Evios, 'she butchered her own man, she–'

'Her man had a gut wound, and would have died slowly and

painfully,' said Thostos, and the Prosecutor-Prime seemed to wither under his glare. 'He was done. The priestess made the hard choice. Thanks to her quick thinking, a warrior remains fit for duty.'

The unfortunate mortal's body crumpled as the vine wrapped ever tighter around his frame, squeezing out every drop of blood like juice from a fruit. As they watched, the dead man's skin turned more and more pale, and the vines of the carnivorous plant swelled and took on a crimson hue.

'We should be gone from here,' said Alzheer, staring expressionlessly at the gruesome sight. 'The blood will draw other creatures.'

'We are nearing the mouth of Splitskull Pass,' said Mykos. 'Prosecutor-Prime, take your men and survey the area. Stay out of sight, and report back to me the moment you come into the contact with the enemy.'

Goldfeather was still staring at Alzheer, who was wiping the blood from her hands with fistfuls of grass and muttering some sort of mantra under her breath.

'Of course, Lord-Celestant,' he said, and gave a curt nod.

'We have no time to give your man proper ceremony,' said Thostos. 'Say your words quickly, and then we must continue on.'

'There is no need,' said Alzheer. 'He came from the earth, and he will be claimed by the sky.'

She gestured at the circling flock, who had dropped lower now, anticipating their next meal. Mykos could see wicked toothed bills, curved talons and piercing, hungry eyes.

'His search is over,' said the priestess.

'Well,' said Goldfeather. 'This certainly makes things interesting.'

An orruk camp of colossal size covered the mouth of Splitskull Pass, a sprawling, haphazard mess of crude huts and tents. It stretched at least a mile in every direction, and Evios could see that it contained thousands upon thousands of broad, heavily muscled figures, some milling aimlessly, others lazing in the heat of the sun. Clouds of dust highlighted several small-scale skirmishes dotted all over the camp – with no enemy in sight, it was only a matter of time before orruks began one of their self-destructive brawls. He caught the glint of yellow from their armour, and upon the seemingly endless stream of banners and totem poles was emblazoned an ugly image of a pair of gauntleted hands snapping a bone in two.

The Prosecutors stayed high, and well clear of the camp, using the clouds for cover. Their resplendent wings did not lend themselves to subterfuge, and if even one orruk happened to look up and see them it could spell disaster for the rest of the Stormcasts. It was hardly as if they needed to get any closer, thought Evios. Any fool could see that this force of orruks outnumbered the Celestial Vindicators' own army several times over.

'I've never seen the like,' said Prosecutor Galeth, who was shaking his head in disbelief. 'How can we possibly triumph against such numbers?'

Normally Evios would have chastised the warrior for such a comment, but in the face of the apocalypse gathered below them, it hardly seemed appropriate.

'We cannot break through that,' said Omeris, and there was no fear in his voice, just simple and unavoidable logic. 'Not if we wish to have anyone left to complete our mission.'

'There must be some other way,' said Galeth. 'Some way to circumvent this.'

'Just keep watch over the orruks,' said Evios. 'And keep out of sight. If they move even an inch, I want to know about it. If this force catches us in the open field, we are lost.'

He turned to let the roaring wind fill his wings and carry him back out across the plain towards the main force of the Celestial Vindicators. The Lord-Celestants would not welcome the news he bore.

* * *

'So the pass is blocked,' said Eldroc. 'That complicates things.'

'How many orruks are camped there?' asked Thostos.

'Many thousands,' said Goldfeather. 'Many, many thousands. We did not get close enough to provide an entirely accurate estimation, but their wretched hovels are thick across the ground. I can still smell the stench from here.'

Stormcasts spent so much time with their faces masked beneath their war-helms that, for a leader like Mykos, reading his warriors' voices was almost second nature. He could tell that Evios was worried. That concerned the Lord-Celestant as much as the grim news, because for all his bluster the Prosecutor-Prime was one of his most eager and unflappable fighters. It must be a mighty force indeed that they faced.

'If we strike hard, before they are ready,' said Thostos, 'can we push through their line?'

'They do not have any lines, Lord-Celestant,' said Evios, shaking his head. 'Just one huge mass of iron. A force a quarter of their size could hold that pass. We would be surrounded and picked apart.'

'Then we examine our options,' said Mykos. 'The mortals. Alzheer says they know every inch of this region. Perhaps they know an alternative route through the mountain.'

'Time runs short,' said Eldroc. 'The God-King stressed the importance of completing this mission as quickly as possible. The longer we delay, the more likely it is that the forces of Chaos will discover our presence and reinforce the dreadhold.'

'Then our choices are limited,' said Thostos.

The Lord-Celestant signalled for the mortals to be brought forward, and in short order Liberator Phalryn had gathered them. They looked even more ragged than when they had first been rescued. The Stormcasts had given them what water and food they could spare, but exhaustion and dehydration had already taken their toll. Their lips were cracked and dry, their eyes bloodshot. Mykos felt a stab of guilt for pushing them so hard, but quickly pushed it aside. Better they were given the chance to survive than left to a certain death out on the plain.

Thostos came forward, approaching the priestess and ignoring her fellow warriors.

'You aided us once,' he said. 'I require you to do so again. A large orruk camp blocks Splitskull Pass, preventing us from reaching our objective. We need an alternate route.'

'You seek the dreadhold, and the gate of fire,' said Alzheer, nodding as if that was the clear and obvious answer. 'The Sky Seekers can help you, son of Zi'Mar. There are ways to reach the fortress.'

'You can lead us there?' asked Mykos.

'The paths through the mountain are dangerous and twisted,' said Alzheer. 'To traverse them, we will require the help of my people. I can take you to our camp, and our scouts will be able to guide you.'

Thostos stared into the priestess' eyes, and again she did not avert her gaze.

'I believe that I can trust you,' said the Bladestorm. 'I warn you, however, that if I sense even the slightest hint of betrayal, you and your people will not live long enough to realise the depth of your error.'

Alzheer nodded.

'The God-King granted me this quest, and I will let nothing interfere with its successful completion. We are clear?'

'We are.'

Before the Stormcasts rose two great towers of wind-scoured, vine-wrapped rock, one shaped like a spear, the other a wide, rough semi-circle that enclosed the smaller formation. Together, they provided a small lee of natural cover from the blazing sun, and in this sheltered valley Eldroc could see the leather coverings of tents and yurts. As they marched closer, they saw no occupants.

'We are here,' said Alzheer.

'Abandoned,' said Mykos. 'Perhaps your people came under attack?'

Alzheer simply smiled, put two fingers to her mouth and gave a series of sharp whistles.

Lean human warriors appeared suddenly from every angle, dropping from cleverly disguised apertures in the walls of the mesa, or bursting forth from tents and thickets of grass.

'Shields,' roared Axilon, and the Stormcasts put a wall of sigmarite between themselves and the mortals. Evios and his warrior-heralds took flight, wings glittering in the midday sun as they readied their storm-called javelins.

'Hold,' yelled Alzheer, breaking free from the line of Stormcast Eternals and raising her hands. She approached the tribes-men, speaking fast and low in a language that Eldroc did not understand.

Two warriors came forward, one male and one female. Both wore chitinous chestplates and greaves, painted with the same lightning-bolt sigil that was tattooed upon Alzheer's neck.

'Priestess,' said the woman, coming forward and lowering a forked spear. 'You bring strangers to our home. Well-armed strangers.'

'Saviours,' said Alzheer. 'Warriors of the Sky God, sister. They slaughtered a greenskin warband as if they were lame dogs.'

Mykos came forward. In his turquoise plate, emblazoned with lightning bolts and the flaming comet of Sigmar, his blue eyes blazing through his unforgiving war-mask, he looked every inch the herald of a vengeful god. Several of the mortal warriors dropped to their knees and traced a lightning bolt down their chests with the first two fingers of their free hands. Most stayed standing, weapons levelled and ready. These people have been battered, but their spirit is not broken yet, the Lord-Celestant thought with some admiration.

The female warrior whistled, and looked to her companion.

'He's a big one, alright,' she said.

The other warrior was a wiry, flint-eyed greybeard, still corded with muscle despite his advanced years and obvious signs of malnutrition. He stepped forward, an arrow nocked on his bow but lowered to the floor, and peered at Thostos' armour.

'This metalwork,' he said, and his voice was full of awe. 'I've never seen the like.'

'Elder Diash is our smith and weapon-crafter,' said Alzheer, smiling warmly at the man.

'By which she means I spend my days tying flint to arrows,' said Diash. 'There's no good, solid metal here, sky warrior, unless you fancy asking the orruks for some of theirs. Mind you, don't seem like you need any.'

'This warplate comes from the forge-castles of blessed Azyrheim,' said Mykos. 'It was crafted from the remnants of a dying world, shaped by the matchless skill of the Six Smiths. It has saved my life a hundred times.'

Diash's eyes went wide. He thought for a moment, and then slapped a palm against the rough chitin of his own chestplate.

'Got this from a sand-crab,' he said. 'Biggest one I ever caught. Devilish, irritable little creatures they are, but smoke 'em right and they make a nice meal.'

There was a pause, and then Knight-Heraldor Axilon laughed hard enough to shake the walls of the mesa. Mykos chuckled too, behind his war mask.

'It seems we have much to teach each other, my friend,' he said.

Thostos came forward, and the mortals shied away from his cold glare.

'Enough. We are here to speak with your leaders,' he said.

Diash and his fellow warrior, the tall, scarred woman called Emni, led Mykos, Thostos and their entourage through the camp. Axilon had stayed with the main force, and he and Lord-Relictor Tharros were now organising them into a defensive screen around the encampment. As the tribespeople filtered out of their tents to stare at these elaborately armoured strangers, Mykos began to appreciate just how difficult life must be out on the plains. Barely a single mortal was unmarked by some sign of combat, and not a single one went unarmed. Grey-haired, weather-beaten elders scowled at them suspiciously as they passed, clutching crude daggers and stone hatchets. The younger warriors were better armed, though not by much. They favoured axes and short, curved sabres. Cavalry pieces, designed for slashing and hacking. He noted only a very few children, scrawny little things that stared defiantly at the Celestial Vindicators as they passed.

A circular clearing in the centre of the camp was home to a few-score tired-looking horses, lazily munching on bundles of tall grass. Behind the enclosure was the largest structure in the camp, a vaguely oval tent with a tapered entrance to the fore, guarded by four warriors. It was tall enough for even the Stormcasts to enter without ducking. Several huge, yellowed tusks anchored the structure at each corner, dug deep into the ground and secured with leather straps. Across the floor were scattered hides of all descriptions – great, thick ursine furs, mottled reptilian skins and strange diaphanous veils. In the middle of the tent a great pit had been dug out of the earth and filled with stones, and in the centre of this pit a fire spat embers out across the gathering hall.

Several figures crouched at the far end of the tent, which lay flush to the side of the mesa. They were wrapped in yet more furs, and the light of the fire flickered across them, giving them an eerie look.

There were seven in total, and as Mykos drew nearer he could see that they were of varying age, though all were weathered and bronzed from a life spent under the harsh sun. Two carried great hornpipes, and a slightly nauseous scent of burning spices filled the tent. Smoke spiralled into the air, lending the place a misty, ethereal quality.

'Who do you bring to us, daughter of Zi'Mar?' said the figure on the far left, pulling back the furs he wore to reveal a wizened, lined face with two milky-white eyes. 'They smell of metal, and of the night sky.'

'The Sky God has sent warriors to protect our lands, Elder Patiga,' said Alzheer. She moved to the ancient figure, and gently lifted him up. Holding his hands in her own, she approached Mykos, and he let her run the elder's liver-spotted hands across his gilded armour, tracing the wondrous lion's-head breastplate and the lightning-and-hammer symbol that he wore upon his pauldron.

'Warriors wreathed in metal,' said Patiga, and he shook his head. 'But not orruks! No, no, no. The wind will cease before those brutes learn to craft such wonders.'

'You come to help us wipe out the greenskins,' said another figure, standing and casting off his furs. This one was tall, for a mortal, well muscled and covered in a latticework of scars and burn marks. Trophies hung from his thick leather clothing, finger-bones, ears and teeth taken from slaughtered orruks. Knives were tucked into his armour, and he carried a short, curved blade at his hip. He had shaved his hair, aside from a ponytail that draped down his back, and his beard was thick and wiry.

'No, we do not,' said Thostos, and the speaker's eyes narrowed.

He was a fierce one, this mortal. Mykos sensed the same ruthless competence from him as he had sensed from Alzheer, but while the priestess was measured and calm, this one did not even bother to conceal his anger.

'So why are you here?' the man snapped.

'They seek a way through the mountains, Rusik,' said Alzheer. 'And you will guide them. You know those paths better than any other warrior.'

The man called Rusik narrowed his eyes at the priestess.

'We are tasked with taking the Manticore Dreadhold, a fortress of Chaos,' said Thostos. 'You must have encountered the men that dwell there.'

'They stay in their holes,' said Rusik. 'They barely venture out on the open plain. Because of the orruks. Those creatures have slaughtered thousands of our people. We were once a proud and numerous tribe. We were lords of this plain. Now we are a pitiful remnant of our former selves, a fading shadow.'

'We are not gone yet,' said Alzheer.

'The orruks despoil the land,' said Rusik, his voice rising in anger. 'They slaughter the herdbeasts, they trample the kishwa plants under their iron boots. Hunger and thirst will kill us while we sit here and do nothing.'

'Our cause is more important than the fate of your people,' said Thostos.

'Your cause?' spat the mortal warrior. 'What does your cause matter to us if we are to die here?'

'If we fail, millions of souls will be lost to the Dark Powers,' the Lord-Celestant continued. 'Whether by the next season or the next decade, your people will fall too. I have seen what happens when Chaos conquers, mortal. Trust me when I say that you would not wish to witness it for yourself.'

'You think you can scare me with dire proclamations?' said Rusik, with a bitter laugh. 'The orruks have already burned everything I held dear to the ground.'

He pointed east. 'You wish to die against the walls of the dreadhold? A half day's ride or so and you'll find the entrance to the Dragonmaw Canyons. Find your own damned way through.'

Rusik made to leave. Before he had gone ten paces Thostos had grabbed hold of the man's leather jerkin and hauled him into the air. The Lord-Celestant's eyes held no fury, simply an implacable resolution.

'You will guide us,' he said, and his voice was as cold and steady as the mountains.

Swords were drawn. The guards raised their spears more in alarm than aggression, but several figures emerged from the shadows with more of those wicked cavalry sabres. These men wore black cloaks of raven feathers, and their armour was of better quality than those borne by most of the tribe. Rusik's men, Mykos guessed.

'Thostos,' he hissed. 'Release him. This is not the way.'

The Bladestorm ignored him.

'You think those little blades will scratch sigmarite armour?' growled Thostos, his war-helm less than an inch from Rusik's face. 'You are welcome to test them. Or you could simply guide my warriors to where they need to go, and I will release you. Either way, I am running short on both time and patience. Choose.'

Rusik held out a hand as his men inched forward to surround the Lord-Celestant.

'Hold!' he shouted. 'Sheathe your blades.'

Reluctantly, his entourage did as commanded. Rusik stared into Thostos' eyes with a mixture of fear and anger.

'We will do as you ask,' he said. 'If you wish to die under the shadow of the dreadhold, I will lead you to its gates. Release me.'

Thostos lowered the man to the floor.

Two of Rusik's men rushed to help him as he stumbled, but he battered their outstretched arms aside angrily.

'Very well, noble sky warriors,' he spat. 'I will gather my men. Night falls, and we had best leave soon if we are to reach our destination before dawn.'

With that he stalked from the tent, retinue in tow. An uneasy silence remained.

Eldroc placed the warding lantern on the ground and kneeled in front of it. The celestial energy washed over him, and suddenly his burdens were lifted and his heart soared as if he was back in the throne room of Sigmar, in the presence of his beloved God-King. Doubts and worries vanished in the soothing luminescence. Redbeak growled softly at his side, and the Lord-Castellant ruffled the gryph-hound's neck fondly.

'What do you make of these people?' came a voice at his side, and Eldroc's hand instinctively went to his halberd. Lord-Celestant Thostos stood in the shadows of a nearby tent. He glanced pointedly at the weapon.

'Apologies, Lord-Celestant,' said Eldroc, shaking his head. 'I did not notice your approach.'

Thostos said nothing.

'I think these Sky Seekers are a brave and loyal people,' Eldroc said, gathering his thoughts. 'To have lost so much, to be torn down and hunted like beasts yet still retain their faith. It is humbling.'

'You believe they can be trusted?' asked Thostos.

'I do. Though I am not sure we have much of a choice in the matter regardless.'

The Lord-Celestant nodded. They stood together awhile, watching the sun dip below the far horizon. Mortals moved quietly around the camp, lighting torches and cooking fires.

'The lantern, it gives you comfort?' asked Thostos eventually.

'It… does,' Eldroc replied, surprised at the question. 'It focuses my thoughts, banishes my doubt. '

'You have doubts,' said Thostos. 'About our purpose.'

Eldroc considered his answer. 'Not our purpose,' he said. 'Chaos must be banished, and the rule of law and justice erected in its stead. I question myself. My role in this war. The true cost of fighting it.'

'I do not remember doubt,' said Thostos, and his voice was a mere echo of his usual harsh tone. 'I simply act. The battlefield shifts, and I move with it. I anticipate, I react.'

'Do you remember anything, my friend?' asked Eldroc.

Thostos shook his head. 'Sometimes an image, a sensation of recollection. Then gone. Like grasping smoke.'

'Sit with me, my friend,' said the Lord-Castellant, gesturing to a spot next to Redbeak. 'Let the lantern's light soothe you. I will tell you of our time in the Gladitorium. It will all come back, if we give it time.'

Thostos hesitated, then took a step forward.

Redbeak rolled upright, feathered ears narrowed to dagger-points, eyes shining in the light of the campfires. He let out a harsh shriek, and pawed and scraped at the ground.

Eldroc and Thostos had their blades drawn in an instant. One did not ignore the warnings of a sharp-eared gryph-hound. From the darkness beyond the ring of tents, dozens of flaming projectiles launched into the air, arcing up high to fall into the camp. The screams began.

'Ready the men,' said Thostos, and his voice was pitilessly calm once more. 'Take Phalryn and his Liberators and secure the camp.'

Without a single glance backwards, the Lord-Celestant charged off through the tents, into the darkness.

Arrows whickered through the air, pinpricks of searing light amongst the darkness. The flaming arrowheads slammed into the rawhide tents, and fire spread across the village as dry brush combusted. More screams rent the air.

Out came the Stormcast lines, Liberators angling their great shields up to intercept the barrage, while the Judicators searched the horizon, looking for targets. The Stormcasts could pick none out in the pitch black, though the arc of the flaming arrows revealed their likely position some hundred yards away from the tribal camp.

'Take them down!' roared Thostos, and a torrent of silver flame rippled away into the darkness as the Judicators loosed. Liberators advanced under the storm of fire, trusting in the skill of their brothers as projectiles whipped past them.

Figures emerged from the gloom. Burly, heavily muscled men in scraps of leather armour and chain, wielding axes and spiked clubs. Their eyes gleamed in the darkness, burning with foul bloodlust.

As strong as the battle-joy of the savages was, the rage of the Celestial Vindicators was equal to it. Of all the Stormhosts of Sigmar, they were the fiercest and most implacable foes of Chaos. Every single one of the turquoise warriors had lost something irreplaceable to the depredations of the Dark Gods, and though the trauma of Reforging had stolen the memory of that loss from many a Vindicator, the white-hot, raging hatred of Chaos remained.

They met the enemy head on, and neither side gave a solitary moment of quarter.

'Death to the servants of Chaos!' roared Thostos, leaping into battle with his sword leading. His blade pierced the chest of a loping warrior, and as the dying wretch collapsed to the ground, the Lord-Castellant spun expertly to crash his hammer into the bare, scarred chest of another.

These were scraps, he realised. Not the heavily armoured, battle-forged avatars of destruction that formed the elite of a Khornate army, but the filthy, gore-drunk masses that comprised its meat. Numbers, and not skill, made such creatures dangerous. This was a raiding party, searching for fresh meat to devour, and not a warband.

Against the roused fury of the Celestial Vindicators, the enemy would be completely outmatched.

Judicators lit up the night with streams of starfire, their bolts and arrows illuminating the carnage of the assault and burning smoking holes through any servants of Chaos unfortunate enough to get in the way. The ripples of glowing ammunition strobed across the darkness, lending a bizarre, dreamlike quality to the battle.

Thostos saw a tall, broad-chested creature barrel towards him, its bloated forearms capped with blood-soaked, rusting cleavers. The afterglow remained etched across his vision as the archers reloaded, and he made a split-second guess as to where he should strike. He held his hammer up defensively and swiped across with his sword. There was a wet impact, and a howl of pain.

Again the battlefield was washed in blinding light as the archers loosed again, and Thostos saw the brute reel backwards, belly opened.

'Leave none alive,' he shouted above the clangour of battle.

Rusik crept through the night, curved blade drawn and readied. He had already cut down two howling, shrieking bloodreavers that had rushed at him from the darkness, swinging their meat cleavers and drooling bloody spittle. He had savoured the scrape of bone as his sword ran down the spine of one, laughed as he took the hand from the second with a savage swipe.

He remembered leaning down beside his stricken opponent, enjoying the fool's last gasps of desperate agony. His blade had come down, again and again and again. Things had gone black for a while, and when Rusik had regained control of his senses there was little more left before him than a gutted, ruptured pile of flesh. He could taste blood at the back of his throat, and his hands were caked with gore.

He shook off his disturbing thoughts. What did it matter how he killed the enemy, so long as the job was done? Leave Alzheer and her rabble to their endless talking. He would do what no one else could. He would protect their ancient lands, against the orruks and against whoever else tried to take what was his.

Rusik came around the side of a burning tent, stepping over two dead warriors. Besik and Tavo. Alzheer's loyal men, so no great loss. Men who would rather run and hide from the greenskins than meet their fate in honest battle. Cowards. Arrows protruded from their chests, still smouldering. Besik had also taken one in the neck. Rusik smelled burned flesh.

He looked up, and he saw her again.

A shiver ran down his spine, and his heart hammered in his chest. There she was, as beautiful and strong as the day they had met.

'Zenia,' he whispered, and the figure turned to him and smiled. Then she faded into nothingness.

'No!' he shouted, scrambling across the carnage of the battle-field towards the spot where she had stood. 'No! Zenia, come back to me!'

With the encampment aflame, the enemy dropped their bows and drew their crude weapons, desperate to shed blood face to face. They charged into the burning camp, expecting, perhaps, to meet beleaguered mortal warriors in battle. Foes that could be hacked apart, torn down and excruciated, their remains carried off to the cooking pits for the night's feast.

Instead, they met a wall of unyielding sigmarite, and the blades of the Celestial Vindicators.

Oh, it was good to match blades against the eternal foe once more, thought Mykos Argellon, smiling broadly as he sliced Mercutia diagonally through the torso of a shrieking berserker. The filth fell apart in two neat pieces, and the Lord-Celestant slammed the pommel of his grandblade into the face of another screaming warrior. The blood-starved wretch spat teeth, and staggered backwards. Mykos followed, crashing the pommel into the man's face again and again. Finally his enemy toppled to the ground, his skull little more than a ruined crater.

This was what they had been created for. This was the honest freedom of battle against a hated foe.

Another volley from the Judicators rippled through the ranks of the blood-crazed enemy, and dozens came apart in a lightning burst of gore and scorched flesh.

She waited for him at the twins. This had been their place, once. They had sneaked away in the night, he from the warriors' tents, she from her father, who had never approved. They had never had much time together. There was always the hunt, always the threat of a warband appearing on the horizon. They had lived their lives in snatched moments, even when the priestesses had blessed them and their son had been born. Even afterwards.

As he clambered onto the taller of the two rocks, he saw her. She turned to him and smiled.

'Husband,' she said. 'Do you remember?'

The figure shifted, becoming an insubstantial cloud of mist. Within its limits Rusik could see the same images that had haunted him every single night since he had lost her. He saw the charging orruks, raising and swinging their jagged cleavers. He saw his son, brave little Achren, fall, trampled under their iron boots. He saw Zenia, her own sword wet with enemy blood, a song of vengeance upon her lips. Spears ran her through from all sides, and she arched her back and screamed in agony. She turned to him. Her dead eyes bored into his own, and Rusik felt her agony, her sense of betrayal. A pair of mighty hands closed around her neck, gauntleted in jagged yellow iron. There was a sickening snap. Zenia fell, and so did Rusik.

'I tried to reach you,' he sobbed, collapsing to his knees. 'I did. I rode my steed until it collapsed, and then I dragged myself for miles across the plains. I was too late.'

'Such bravery, husband,' his dead wife snarled. She lay in a pool of blood, her head swivelling on a broken neck with a groan of creaking cartilage. 'Tell your dead son how you tried so hard to reach him. Tell your fellow tribesmen, left bleeding and broken.'

'Zenia, please,' he begged, hot tears running down his cheeks.

'You were weak,' she snarled, beautiful face twisted with pain and hatred. 'You let them die. Worse, you left them unavenged.'

'I have killed so many of them,' said Rusik, shaking his head.

'You think cutting down a few scouts assuages your sins?' Zenia spat. 'You think our tortured souls can be soothed by such paltry offerings? No, *husband.*' She made the word a curse.

'Only when the plains run red with orruk blood will we be calmed,' she continued. 'And your pitiful Sky God cannot give you the strength to do this. He has abandoned you, husband. You know it to be true.'

'He sends warriors,' said Rusik. 'Giants in fine metal armour.'

Zenia was silent for a moment. 'And these warriors have pledged their aid to you in destroying the orruks?' she asked.

'No,' growled Rusik. 'They refuse to aid us, and say they have their own mission here.'

'Then they are no servants of Zi'Mar,' said Zenia. 'They are impostors, and they mean to use our people to achieve their own ends. They are not to be trusted. There is only one power in the realms that can offer you what you seek.'

'Tell me,' pleaded Rusik. 'I will do anything to avenge you, my love.'

Zenia smiled a blood-red smile.

Eldroc strode through the wreckage of the camp, Redbeak at his side. The Lord-Castellant's anger rose as he passed fallen mortals riddled with arrows and burned by the rising flames. The surviving tribespeople stared out from the ruins of their tents, faces blackened by smoke. He saw no fear or anger on their faces, just the weary resignation of a people worn down by constant war. He leaned down and gathered up the body of a fallen youth, pale hands clasped around the wicked arrow shaft that had pierced his belly.

The Lord-Castellant laid the corpse down in a row next to a score of other casualties. The boy's dead eyes were wide with pain and shock. Eldroc brushed them closed, snapped off the arrow shaft, and crossed the dead youth's hands over his chest in the same manner as his fellows. He caught Elder Diash's eyes, and the old man nodded gratefully.

'I am sorry for your losses,' said the Lord-Castellant. He felt as if he should say something more, but words escaped him. He was not used to dealing with mortals.

'We will commit their flesh and their souls to the Sky God,' said Diash. 'They will return to the earth, where they will remain with us, always.'

Eldroc bowed, intrigued by the strangeness of the nomads' rituals. Stormcasts were deeply faithful, but that faith was rooted in the physical presence of a living, breathing god. These mortals had survived centuries without a glimpse of their deity, and even in the midst of terrible loss and hardship, they still believed. That impressed and terrified him in equal measure. Would he fight so hard in Sigmar's absence, he wondered? He supposed he had, once. That was the hallmark of a Celestial Vindicator's ascension, after all.

The Lord-Castellant was shaken from his musing by the sound of armoured boots. He turned and saw Mykos Argellon approach, wiping his grandblade clean of gore with a few strands of grass.

'They have scattered,' he said. 'The scum didn't put up much of a fight.'

'I don't believe they expected to find us here,' replied Eldroc. 'They meant to draw the tribespeople out. To capture as many of them as they could.'

'For what reason?' asked Mykos.

'Who knows?' replied Eldroc. 'Perhaps they require slaves. Perhaps they require food.'

Mykos shook his head in disgust. 'Cannibals. How does a man fall so far?'

'I have long since ceased asking myself that question,' Eldroc replied. 'Where is Thostos?'

'Somewhere out there,' said Mykos. Eldroc could tell his friend was attempting to keep his tone neutral. 'He took a score of warriors with him in pursuit of the fleeing enemy. He wants them all dead, so none can reveal our presence to the main host.'

'Sound strategy,' said Eldroc.

'I suppose so,' replied Mykos.

Eldroc sighed. 'Speak, brother, I beg you. I have suffered enough brooding silences of late to last me several lifetimes.'

'You wish me to talk directly?' said Mykos, a hint of anger in his voice. 'Very well. The Bladestorm is a danger to his men. He is no longer the hero that led your chamber to victory at the Eldritch Fortress. You must see it.'

'I see a man traumatised by the torture he has suffered in pursuing a just cause. I see a man who has survived unthinkable agonies, and yet continues to fight against the darkness with all the strength he can muster.'

'Lord-Castellant–' Mykos said, shaking his head.

'With respect, Lord-Celestant,' said Eldroc, 'you are yet to experience the true cost of this war we fight. You have not been reforged a second time.'

The Lord-Castellant stared out across the field of corpses.

'Agony,' he said at last. 'An infinity of torment. And at the centre of it all, a sure knowledge that you will never be the same even if you survive. It almost broke me, Argellon.'

'Yet you remain calm. Thoughtful,' said Mykos. 'You do not carelessly risk your life or those of our fellow warriors.'

'I can afford to be the voice of reason. Thostos must lead. He must be the epitome of what every Celestial Vindicator aspires to be. That is no easy task, especially for one suffering as he is. Yet despite your concerns, Thostos has not led us astray.'

'He has been reckless,' insisted Mykos.

Eldroc turned to the Lord-Celestant.

'Are you sure it is the Lord Bladestorm that concerns you, my friend?' he asked, softly.

Mykos bristled. 'What do you imply, Lord-Castellant?'

'Thostos unnerves you because you know that in time every Stormcast Eternal will fall in battle. Including you.'

'I do not fear death,' said Mykos.

'But we do not talk of death, do we?' Eldroc replied. 'You are a man who prides himself on his humanity, and the thought of losing your grip on that is what you fear.'

Mykos said nothing.

'I tell you truly, my friend,' said Eldroc. 'The Reforging was a crucible that almost destroyed me, but I came out of it a stronger man, and a greater warrior. Thostos will too.'

Mykos shook his head. 'I hear your words, my friend, but I know you do not believe what you say. I see the way you look at him. I hear the concern in your voice when you speak his name. You are as afraid at what is happening to Thostos as anyone.'

Varash heard the sorcerer's cackling before he even entered the grand tower. It was a high-pitched, joyless sound, and he had only ever heard the stunted whelp utter it when he was taking some poor wretch apart on the ritual tables. It echoed around him as he climbed the circular steps that wound towards the battlements. Even now, before they had begun the ritual proper, blood was dripping down the central shaft of the tower, pooling in the recesses of the great bronze skull that adorned the ground floor chamber.

'Yes, yes, yes!' came that voice again. 'Scream and curse all you like, for all the good it's going to do you. You cannot halt progress, my unfortunate friend.'

Reaching the top step, Varash swung the wrought-iron door open and stepped out into a scene of butchery.

The gorepriests were busy removing the innards of the latest unfortunates to be chosen for Xos'Phet's haruspicy. They worked in silence, mouths stitched closed – the sorcerer hated any noise while he worked, save for his own blathering – and dirty smocks stained red and brown with dried viscera.

The centre of the tower was slightly concave, forming an oval bowl into which drained the blood of the slaves and prisoners that had been sacrificed in the name of the sorcerer's work. Running around the outside of the tower were cages, and as Varash passed he saw dead-eyed mortals stare out at him. They no longer screamed or begged. They knew that doing so would only mark them as the next to be given to the gorepriests.

Xos'Phet stood on the other side of the charnel pit. Before him was a wooden rack, upon which was impaled the hulking, green-skinned figure of an orruk shaman, its eyes and mouth stitched shut. The sorcerer turned.

'Lord Sunken-Eye,' he chirped, in that obsequious squeal that made Varash want to crush his skull to dust. 'We have made much progress today, much progress.'

The sorcerer was hardly an imposing figure. A stick-thin sliver of a man wrapped in blood-stained purple robes, he hardly reached past Varash's waist. He was bald and ill-looking, with watery eyes and a mouthful of yellowed teeth. The right side of his face, from temple to chin, was covered in iridescent scales like those of a fish, no doubt the result of some sorcerous accident. Varash despised every inch of the man.

'You will make this work,' he said, and it was not a question.

Xos'Phet wiped blood from his face with the hem of his robe, and gave a grin that turned his sallow face into a leering skull.

'Oh yes,' said the sorcerer. 'So much power here. The gate of the Manticore, it has been doused in blood, saturated in it. They sense it. They taste it. All that is left is to send the invitation.'

'You asked for more slaves for the sacrifice,' said Varash. 'I have already dispatched a raiding party, and they should return soon with fresh mortals.'

Xos'Phet giggled, and foamy yellow froth formed at the corner of his mouth.

'Oh, I'm afraid not, Lord Varash,' he said. 'I'm afraid your little man-eaters have run into some trouble.'

He made a series of intricate gestures with his wrinkled hands, and the blood pooling in the grooves of the stone floor dribbled into the air, coming together to form a flat, circular disk. The blood-mirror shimmered, and an image formed like a reflection on the surface of a lake. It was dark, and hard to pick out, but Varash saw dozens of torn and broken corpses scattered across a field of grass. They wore scraps of leather and chain, and their flesh was marked and seared with both old ritual scars and fresher wounds. His men, he realised.

'Dead,' he growled. 'Orruks?'

'No,' replied Xos'Phet. 'Something far more interesting. Observe.'

As the sorcerer gestured at the image, a towering armoured figure stepped into view. This warrior was broad and tall, his imposing physique exacerbated by wondrously crafted warplate decorated with lighting bolts and the angry maw of a lion. His helm was a stern mask of cold fury, and he carried a warhammer and longsword of equally magnificent quality as his armour.

'Sigmar's whelps,' snarled Varash, and cursed.

'They fight impressively,' said Xos'Phet. 'Perhaps as well as you and your chosen warriors. None of your scouts will return, and they will bring with them no fresh meat for the sacrifice.'

Varash grabbed one of the gorepriests around the neck, and smashed the mute creature's head into the table upon which he was working. Once, twice, three times. He felt its skull collapse and let the dead thing fall to the ground. The Stormcasts, these warriors called themselves. They had fallen to earth on bolts of lightning in all corners of the realms, taking the fight to the bastions of Chaos with the sickening fervour of the righteous. At any other time, Varash would have welcomed their appearance and the opportunity to match blades with the preening upstarts, but the timing here was too delicate for such complications.

'Do not be concerned, Lord Sunken-Eye,' said Xos'Phet. 'I have taken steps. We will have our sacrifices.'

'Explain.'

The sorcerer's eyes flared suddenly, and his smile disappeared. Xos'Phet might be a stunted weakling, but he was not used to being spoken to in such a manner.

'The human tribes that dwell here are on the verge of extinction,' the sorcerer said. 'They are weak and near broken, and in the absence of hope all that is left to them is shame and regret. Easy emotions to prey upon.'

He waved a pallid hand, and the blood-mirror warped and twisted again, now showing a solitary mortal warrior kneeling amongst several corpses. The man shook and wrapped his arms around himself, and Varash realised he was sobbing.

'In truth I am not so skilled at the more delicate uses of magic,' said Xos'Phet, considering the weeping figure. 'This one, however, barely needed any prodding at all. It is all in hand, Lord Varash. I will have my subjects and you will have the opportunity not only to wipe out the orruk threat, but to take care of these new interlopers as well.'

He snapped his fingers and the blood-mirror collapsed. The sorcerer crossed to the inner wall, and Varash followed. They looked out across the courtyard, to the rear wall where the fortifications met the mountain. Rough stone steps wound into the rock, leading up to the hollowed-out platform upon which the gigantic Manticore Realmgate stood. Tendrils of baleful red light lashed across its rune-scarred surface, bathing the rear of the fortress in a crimson glow. Above the gate, crouching with wings outstretched and so intricately carved and engraved it seemed perpetually on the verge of bursting into life, was the gate's namesake, a monstrous, bat-winged fiend with a leonine head.

'See how it hungers, Lord Varash?' whispered Xos'Phet, staring at the portal like a starving man at a grand feast. 'Such incredible power. This realmgate is different. It has been awakened, weaned on blood and fear. Given the proper sacrifice, it will birth a legion that will drown the Roaring Plains in blood.'

The sorcerer looked up at him, crimson light shimmering in his eyes and across the iridescent scales that marked his face.

'I will unlock the secrets of this realmgate, and you will have your army. And together we will tear the Mortal Realms apart.'

CHAPTER THREE

The Manticore Dreadhold

They said goodbye to their dead upon the dawn. There was little ritual to speak of; a score of tribespeople slain in the raid were carried out of the town to a cluster of flat-topped rocks stained a vibrant green with moss and lichen. While several of the elders droned a deep, sonorous prayer, the bodies were laid gently upon the stone, hands crossed over their hearts and eyes open towards the sky.

As the funeral party made their way back to town, the carrion birds began to descend, in a flock thick enough to blot out the early morning sun. They whirled and circled, a murmuration of black and grey specks that was oddly beautiful despite its predatory intent.

'There's a savage sort of poetry to it,' said Knight-Heraldor Axilon, glancing back. 'Though I'm not sure I would choose to be devoured by crows upon my death.'

'Death feeds life,' said Alzheer, priestess of the Sky Seekers. She still wore her leather armour, and carried a curved blade at her hip. 'We return our bodies to the sky, and begin the circle anew.'

'I am sorry for your losses,' said Lord-Celestant Mykos Argellon.

'They would be much greater if you had not been there to defend us,' said Alzheer. 'We will not forget this.'

'I wish I could promise your people more than further battle and bloodshed,' said Mykos. 'I wish I could say that the armies of Azyr will pour into this realm and make it safe for humanity once more, let you hunt the plains and grow your crops in peace.'

He shook his head, and lifted his war helm. It was the first time he had done so in her presence. His skin was a rich, dark black, almost perfect in complexion, unmarked at all by the many battles he must have fought. He had a round, boyish face, topped with a strip of shaved hair that ran down the centre of his skull.

She looked upon him, and for a moment she was surprised that she pitied him. His fight would never end, she knew. There must be uncounted realms that were equally stricken as this one, endless, shattered remnants of humanity praying desperately for relief from the long darkness. Mykos and his warriors would likely never see their task completed. How could even warriors as brave, as skilled as this defy so great an evil as the shadow that lay across the world?

'I can only promise that the Celestial Vindicators will make our enemies pay,' he said, and there was a fire in his voice that she had not heard before. His stark brown eyes bored into her. 'We will seek them wherever they hide, in their fortresses where they think themselves safe from justice. We will tear down their walls, and we will put them to the sword. They will die as their victims did, begging for a mercy I shall not grant them.'

As quickly as it had flared, his rage was gone. He blinked and swallowed, and looked almost surprised at his own vehemence. She smiled sadly, and traced her fingers across the lion carved upon his breastplate.

'Your vengeance is Zi'Mar's justice,' she said. 'But do not lose yourself in it, my friend. You are a good man, in a world where few exist. Do not let revenge define you.'

They did not spare much time for grief. Led by the warrior Rusik's horsemen, the Celestial Vindicators made good time to the mouth of the Dragonmaw Canyons. It was easy to see how they had earned their name. Jutting out of the low range of mountains like a snapping jaw, the entrance was a jagged cluster of sharp stone that seemed almost impassable, a twisting spiral of serrated rock keen enough to draw blood. As the Stormcasts approached, a thunderous rumble shook the earth beneath their feet. It was a drawn-out, grating roar, the sound of a hundred fortress walls collapsing.

'The earth here, it moves and shifts,' said Rusik. 'One moment the path through the mountain may be clear, the next it is a forest of razor-sharp stone.'

'Then how in Sigmar's name are we going to march several hundred plate-armoured warriors through it?' snapped Prosecutor-Prime Goldfeather.

'We will pass through because I know this land well, and I know when it is about to betray me. Priestess, I will need your riders,' Rusik said. 'We will scout ahead on horseback, find a route through. Once we are sure, we will send back a rider to signal that things are safe and guide you in.'

'You require every single rider?' asked Lord-Celestant Argellon.

Rusik nodded. 'These canyons are vast, and not friendly to trespassers. Many dangerous creatures hunt within.'

Alzheer's force numbered around a hundred mortals, fifty or so on horseback and the rest lightly armoured skirmish troops carrying bows and simple hatchets. Rusik led another fifteen horse riders – dour, battle-scarred men who eyed the Stormcasts sullenly. Clearly their leader had not extolled the virtues of the Celestial Vindicators to them after his treatment at the hands of Thostos.

'Be careful, priestess,' said Mykos as Alzheer made her way over to Rusik's band.

'I am always careful, my friend,' she replied. 'And besides, I would not miss the chance to see you and your warriors in battle once again.'

As she and the rest of the riders filtered into the maze of jagged rocks, Mykos Argellon got the uneasy impression that those had been the last words he would ever hear her speak.

Diash felt the hard ground beneath him clatter his old bones with every step taken by the ancient, rheumy horse that carried him. Not for the first time he wondered why he had decided to join this damned fool expedition. He had never intended to. Then that foul-tempered troublemaker Rusik had opined loudly that it was good he was not coming, as coddling old, frail warriors past their prime would only slow them down. Well, he could hardly stay after that, could he?

They had been travelling for almost an hour now, and the sunlight of the plain had given way to a gloomy darkness as the canyon walls loomed overhead, knotted together far above with a canopy of twisting vines. As they rounded a sharp turn, dust fell from the canyon wall, and another loud groan echoed around them.

This was a cursed place, as the tales said.

'Stay close,' growled Rusik, at the head of the line. 'Another five hundred yards and we will send back a rider to the sky warriors.'

As he spoke his men, identifiable by those ragged, crow-skin cloaks, dropped back to the flanks. Their hands rested on their curved sabres, ready to draw at a moment's notice. Diash frowned. A lot of good that would be in such tight quarters. It would take a single rockfall or a few good bowmen to end this little expedition in short order.

'I do not like this place,' said Emni, riding at his side. 'It has an ill feeling.'

They emerged from the tight canyon into a small, oval clearing, mottled with fallen sunlight. Vines wrapped around the edges of the space, pouring forth from the pockmarked and crumbling walls. Here the canyon forked left and right, and Rusik's men spread out to guard each exit.

'We are stopping here?' asked Alzheer. 'We should send back a messenger to inform the Stormcasts that it is safe to progress.'

A blood-curdling roar split the air, echoing loud enough that Diash cursed and covered his ears. Then, the sound of dozens of iron boots rattling on stone.

'Orruks!' shouted Alzheer, drawing her sword.

'No,' said Rusik softly. His own blade was in his hand. He sliced it into the neck of Alzheer's horse, and the animal gave a horrifying shriek, rearing and kicking out as arterial blood fountained into the air. Alzheer gasped and toppled from her mount, and the beast collapsed on top of her, writhing and whinnying.

'We are betrayed,' shouted Diash, scrabbling for his own blade.

'To the priestess!' shouted Emni, but it was already too late.

Ragged, filthy warriors came towards the Sky Seekers from all sides, hurtling from hidden gaps in the canyon wall, brandishing cleavers and wicked, serrated blades. They leapt at the surprised riders, slashing, hacking and dragging them from their mounts.

Emni was already in motion. She hefted her spear, aimed and hurled it in one fluid motion. It sailed through the air, hitting one of the reavers in the gut and dropping him screaming to the floor.

'Come on, old man!' she shouted, drawing her sword and gripping the reins of her horse as it reared in panic. 'We must break through.'

Diash was still fumbling with his blade, which he had tangled awkwardly in his reins. He got it loose, and slashed at a warrior who was charging at him with blood-flecked saliva dropping from his screaming mouth. The blade sliced flesh and scraped across teeth, and the weight of the blow flipped the attacker to the ground like a ragdoll.

'Run, Diash,' screamed Emni, and through a blur of sweat and blood he saw her fall, unhorsed by a wicked, hooked glaive. 'Warn them!'

Someone struck her in the face, and she spat blood before she struck back. Her assailant howled, and as he spun around Diash could see the knife Emni had left in his eye.

'Run, you old bas–' she yelled, and her voice was cut off as someone struck her with an axe haft from behind.

Grinning, gore-streaked faces turned to him, and fear cut through the haze of pain and confusion. He wheeled his horse around, saw a spear arc through the air and miss his head by only a hair's width. He kicked the beast into motion, making for the path they had entered from, angling his mount away from the screaming reavers that were bludgeoning and battering his fellow warriors into submission.

Something punched him hard in the chest, and Diash reeled, almost toppling out of the saddle. Gods, but it hurt. Whatever was attacking him struck his leg, in the meat of his calf, and scratched at his cheek. His vision blurred, and he hacked and coughed blood. Desperately, drunkenly, he kicked his horse forwards, leaning down low as the creature built up speed and barrelled through a cluster of painted warriors wielding barbed axes.

He was dimly aware of a jolt in his gut as his mount leapt over another obstacle, and the clattering of spears as more of the enemy sought to strike him from his saddle. Then the horse was running free, every single step taking him closer to the Stormcasts and hammering a nail deeper into his chest.

'Lord-Celestant Thostos,' came the cry from one of Goldfeather's Prosecutors. 'A rider.'

A pale horse broke free from the teeth of the cavern at a

gallop, carrying a solitary figure upon its back. The rider was slumped low in the saddle, and as the beast drew closer Eldroc could see arrows protruding from his chest. Within his bloody, matted hair could be seen streaks of silver-grey. It was the old warrior, Diash.

The Lord-Castellant rushed forwards, placing himself before the terrified horse, which was frothing at the mouth with pain and fear. It came to a stop, and made to rear back, but Eldroc grasped its reins and placed a calming hand upon its panting chest.

'Easy, my lad,' he whispered, 'easy there. Your task here is done. Be at rest.'

The creature whinnied and shook, but allowed him to gently lift Diash free and lay him on the floor. He was in a bad shape. Two arrows had struck him, one in the shoulder, just under the collarbone, and another between his ribs.

'He's lost a lot of blood,' said Eldroc. 'Removing the arrowheads may kill him.'

'Let me see,' said Yereth, the leader of the tribal infantry that had remained behind with the Stormcasts. He was a squat, bull-ish man of middle years, with a shaved head covered in intricate tattoos. He knelt down beside Diash, and studied the wounds, then reached for a pouch at his belt.

'You can help him?' asked Mykos.

'I can clean the flesh and numb the pain, but these are deep wounds,' Yereth said. 'He will likely not survive.'

Diash's eyes snapped open, and he gasped and choked for air.

'Easy, old man,' said Yereth. He dipped his fingers into the leather pouch, and when he withdrew them they were covered in a thick, green paste. He began to apply the ointment to the arrow wounds on Diash's chest.

'They... they,' gasped Diash. He coughed blood.

'Do not speak, friend,' said Eldroc. 'Rest now.'

The old man shook his head furiously, and looked fiercely at the Lord-Castellant, reaching out to grasp the warrior's arm in one trembling hand.

'We were... betrayed,' he whispered. 'Rusik.'

'The others,' asked Mykos, 'where are they?'

But the old man's eyes had lost focus, and his hand fell limply to the ground. Yereth shook his head and cursed.

'Bury your dead,' said Thostos, 'and return home.'

Yereth opened his mouth to protest, but the Lord-Celestant ignored him and turned to Mykos.

'We must make haste,' he said.

Unheeding of their own safety, the Stormcasts hurled themselves into the depths of the pass. Each dark corner of the path promised an ambush that did not come. There was little time for an ordered, safe advance. Instead they marched apace, in loose formation, shields raised, while Prosecutors swooped overhead with celestial hammers and javelins raised and ready.

After some time they emerged into an oval clearing, where dead mounts and shattered weapons covered the floor. Blood was spattered liberally across every surface, though only a few bodies littered the ground.

'Reavers,' spat Axilon, turning one of the corpses over with his boot. 'Flesh-hungry savages. Chaos filth.'

'No tribal corpses,' said Goldfeather, scanning the scene. 'This was a swift and well-planned ambush. They intended to capture, not slay.'

'Food for their vile feasts,' spat Axilon. 'No loyal mortal deserves such a fate. We must pursue this raiding party and crush them beneath our boots.'

The Lord-Relictor Tharros Soulwarden knelt, examining one of the dead horses. It had been run through with a barbed spear, and hacked apart with axes. Pointless barbarism of the sort that the enemy hordes delighted in.

'There were fifty warriors here,' he said. 'Blood-crazed reavers would have not the wit or self-control to capture every one of them. So why are there no mutilated remains?'

'Perhaps they desired prisoners?' asked Mykos.

'Then why not just take a few, and kill the rest?' said Thostos. 'No, this has the stench of something darker about it.'

There was a silence. Each Celestial Vindicator was imagining in horrifying detail why a servant of Chaos might require a few dozen living prisoners.

'We march,' said Thostos at last. 'These are no aelves – they will not pass without leaving a trace. We follow them, at pace, and when we find them we kill them.'

'And if they make it back to their cursed fortress before we catch up with them?' asked Mykos.

'Then we attack. With full force, and no quarter,' said Thostos, raising his voice so that every Stormcast in the clearing could hear him. 'Let the might of our Warrior Chambers be unleashed. Let the enemy see what doom awaits them. No more waiting. We tear that place down, and we put every single one of its cursed defenders to the sword.'

Both the Argellonites and the Bladestorm had brought the greater number of their Warrior Chambers into the Roaring Plains, some five hundred warriors in total. A fighting force strong enough to tear down all but the most redoubtable bastions of the enemy. The Stormcasts roared, and songs of vengeance and of the glory of Sigmar shook the walls of the Dragonmaw Canyons. Lord-Celestant Mykos Argellon nodded.

'For once we agree, Lord Thostos,' he said. 'No waiting to discover what fell purpose the enemy intends to use those captured warriors for. We fall upon them in full force.'

The Manticore Dreadhold was a cancer nested in the midst of the mountains, a brutal, imposing wedge of iron that comprised three grand towers and a semi-circular perimeter wall. As the

Stormcasts broke out through the canyon and into the valley that housed the fortress, each of them felt the oily, nauseous touch of fell magic. The grand statue of the hated Everchosen, Archaon, loomed over them, cut into the heart of the mountain itself, casting a great shadow across the valley floor. Thostos felt the pitiless eyes of the monument bore into his own.

Build your self-aggrandising statues, Chaos filth, he thought. Watch as we hunt them down and shatter them beneath the lightning storm of Sigmar.

'They are at the gate,' shouted Goldfeather, high in the sky above the Vindicators' position, accompanied by his Prosecutor retinue. 'They have the prisoners!'

'Then we are not yet too late,' said Mykos. His grandblade Mercutia was already in hand, and Thostos could feel the man's eagerness for battle. It very nearly rivalled his own.

'We promised them hope, brother,' Mykos continued, 'and we let them all be taken. We failed them. I cannot accept that. I will not.'

'We will rescue those we can,' said Thostos. 'But remember our mission, Lord Argellon. You know the consequences if we fail to secure that realmgate.'

'Prisoners, Lord Varash,' boasted the leader of the Bloodreavers, a balding, anvil-jawed creature with putrid, yellowed teeth. 'Meat for the fire!'

Varash backhanded the wretch as he passed, sending him flying into his fellows, unconscious and drooling blood.

'There will be time enough to fill your bellies later,' he bellowed. 'These ones are for the ritual tables. Slaadh?'

The Slaughterpriest loped over, his perpetual, razor-toothed grin etched across his face.

'You see a man here touch one of these slaves without my permission, you give him a meal. Feed him his own lungs, and make sure he's still alive so he can savour the taste.'

Slaadh chortled. 'Yes, Lord.'

They were interrupted by the sound of a deep, booming horn, which emanated from the central tower. Almost at once the atmosphere inside the fortress changed. Warriors who had been gleefully taunting the captured tribesmen drew their axes and blades at once, and rushed off to form into their kill-packs.

The Bloodreavers began to holler and howl, like dogs promised fresh meat. Memno, one of Varash's chosen Blood Warriors, hurtled from the tower, pulling on his horned, grilled helm as he ran.

'Lord,' he said, and his eyes were shining with joy. 'Warriors in turquoise armour. Not orruks, but larger than men.'

Varash cursed. 'Sigmar's whelps,' he spat. 'Very well, let them come. To the walls.'

By now the inner courtyard was swollen with blood-mad killers, twitching and growling as the voice of the Lord of Skulls filled their heads with promises of torn flesh and spilt blood. The blood-lust was so thick about the fortress that Varash could almost see it as a tangible cloud over their heads. His ruined eye ached, and he delighted in the pain. It promised much.

He ascended the stairs of the central tower, pushing past the dull creatures that Xos'Phet used as his servants. He despised the things. They stank of the sorcerer's weakling magic. One blocked his way at the iron door leading out onto the tower, so he grasped its head and snapped its neck with a satisfying crunch, then hurled the broken thing down the stairs.

Out on the battlements, Xos'Phet was putting the finishing touches to his twisted masterpiece. Three orruk shamans had been crucified at the far end of the tower. Over the course of several weeks they had been mutilated and otherwise prepared according to the profane texts.

'They live, still?' said Varash, as one of the things gave a low groan.

'Oh yes, most resilient creatures,' said Xos'Phet. 'And powerful, of course. Their latent magic is degenerate and savage, but it will serve my purpose. There.'

The sorcerer finished cutting into the orruk's flesh, and stood back to admire his work, wiping a bloody knife on the hem of his robe. The creature's tough, green hide was now covered in runes and symbols that meant nothing to Varash, but still set his teeth on edge. The work was fine, as legible and neatly inscribed as any book. Xos'Phet was nothing if not a perfectionist.

'The enemy comes,' said Varash. 'Are you done, witchkin?'

The sorcerer gave him a sickly, yellow-toothed smile.

'Indeed, Lord Varash,' he said. 'Let us begin.'

Varash felt a surge of excitement. This was it, his chance to end the threat of the orruk tribes and to earn the favour of the Everchosen. He had seen Archaon's fury when the Dreadhold had been overrun, when the great statue erected in his honour had been defaced with the image of the greenskins' idiot gods. When the burning hooves of the Blood God's eternal servants burned the grasslands of the Roaring Plains to cinders, then the name of Varash Sunken-Eye would be spoken of in awe in the halls of the Varanspire itself, the dread fortress of Archaon. Perhaps such a feat would even earn him his rightful place in the Varanguard.

He stood at the wall of the tower, overlooking the inner courtyard. From here he could see the hateful glow of the Manticore Realmgate, the ravenous essence that dwelt within its shifting, roiling depths already sensing the promise of spilled blood. Soon the sorcerer's ritual would draw the full power of the ancient structure forth, and he would have his grand army. Let the weakling minions of Sigmar be the first to fall before him.

As the Stormcasts rushed towards the fortress wall, the first of the missiles began to fall. The crude projectiles of the human defenders, javelins and thrown axes hurled from the battlements, did little against the fine armour and shields of the Celestial

Vindicators. Yet as they drew closer, the Dreadhold's true defences roared into life.

The leering daemonic skulls carved into its surface began to smoulder, eyes burning with baleful light. This light grew in intensity until it burst forth from the carvings in a shower of white flame. Arcing jets of molten fire spat into the midst of the Stormcasts, searing and melting sigmarite, enveloping warriors in shrouds of flame. Celestial Vindicators went down, screaming in agony as the daemonfire devoured bones and turned their flesh to cinders.

In response, the Judicators knelt and loosed the latent celestial energy that coursed through their heaven-forged weaponry. Great, glittering arcs of lightning smashed into the tower, crumbling the cursed stone and sending chunks of shattered masonry tumbling to the ground. While those warriors wielding powerful boltstorm crossbows turned the fortress's deadly defences to rubble, skybolt bows sent a cascade of light pouring over the perimeter wall to find its home in the tainted flesh of the Dreadhold's defenders. Smoke rose from the battlements where the devastating barrage of lightning scorched and burned the unworthy.

Shields raised and clattering under the incessant rain of projectiles, the Liberators pushed towards the great gate of the Dreadhold. The sky boiled above them, blood-red clouds swirling and reforming furiously, thunder bursts rolling across the battlefield, almost drowning out the calamitous sounds of battle. Then a sudden, violent crack split the air, louder even than the hammers of the great forges of Azyrheim. Tendrils of violent scarlet energy trailed across the main tower of the Dreadhold, wrapping around its surface like a cluster of vines. Mykos Argellon turned his eyes to the heavens, and felt a soft tapping sound on his mask and across his armour.

The blood rain fell. Inside the Dreadhold, the warriors of Khorne whooped and shrieked with joy at this sign of providence from their monstrous master. They turned their faces to the sky and let the iron taste roll down their tongues. They beat their chests and brandished their weapons and howled. Above them, the sky darkened and swelled, and the tendrils of fell energy crept over the edge of the tower. The sorcerer Xos'Phet stood upon the battlement, laughing in delight.

'It begins!' he chortled. 'The gate swells in power. Now we must feed the link between this world and the other.'

He looked at the prisoner that the gorepriests held, a straggle-haired man with wide and frightened eyes. 'This is your task, my friend. You are truly blessed.'

The knife was in his hand in a flash, and he cut the man's throat with one swift motion. The prisoner's eyes rolled back in his head, and the gorepriests hurled him into the oval pit at the centre of the tower. Blood spilled, and seeped through the grilles cut into the floor.

'Fetch me another!' said Xos'Phet, grinning widely.

Despite the rain of projectiles and the blood that now churned the earth and bogged them down, the Celestial Vindicators pushed to the main gate, a monstrous slab of iron covered with foul symbols and wrapped in dust-dry human skin.

Here the phalanx of shield-bearing Liberators peeled apart, allowing the breaching teams to rush through. First came the Knight-Heraldor Axilon, and the men cheered to see him raise his war horn, the blessed instrument of Sigmar that all of his rank carried.

'What say we play an old Azyrheim tune for this Chaos filth?' he roared above the clatter of weapons and the belching fire of the wall defences. He raised the horn to his lips.

The note that issued forth was one empowered by the fury of Sigmar's storm, a pure wave of destruction that swelled the heart of the faithful and echoed in the ears of the damned as a promise of obliteration. The strong metal of the castle gate crumpled in the face of its awesome power, as if struck by the armoured fist of a towering giant. The gate was bound and reinforced, and it was not breached, but in the wake of Axilon's strike, the tall warriors of the Paladin retinues that carried wondrous starsoul maces came forwards, and began to beat a furious rhythm on the ruined surface. Explosions of storm-light marked each strike. Shards of metal and chunks of stone fell, and the gate groaned under the assault. Axilon even found time for a theatrical bow as the Celestial Vindicators beat their shields and chanted his name.

Rusik watched as, one after another, his people were led to the slaughter. This next one was of his own retinue, and his eyes were full of terrified anger as the pallid, nightmarish creatures that served the sorcerer dragged him over to the pit of corpses.

The knife tore flesh, and Rusik did not look away.

'Betrayer,' hissed a voice at his back, and he turned to see Alzheer, leg bloodied and one eye swollen shut with blood. She gripped the bars so tightly that her hands were white. 'Faithless, murdering scum.'

He turned away as the next prisoner was dragged forwards.

'You are right,' he said. 'I am faithless. My faith died along with my family and my friends.'

'And murdering others gives you peace?'

'There is no peace,' he spat. 'Nowhere. There is only war and bloodshed. An eternity of slaughter that will not cease and cannot be quelled. Varash and his men understand that, and so do I.'

'Zi'Mar sends his heralds,' Alzheer said. 'You see them for yourself. We are not alone. The light of humanity shines on, even in such darkness.'

Rusik whirled, his dark eyes burning with rage.

'They come now, when we are already lost,' he shouted, and he could taste the blood rain seeping into his mouth. 'We are already dead, woman, you are just too blind to see it. I will no longer hold on to what is lost. If this is our future, I embrace it.'

Under the combined assault of Knight-Heraldor Axilon and the hammers of the Retributors, the gates fell inwards, and the Celestial Vindicators met the enemy face to face. The true enemy, not the simple-minded bloodlust of the enemy's reavers, but warriors who had fully embraced the touch of Khorne. These were hardened killers, tall and broad, encased in ornate plate armour of imposing design and wielding vicious, jagged axes. They did not fall before the charge of the Stormcasts, but leapt and charged into the mouth of the storm, hacking and slicing, songs of devotion to their twisted god upon their lips.

The two waves crashed together, the gleaming turquoise of the Celestial Vindicators and the spoiled-meat red of the Bloodbound warriors, and the carnage was total.

Many Stormcasts fell in that initial clash, even their mighty warplate unable to defend them from the enemy's wild, delighted frenzy. A screaming fiend with a bronze crest took the head from a Liberator with his twin axes, then was crushed under the heavy swing of a sigmarite hammer. Drooling and chortling, a warrior wearing a flayed orruk-hide cape ground a Celestial Vindicator's face into the ground, hacking at the stricken figure's back with a wide-bladed gladius as he did so.

Mykos Argellon put his blade through the warrior's back. The man gasped and choked, and Mykos kicked him free to sprawl in the dirt.

'Push forwards, brothers,' he shouted above the grind of battle. 'Forge a breach!'

They were in the gatehouse tunnel, which stretched for a dozen yards ahead, culminating in a wide staircase that led up. Dull red light shone down those stairs, telling Mykos that if they could push the enemy back they would emerge in the fortress courtyard, below the main tower. Easier thought than achieved. The forces of the Dreadhold outnumbered the two hundred fighters that Mykos commanded at least four to one.

'They're thick as a rat swarm in here,' Axilon shouted, his own broadsword wet with gore, and a great rent torn across his breastplate. 'We'll not get past them easily, and more are on their way.'

'Come on, Bladestorm,' Mykos said, searching for a gap in the line where he could bring his sword to bear. 'Where are you?'

Up came the Prosecutors, over the wall of the Dreadfort, nimbly weaving past the poorly aimed missiles that were hurled their way. First, they cleared the ramparts with a flurry of their own. Lightning swept aside the throng of bloodstarved that garrisoned the wall next to the central tower. Celestial hammers and javelins hurled Chaos-warped figures to the courtyard, where they broke upon hard stone.

No sooner had they struck than the winged warriors were on the move again. This time they dropped over the perimeter wall, swooping low to pass over the heads of the defenders, releasing more lightning-wreathed javelins. Howling in outrage, the Bloodbound charged after this new quarry, abandoning their attempts to get at Mykos' force currently pushing through the main gate. It also drew their attention from the wall itself.

Thostos Bladestorm and the ten-score warriors of his chamber hauled themselves up the grappling ropes, using the indentations and ornaments that covered the face of the Dreadhold to ease their ascent. Belatedly, they were spotted by the remaining defenders, who rushed to the spot on the wall that the Prosecutors had cleared and began to hack and tear at the ropes, and hurl spears down at the ascending Stormcasts in an attempt to dislodge them. Several of Thostos' men were taken down by the volley of missiles, dropping like stones to land with a bone-shattering clatter on the hard earth below. Others were unfortunate enough to pass too close to one of the daemonic mouths, and burst into flame as the deadly trap covered them with flammable liquid.

Try as they might, however, the defenders could not dislodge the heavy grapples or hack through the thick rope. Their blades met looping wires of hard metal woven into the hemp, which turned all but the heaviest axe blades. Spitting with frustration, the Chaos warriors hurled their last few missiles and waited for the heads of their foes to emerge above the parapet.

Before they had a chance to strike, Goldfeather and his Prosecutors returned with another volley of storm javelins. Yet more defenders fell shrieking and burning to the floor, and in the confusion Thostos and his warriors hauled themselves over the lip of the wall. The Lord-Celestant whirled his hammer as he pulled himself up, crushing an opponent's hand into pulp against the wall, and rolled over onto the rampart. He drew his blade, and began to hack his way through the staggered enemy towards the nearest stairway down to the courtyard.

A reaver came at him, swinging a glaive at his neck, and the Lord-Celestant managed to get his hammer up in time to block. He reversed his grip on the weapon and struck low, and the man's knee bent backwards. His opponent screamed and fell, and Thostos drove his runeblade into his chest.

The lines had broken. Battle had dissolved into a wild melee, aside from a few pockets where the Stormcasts had managed to maintain a semblance of discipline. While Thostos' warriors hacked into the rear of the Blood Warriors holding the gatehouse, the Argellonites pushed forwards relentlessly. Caught between the pincers of the two Stormcast forces, the defenders were forced back into the courtyard proper. Yet despite the Celestial Vindicators' impressive gains, the enemy was not done. More and more reavers poured from the cliff tunnels behind the fortress, swarming around the huge realmgate itself and crashing into the press of bodies, straining to get at the enemy.

'Thostos!' came a cry, and he turned to see Mykos at the foot of the wide stairs that led from the gatehouse into the courtyard. His fellow Lord-Celestant despatched an enemy warrior with a backhand swipe, and gestured to the main tower. The sky was now a patchwork of striated red lightning, broken only above the tower, where there now hung a circular vortex around which the baleful energy swirled. The build-up of pressure in the air was a physical ache that spread across the battlefield, a drying of the mouth and a ringing of the ears.

As they watched, the vortex vomited a torrent of blood, a coruscating pillar of viscera that swirled and lapped at the edges of the tower, but remained in place, enclosing the structure like a gauntlet over a fist.

'We must break through,' yelled Mykos, above the cacophony of roaring liquid. 'We must stop this, brother.'

Thostos stood. He swayed to his left as a raging berserker hurtled past, narrowly missing the Lord-Celestant with a swipe of his dual axes, and barrelled into the thick of the battle, battering his way through to the steps leading up to the tower.

Leering faces pressed against his war helm, and he hacked and smashed at them with warhammer and blade. He shoved, strained, kicked and levered bodies aside, accepting a dozen minor hits in his haste to break free. Suddenly his path was clear, and he saw the steps arc up over the gatehouse entrance towards the central tower. He leaped up them two at a time, lifting a filthy, tattooed mortal over his shoulder as he went, pitching the man over into the swirling melee below.

On the other side of the gatehouse, Mykos Argellon made his own ascent. As he reached the tower entrance, a shadow fell across him. The figure was something from a nightmare. Impossibly tall for a mortal man, thin and long-limbed in a manner that made it look entirely unnatural. Its neck was stretched and corded with muscle, and a burnished skull on a chain of brass dangled over the creature's chest. The monster held a great, two-handed axe in pallid, scarred hands.

'You should not have come here, son of Sigmar,' the Slaughterpriest hissed, and then he grinned wide enough to expose bloodstained, razor-sharp teeth. 'But I am glad that you did.'

'Silence, creature,' said Mykos, raising his grandblade high. 'Your bleating offends me.'

The blood priest's eyes narrowed, and with a bellow of rage he exploded forwards, axe swinging at Mykos' neck. The Lord-Celestant stepped backwards and, rather than blocking, angled Mercutia to push the axe blade aside. Against any normal foe this would have opened up an opportunity as he struggled to get that heavy great axe back into position, but this creature was blindingly fast. He rotated the axe, jabbing with a spike attached to the bottom of the haft, and in an instant had it up and swinging again, this time a wild swipe at Mykos' midsection.

The Lord-Celestant picked that blow off too, and there began a series of lightning-fast parries, dodges and blocks. After several seconds the momentum played out, and each warrior took a step back, breathing heavily.

'You fight well,' said the blood priest, wiping blood from a gash than ran down the side of his angular face. 'You would reap a fine skull-tally for the Blood God.'

'I spit on your wretched god, vermin,' growled Mykos.

'You will join the tide, or drown in it,' said the Chaos priest, gesturing at the torrent of gore that spiralled around the tower. The heat of it was astonishing. Where it met the ground steam rose, a boiling vapour that billowed out over the surrounding melee.

'The blood is life,' he said, and his smile was wide. 'Let me show you.'

One hand reached out at Mykos, a claw aimed at his heart, and the priest spoke eight profane words.

Mykos screamed as his blood began to boil.

Thostos saw his fellow Lord-Celestant fall to the floor, writhing in agony. A twisted, misshapen blood priest advanced upon him, chanting in a dread tongue. He was too far away. Thostos could not possibly reach him in time. He smashed a fist into a jaw, felt it snap and battered another foe aside with a sweep of his hammer. A dozen paces now, but still too many of the enemy in his path.

'Argellon,' he roared. 'Get up, brother!'

Mykos Argellon's world was a storm of crimson agony. He could not see past the blood that poured from his eyes, could not feel anything but the fire that devoured every inch of his body. Distantly, as if from the other side of a rushing waterfall, he heard a voice he recognised. There was laughter too, deep and pitiless.

Endless, burning agony and the laughter of cruel men. The vow, the screamed oath. Then, the storm, the lightning. The rage, tempered and focused. Hope and duty flowing through his veins. The knowledge that he would never again feel so helpless and weak, and would let no other good-hearted soul feel that way if it was in his power.

Through the wave of torment, one thought coalesced. He would not fall here. Not when there were people counting on him.

Slaadh watched the stricken Stormcast with amusement. These fools. They thought they had power within them to rival the Lord of Skulls. They thought a set of shining armour and some heaven-wrought weapons gave them license to defy the true power in the realms. Their arrogance had not only doomed them, it had revealed the presence of the last bastion of humanity. Gates opened two ways.

Astonishingly, the warrior in sea-green and gold armour was still moving, despite the blood that boiled in his veins. Slaadh felt his heart sink. These were such worthy foes, but someday soon they would all be dead, their idols cast down and their cities burned around them. Who would be left then to challenge the might of the blood-chosen? It was almost a waste.

Still, there was a tally to collect. He raised his axe for the killing stroke.

Mykos could not see through the haze of pain, but he could hear the heavy steps of the scarred warrior coming towards him and could smell his rancid, rotten-meat stench. He wrapped his fingers tightly around the hilt of his grandblade, which lay in the dirt only a few inches from his face, and waited. He would only have one chance.

'Blood for the Blood God,' came the creature's ragged, eager hiss. Too close.

Mercutia sang as she whipped through the air.

The blade swept across so fast that Thostos could not see if it had struck home. Through the rain of blood he saw the Chaos priest standing before Mykos, axe raised and ready to strike.

The brute's head slowly slid free, tumbling down to splash in a puddle of gore, a grin still etched across its savage features.

Mykos was struggling to his feet, digging his grandblade into the earth to lever himself upright. Thostos hacked another enemy down to the ground, finished him with a crushing blow from his hammer, and ran to his fellow Lord-Celestant. Argellon was staggering towards the curtain of blood that enclosed the tower. One hand was outstretched, and Thostos could see the sheer heat of the sorcerous power begin to melt the sigmarite.

'Hold, brother,' he shouted over the roaring, boiling sound of the bloodfall. 'You cannot pass.'

'Someone must,' said Mykos, collapsing to his knees. His voice was little more than a ragged whisper. 'We must end whatever is happening, and I am near dead already. Let me go.'

'This is my task,' said Thostos. 'You will stay, and you will lead our men to victory.' He grabbed the man around the shoulders, and locked eyes with his brother. 'They must reach the muster point. You must lead them there, as Sigmar ordered us. You will do this.'

'Thostos–' Mykos said, but the other Lord-Celestant was already moving.

Without a moment's hesitation, he stepped into the curtain of boiling blood.

Where it fell, the acidic gore ate through sigmarite and flesh with contemptuous ease. Thostos could feel his glorious armour, forged to deflect the blows of Chaos-forged axes and deny the spell-fire of twisted wizards, coming apart around him. The finely wrought image of the lion that he bore on his chest melted away. The icons of his beloved Warrior Chamber were obliterated. Yet Thostos did not fall.

Where once his flesh had been pale-white, now it glinted with the strength of purest sigmarite. A gift from the sorcerer Ephryx, the Ninth Disciple and lord of the Eldritch Fortress. Where once it had nearly destroyed him, now it saved his life. The blood ate away at the metal of his flesh, searing and scarring him, but where soft flesh would have been utterly destroyed, his new form endured. Soon he was through the burning bloodfall, and he collapsed to a hard iron floor.

He growled, trying to fight back the waves of agony that enveloped him. Smoke rose from his mutilated body, and melted sigmarite dripped free to spark and smoulder on the ground. Gritting his teeth and roaring in defiance, he punched one gleaming metal fist down, and forced himself to his feet. He staggered and almost fell, but reached out to grab a wrought-iron sconce shaped in the image of a screaming face. Through the blue-red haze of his vision, he took in his surroundings.

Inside the tower a circular staircase wound to the upper floors, while a steady stream of blood, shed naturally rather than summoned from some hellish realm, fell to pool in the indentations of a great bronze skull engraved upon the floor.

There was a sharp hiss, like the sound of a punctured lung, and Thostos heard movement above him. From an upper landing, two creatures bounded down the iron stairs to meet him. They were tall, spindle-limbed, with bloodied, bandaged faces and smocks stained with gore. One clutched a short, rusted bone-saw, while the other wielded two thin-bladed knives.

Thostos pushed away from the wall, and set himself upon the lowest stair. As the saw-wielding creature drew close, it leaped down at him. As it fell, Thostos could see the stitches that bound its mouth and eyes closed. Blood flecked its maggot-white skin as it hissed in fury.

He raised his blade, shifted to the side and let the thing impale itself. It groaned and wailed, yet still tried to hack at him with the saw. He let it slide free of his sword, and brought his hammer up to fend off the second creature. Somehow it got a knife past his guard, but it skittered off his metallic flesh. He stuck his sword through its chest, and as it gurgled he brought the hammer down to crush its head in a splatter of bone fragments and pink meat. The first attacker had staggered upright, so he spun and planted a boot in its chest. Bones shattered with an audible snap, and the thing flew away to land with a splash in the pool of blood at the tower base.

Thostos turned, and began to ascend the stair.

Mykos Argellon could barely stand. His entire body was aflame, and the slightest motion sent a ripple of torment through his wracked body. Around him the battle raged. The Stormcasts had established a defensive position in front of the gatehouse, but even as they hacked down scores of Bloodreavers, more rushed from the depths of the fortress or around the rock formation upon which stood the Manticore Realmgate. They could not hold here forever. Unless they could break the back of the enemy, they would be slowly picked apart.

The great relic-staff of Lord-Relictor Tharros was a blazing totem of celestial energy at the rear of the formation, but even the waves of healing energy that emanated forth and closed the wounds of stricken warriors could not reach every corner of the battlefield. Despite the attempts of the Prosecutors to clear the wall, more and more axes were being hurled down into the ranks of the Celestial Vindicators, and Mykos could see explosions of light all across the field as fallen warriors were called home by the storm.

He staggered down the steps, where a band of Argellonite Liberators held the stair leading to the central tower. They fought as one, shields intercepting the frenzied strikes of the enemy and opening just long enough for the warriors to thrust their runeblades through chests, stomachs and throats, or crush skulls with their heavy warhammers. In front of their formation lay a carpet of ripped and torn bodies, but the Stormcasts' numbers were steadily dwindling. As Mykos stumbled forwards to join them, a flaming anvil head attached to a wicked, barbed chain sailed over the top of a Liberator's shield, caving in the man's helm with a splatter of flesh. Booming laughter echoed over the din of clashing blades as a broad warrior with bare, burn-scorched arms barrelled into the Stormcasts, whirling and rattling skull-tipped chains. He brought the anvil and chain around in a full circle, and swept it low, underneath the shield of another Liberator, who went down with a cry as his leg folded sideways.

'Come, little warriors,' roared the man, a mocking leer visible underneath a towering horned helm. 'Give your skulls to me!'

Mykos half-staggered, half-ran forwards, and ducked as the warrior swept his burning anvil back around. He felt the heat of it as it rushed past his head, and brought Mercutia up in a thrust aimed for the fiend's throat. His opponent ducked back, spinning with unsettling grace for one so large, letting his momentum add to an overhead swing that had Mykos scrambling backwards, falling to the ground with his blade out of position. The warrior flicked the chain back up, and the anvil smashed into the bottom of Mykos' war-helm. He felt the bones in his jaw come apart, and sprawled backwards, head spinning.

The brute stalked forwards, laughing.

'Well fought, little general,' he chortled. 'You have earned a place on my trophy belt.' He gestured to a row of chipped and broken skulls that had been bronzed and arrayed on a chain around his midriff.

He raised the flaming anvil.

A thick blade punched out from the front of his throat. The warrior glanced down in surprise, and blood poured down the front of his battered iron armour.

Lord-Castellant Eldroc retracted his halberd, switched his grip on the long haft and swung it sideways at the Skullgrinder's neck. His head tumbled free as his body collapsed awkwardly and rolled down the stairs. The Gryph-hound Redbeak spat a clump of flesh from his jaws and trilled briefly in appreciation.

Mykos watched, blearily, as the Lord-Castellant rushed over to him.

'Do not move, my friend,' he heard, as the cloud of darkness at the edge of his vision threatened to engulf him. Suddenly the blackness was washed away in the face of a soothing beam of light, like a breaking dawn.

'Come back to the light, brother,' he heard Eldroc say.

Thostos kicked open the door, his metallic skin still dripping molten sigmarite and hot blood, and emerged into a storm of profane magic. Coils of twisted, baleful light spiralled and curled around the tower summit, enveloping three forms that were raised above the fortress wall on jagged iron crosses. These figures flickered and jerked spastically as the onslaught of fell energies wracked through them. In the sky above clouds rolled back, exposing a dark vortex that crackled and howled. Thostos could see shifting, roiling shapes within. A terrible sound echoed in his ears, the laughter of something impossibly old and unimaginably vast. The veil between the realms was being torn apart.

Before him stood a tall, powerful man in ridged black armour, hands resting easily on the pommel of a bastard sword with pulsing veins running through its obsidian blade. On one side the man's face was almost concave, and where the eye should be there was instead a red jewel that wept blood. The man smiled.

'My name is Varash Sunken-Eye,' he said, in a measured, almost soft voice that seemed at odds with his fearsome appearance. 'I am lord of this Dreadhold, and I will claim your skull.'

'I am Thostos Bladestorm, and you are welcome to try.'

'I knew you would meet me here,' said the warrior, circling around the pit of bodies with a wide grin on his ruin of a face. He gestured to the boiling skies. 'Symbolism. Ritual. This confrontation was inevitable, as soon as you arrived in the Roaring Plains.'

'It was,' said Thostos, settling his weapons in each hand and fighting away the waves of pain that threatened to bring him to his knees.

A small, pallid rodent of a man dressed in garish purple robes appeared from behind the Chaos Lord and glared at Thostos, seemingly more in irritation than anger. He clutched a small, serrated blade and inched towards the cage on the far left side of the tower, where a clutch of blank-eyed human prisoners crouched. They were guarded by more of the bandaged, stitch-mouthed monsters that Thostos had fought in the tower below.

'There must be no interruptions,' the small man said. 'Finish this thing quickly, Lord Varash. It disturbs my work.'

With a roar, Varash leaped across the pit of blood, his flayed-skin cloak spreading out behind him like the wings of a bat and his obsidian blade reaching for Thostos' throat.

'Lord Thostos,' Alzheer whispered. She could hardly believe that the twisted, melted thing before her was the grand and imposing Lord-Celestant she had met on the plain. His armour was a smouldering wreck, and his exposed flesh was a dull, ash-covered gold. He moved slowly, shorn of the terrifying speed and surety he had displayed in battle against the orruks. The Chaos warrior that faced him was smiling as he ducked and wove out of the path of the Lord-Celestant's attacks, occasionally dragging his blade across an exposed flank or knocking Thostos off-balance with the heavy pommel.

'He will fall,' said the warrior Emni. Her dreadlocked hair was matted with blood, and her scarred face was bruised and swollen where she had been struck. 'Look at him. He is done. We must escape, priestess.'

'There is no escape from that,' said Alzheer, nodding at the boiling blood that rushed past the edge of the tower.

'Then we kill as many of those monsters as we can,' Emni replied fiercely. She nudged Alzheer, and gestured down. Though she kept her hands together, the priestess could see that her friend's bonds were cut. She wondered how Emni had done it, then saw the dead prisoner behind her, bone protruding from a shattered leg.

'One of Rusik's lot,' whispered Emni, and she was grinning. 'Cursed traitor at least managed to serve us in death.'

'Hush,' said Alzheer. The wizened man was returning, and as he gestured, two of the bandaged servants bent to unlock their cage. Alzheer held her breath, and gripped her claw-hound tooth necklace tight enough to draw blood. She had taken the trophy from her first kill, and the fang was still sharp, after all these years.

'Take me, you filth,' shouted Emni, as one of the figures reached for a man with one ear missing and started to drag him out, kicking and screaming.

Its foul head snapped around, eyes weeping, stitched-together mouth drooling. It grabbed Emni, and began to haul her free of the cage.

The warrior let the creature drag her until she was half-in, half-out of the cage door. Then, in one fluid motion, she pulled the thing off balance and wrapped her legs around its neck. It struggled and moaned, but Emni made a dagger of the first two fingers of her right hand, and jabbed them into one rheumy eye. Stitches tore free as the creature gave a strange, ululating howl. Emni grasped the corpse-knife that the thing carried in its belt, and drove it into its neck.

'Insolence!' roared the sorcerer. 'Grab her! She will be the next to bleed.'

Another of the bandaged servants reached at Emni. Alzheer tucked in her legs, forced her bound arms underneath, and rolled them free. As the creature grasped at her friend, the priestess clenched the claw-hound tooth between two fingers, and punched it in the face once, twice, three times. It screeched and reeled back.

The two women crawled free, and the other prisoners, given fresh hope of escape, scrambled after them.

'Enough!' shrieked the sorcerer, and gestured at Emni. A white-hot bolt of energy spat out from his finger and burned into her chest. She screamed and fell to the floor.

Alzheer did not have time to worry for her friend. She scooped up the knife as it clattered to the floor and charged the mage. He laughed, stepping backwards and weaving another spell. She felt her muscles constrict, and suddenly she could not move at all.

'Oh, very good,' he giggled. 'Very brave. But you cannot stop what is happening, girl. No, in fact you will watch. I will slaughter all your friends, and then, at last, I will allow you a slow death.'

More prisoners scrambled across the blood-slick stone to get at the sorcerer, and he cackled and waved a hand at them. A curtain of flame enveloped them, and a dozen men and women went down, burning and screaming. Alzheer felt a finger twitch. The sorcerer took a pace backwards, stepping out of the way as a blazing figure collapsed in front of him.

That step brought him too close to one of the other prisoner cages. Hands reached out of the bars, grasping at his robes, pulling at his hair.

'No,' he screamed. 'Release me!'

Alzheer took a step forwards. She stumbled as the spell released her from its control. Her legs ached as if she had just run a thousand leagues, but she did not stop. She took another step, then another, then she was sprinting. The sorcerer brought one hand up to fend her off, and she could see the fear in his eyes. She stabbed the blade in between his ribs. He squealed like a dying rat, and his eyes were wide with terror and pain as she twisted the knife. Then he was writhing and melting, falling in upon himself with his last scream still echoing in her ears. The purple robes fell to the floor, with no body to be found.

Thostos could not win. He had known this from the moment he matched blades with the Lord of Chaos. His opponent was too fast, too fresh. His own reflexes were slowed by pain and exhaustion. Each step backwards, each block and parry sent a sheet of lightning roiling through his body.

He blocked a downwards swing on his blade and swept his warhammer around at Varash's side. The man turned and spun, neatly avoiding the strike, and flicked his blade along Thostos' arm. Whatever twisted, Chaos-tainted alchemy had forged that obsidian blade, it had imbued it with astonishing power. It cut deeply into his transmuted sigmarite flesh, and the pain caused him to open his hand. His warhammer bounced away on the hard stone.

Thostos tried to step back, to gain some space, but the Chaos lord was too fast. His bastard sword swept out and cut across the Lord-Celestant's leg, and as Thostos stumbled, a backhand swing tore a shard of metal from his face and snapped his head violently to the side. His vision swam, and he felt himself clatter to the floor.

'I had expected more,' said Varash, wiping bloody tears from his ruined eye. 'This is a disappointment, truly.'

There was only one chance, only the briefest of opportunities as the monster standing before her revelled in his apparent victory. Alzheer knew that taking it would in all likeliness mean her death. She had never been concerned by that possibility before, despite living every moment of her life in some form of life-threatening danger. As fervently as she had preached the wisdom and benevolence of Zi'Mar, she had always believed that her people were dying, and her god was gone. The sacred words and rituals were simply fragments of a better past that she could not quite let go.

That was until they had come, these warriors in burnished plate. These demigods who spoke like men. Now, she had a reason to live. They all did. Hope. Hope that they would see this new future that the Sky God had offered them, hope that the orruks and the forces of the Dark Gods and all the other cataclysms that had seemed so insurmountable could in fact be resisted – could even be defeated. She wanted so badly to live to see that future, and conversely that made her choice so much easier. Life meant something now. Life, and what she chose to do with it.

She did not waste her opportunity.

Staggering across the gore-slick ground, she jumped onto a table covered in the innards of unfortunate prisoners, and from there leapt onto the creature's back, scrabbling for purchase on the trophy-racks and chains that wrapped his gore-encrusted plate armour. He was lightning fast, snatching at her with a spiked gauntlet that ripped into her flesh, but she had surprise on her side and a hunter's instinct for the kill.

The claw-dog tooth she held in her fist sank into the Chaos Lord's eye, and she twisted and dragged it, screwing it deeper and deeper. She returned the pain that ran through her a hundredfold, screaming a prayer of vengeance for her fallen friends.

He roared in agony, and suddenly she was flying through the air. Something rushed forwards to meet her, and the world went blank.

The Chaos lord staggered back, cursing and pawing at his face. There came the sound of shattered earth, of rushing water, of a thousand siege-stones striking a thousand castle walls.

The sky opened once more, but this time it was not the bloody horror of Chaos that issued forth, but the searing righteousness of the storm that was Sigmar. A fork of lightning as tall and wide as a mountain blasted into the vortex, exploding in a coruscating web of blue energy that arced across the sky. For a moment it seemed as if Sigendil itself, the High Star that bathed blessed Sigmaron in purifying, celestial light, had descended over them.

That purifying bolt of light turned the rain of blood to mist, banished the darkness that had fallen across the Dreadhold, and fell to strike Thostos Bladestorm in the chest.

Thostos screamed as the storm enveloped him. It tore him apart and reassembled him. He felt the agony of transformation as armour and sigmarite flesh moulded and reformed around his body. With the pain, the honest, cauterising pain, came memories. He remembered the agony as the vile minions of the Dark Gods cut into him. He remembered the sorrow of loss, the ecstasy of his grief as he looked for the last time upon the smoking ruins of his lands. He remembered the helplessness, and the shame of knowing that his people had counted on him to protect them, and that he had not been there in their hour of greatest need. Thoughts and memories seared through his consciousness, too many and too vivid for him to process.

As quickly as it had come the storm was gone. Varash blinked as the flare slowly receded from his vision. His eye burned as if molten steel had been poured into the socket, but from somewhere in the haze of torment a figure swam into view. The storm warrior still knelt before him, but where once his warplate had been melted and seared, it was now resplendent in gleaming turquoise. There was not a mark upon its surface, and it shone as if it was freshly polished. The figure, despite its miraculous transformation, showed no sign of movement.

'A clever trick,' spat Varash, 'but it makes no difference. You will die now, and know that every one of your warriors will die with you.'

As he spoke, he brought his bastard sword up and over, rolling his shoulder in a circular motion, adding furious momentum to the killing strike.

Thostos Bladestorm, warrior of Sigmar, who once had been the mortal warrior Prince Caeran of Wolf Keep, reached up and caught his enemy's hands as the sword fell. The blade came to rest an inch from his eye.

'No!' shouted Varash, and his ravaged eye widened with shock.

Thostos stood, and as he stood he brought his runeblade up, roaring in defiance as he tore its edge through the Chaos Lord's thick mail armour, cleaving devotional totems and skulls in half as he cut a bloody, vertical line into the man's pale flesh. He ripped his sword free, and a mist of blood covered his armour.

Lord Varash stood, eyes fixed in astonishment at the ruin of his chest. As he swayed, he turned his gaze to Thostos.

Blue eyes bored into his skull, not the emotionless reservoirs of cold fury that they had been, but alive with righteous fervour, the eyes of a man who fought for a cause that he embraced with every fibre of his being.

'Tell your gods that we are coming for them,' said Thostos, 'and that their realms will burn as ours did.'

Varash Sunken-Eye, master of the Dreadhold, collapsed in two separate pieces, toppling to the floor of the tower in a shower of gore.

The bloodstarved hordes were no cowardly ratmen, and their resistance did not end with the death of their master. When Thostos Bladestorm emerged from the great tower with his rune-blade in one fist and the severed head of Varash Sunken-Eye in the other, more than one crazed warrior hurled themselves at him in desperation to claim a worthy skull.

None landed a blow. Thostos was renewed, healed and imbued with fresh purpose. He spun, whirled and sliced, a whirlwind of destruction that cut deep into the enemy ranks. Emboldened at the glorious sight of their Lord-Celestant and the death of the enemy lord, the flagging Stormcast offensive surged once more. Judicators lined the inner wall, using the higher ground to their advantage now and loosing devastating volleys into the Bloodreavers.

'Bring down the icon-bearers,' shouted Evios Goldfeather, hefting a javelin and sending it soaring down to burst through the back of an obese brute wielding a heavy chain and flail. The missile flared with white-blue light as it struck, and the man toppled to the ground, his back a smoking ruin.

In the courtyard the sheer might of the Retributors was beginning to tell. In such close quarters their heavy hammers reaped a horrific toll, smashing in breastplates and caving in skulls with furious precision. The ground was slick with gore, and the Bloodreavers were so hemmed in by the aggression of the Stormcasts' assault that as many slipped and were trampled by their fellow warriors as were slain in honest battle.

For the majority of the defenders there was no retreat. Neither the tight confines of the Dreadhold nor the single-minded battle-lust of its defenders allowed for even the thought of it. They died hard, hacking and slashing and screaming with the pure joy of the slaughter even as the tide claimed them.

Only a few battered survivors scattered, rushing into the cave passages that wound into the mountains behind the realmgate, choosing a long, dangerous trek through the darkness in favour of the vengeance of the Celestial Vindicators. Rusik paused as he made the entrance of the cave, and looked out across the inner courtyard at the shining warriors who had denied him his chance for revenge. Then he turned, and raced away into the shadows.

As the sun began to fall, a soft pink glow fell over a scene of devastation. As it had so many times down the centuries, the Dreadhold ran red with blood.

Thostos Bladestorm stood in front of the Manticore Realmgate, staring into the pulsing, warping maelstrom at its centre. He could feel its hatred and cruel malice, its rage at being denied so many souls.

'What will you do now?' came a voice from behind him. He turned to see the priestess Alzheer, limping and heavily bandaged, one eye wrapped in a poultice. She stopped at his side, and gazed into the portal herself. Red light played across her face, and she winced at the hateful power of it.

'Sigmar's plan for the next stage of the great war is unimaginably complex, and the Celestial Vindicators have their part to play,' said Thostos. 'Through this realmgate lies our true goal. But first it must be cleansed, made safe for our passage. Until then, the fortress must stand.'

Roaring and snuffling with barely constrained fury, the beasts raced across the broken earth towards the fortress of the statue, from which the sounds of battle had been heard. These were not agile creatures. Where more graceful animals would nimbly jump from rock to rock, navigating the tortured highlands with precision, these beasts simply smashed and ripped their way through. They lowered the horns that jutted from their snouts and hurtled into stone formations, blasting them into fragments as they hauled their great bulk through the gap they had created.

Barely holding on to the crude iron bands that served as saddles, the beasts' riders whooped and hollered, beating their mounts with axe hafts and clubbed fists in an attempt to push them further and faster.

Eventually the riders came to the end of the mountain ridge overlooking the canyon below and behind, and the valley plain that stretched out before them. To their right was the fortress of the red-iron men and the colossal monument that loomed over it – the statue of the warrior with the horned helm and the pitiless gaze.

There had been a battle, that much was obvious. Corpse-fires were visible within the interior of the fortress, and the ground surrounding the structure was stained red like an open wound. More interesting still was the fact that the tiny figures within wore not the red-and-black iron of the expected defenders, but a rich sea-green trimmed with gold that glittered in the midday sun. New banners flew from the fortress walls, proudly displaying a hammer wreathed in lightning bolts.

From here the beast riders could not pick out the specifics of the enemy force, but one thing was certain. If they had managed to dig the red-iron men out of their hole, they were a worthy foe.

The riders shared an eager, toothy grin.

Then they wrenched on the reins of their mounts, and raced off back the way they had come, leaving a trail of dust and shattered stone in their wake.

CHATER FOUR

Iron Tide

'Lord Thostos,' said Alzheer, running after the Stormcast as he made his way across to the realmgate. 'I would ask a favour of you.'

He turned, and looked at her. To her surprise he gave her a quick salute, beating one gauntlet upon that fabulous gilded chestplate. She still did not understand how it had been repaired so thoroughly. The Lord-Celestant had been a half-melted ruin before the coming of the storm, and the renewing light. Alzheer's faith had always been strong, but it had never blazed brighter than when the lightning cleared and she saw Thostos stand, restored and defiant.

'I am aware of what you did upon the tower, priestess. Your bravery saved my life. You have my thanks.' He paused. 'If what you request is within my power to grant, I will do so.'

'I aim to hunt the traitor Rusik down,' she said. Even saying his name filled her with bile. 'He must die for what he has done.'

'And you wish me to provide you with a cadre of warriors,' said Thostos, understanding immediately. 'I am sorry, priestess, that is not something I can allow. Our mission is only just beginning, and I cannot afford to spare a single one.'

Her heart sank, but she would not give in that easily.

'I heard what you said at the Manticore Gate,' she continued. 'That portal will take time for your people to restore. In the meantime, the cave systems that open out into the back of this fortress remain vulnerable. If the enemy stages a counter-attack, they could tear into your force before you know they are upon you.'

Thostos considered this.

'It is a potential weakness,' he admitted. 'What do you suggest?'

'Lend me just six of your warriors,' she said. 'They will join the thirty fighters I still command. My people are fine trackers. We will find Rusik and whoever else managed to escape with him, and we will make sure they do not pose a threat to you any longer.'

'I can afford to give you three,' said Thostos. 'I will not risk my mission and the coherence of my fighting force by offering any more than that.'

Alzheer considered this. 'Three men will do,' she said. 'A small force will be able to move more quickly through the tunnels. Thank you, Lord.'

'Thank me by bringing my warriors back in short order, priestess,' said the Lord-Celestant. 'By rights I should not grant your request, but you have aided me and my men well and deserve your chance at vengeance.'

He glanced across the courtyard, which was carpeted with enemy dead.

'And if there is one thing the Celestial Vindicators understand, priestess, it is vengeance.'

Lord-Castellant Eldroc led the detachment of Celestial Vindicators that were tasked with disposing of the corpses left in the Manticore Dreadhold's main courtyard. In places the piles were knee-deep. It had been an inglorious slaughter at the end, when the ranks of blood-starved warriors had finally begun to break and flee. No Celestial Vindicator had given the foe a moment of mercy. They were tainted. They were traitors. There was no question of quarter. The men had killed with a song and a smile upon their lips.

Perhaps the Hallowed Knights would shake their heads at such joyous slaughter. Perhaps the Hammers of Sigmar would see it as beneath them. So be it. Let their brother Stormhosts be the proud and noble warriors. The Celestial Vindicators would fight as they had always done – with the fire of vengeance burning in their hearts.

Lord-Celestant Thostos approached.

'A fine tally,' said Eldroc. 'Many have been avenged this day.'

'This is but a taste of what awaits us,' Thostos replied. 'But yes, it will do for the moment.'

The Lord-Castellan studied his friend. It was hard to describe the exact difference in the Bladestorm's mien, but something had certainly changed. He remained reserved and distant, but where previously being around the man had made one feel awkward and uncomfortable, as if he radiated a cloying sense of unease, now there was simply a quiet intensity.

'What happened on that tower, Thostos?' asked Eldroc.

His friend did not answer for a long while.

'Truly, I do not remember,' he said at last. 'Sigmar reached out to me, that much is clear. I was broken, defeated. He restored me. The rest is but a fragment of a dream. Images, emotions.'

He shook his head. There was an element of frustration in that movement, but also, it seemed to Eldroc, an acceptance.

'I have never heard of such a thing, of the storm of Azyrheim reaching out to restore a warrior in the midst of battle,' said the Lord-Castellan.

'Nor I,' said Thostos. 'Yet you saw how the retrieval of Ghal Maraz ignited the fire within the God-King. Do any of us truly know the limits of his power, especially now that he is reunited with that marvellous weapon? Whatever the storm revealed to me was lost in moments,' Thostos continued, 'but the echo of it remains. I do not remember the life I have lost, but I recall the vows that I made. That we all made. If this is now what I am, the fury of those oaths wrought in sigmarite and unleashed to destroy the taint of Chaos wherever it may be found, then I embrace it.'

Eldroc opened his mouth to say something, but Thostos raised a hand to cut him off.

'We will speak of this again, but not now,' he said. 'Lord-Relictor Tharros requires our presence at the realmgate. We still have a mission to complete.'

The Manticore Realmgate no longer spewed out tendrils of eldritch fire, but it still resonated with ill intent. The monstrous carving that topped the archway of rune-carved black stone glared down at the Stormcasts, its leonine head promising obliteration to anyone who dared trespass upon its territory. Lord-Celestant Mykos Argellon made the mistake of staring too long at the symbols carved into the unyielding stone of the structure, and immediately regretted doing so. His head ached, and sour bile filled his mouth.

'We must pass through this gate,' said Thostos. He could see that no one present relished the prospect. 'You all know the part we have to play in Sigmar's grand plan. Our task was to secure this path to the mustering point, where we shall join a host the like of which the realms have never seen. The God-King aims to bring the war to the Everchosen's doorstep, but unless every piece is on the board at the allotted time, that cannot happen.'

'The Allpoints must fall,' said Eldroc, softly.

The Allpoints. The nexus through which was linked every single Realmgate. An island adrift, set apart from the Mortal Realms yet intrinsically linked to them through its web of eldritch passageways. As long as the forces of Chaos controlled the mighty fortresses that guarded these portals, the enemy's great armies of daemons and dark warriors could be sent forth anywhere in the realms to burn and despoil.

'It must,' agreed Thostos. 'But first we must shatter the formidable defences that guard it. That is our task, and the Manticore Realmgate will lead us to the Crystal Forest of Chamon, and to the next stage of the war.'

'These gates – the magic that binds them is strong but easily warped,' said Lord-Relictor Tharros Soulwarden, leaning on the ornate staff that was his mark of office. 'The fell powers can easily twist them to their purpose, redirecting and refocusing the latent energy to their own dark ends.'

'We had actually noticed that,' said Evios Goldfeather. The Prosecutor-Prime was perched on a rock cluster slightly above the ancient structure, staring grimly down.

'Don't interrupt,' snapped Tharros. 'My point is that we cannot trust that this portal will not drop us in a lake of fire, or a pit of blood demons. Throne of Azyrheim, we could even end up in the court of the Blood God.'

The realmgate stood at the rear of the fortress courtyard, on a raised platform built against the great mountain wall. Around it was a cluster of jagged rocks, and to each side of the stone-carved dais were tunnels that led deeper into the mountains. To hold this position, one needed to control both the fortress and the gate. At any moment, they all knew, fresh reinforcements could come pouring through this portal to smash into their exposed flank.

'How long will it take for you to purge the taint, Lord-Relictor?' asked Thostos.

'How long will it take me to restore this realmgate to its original state? How long will it take a man to unravel the dark enchantments and twisted blood rituals that have fed this thing for centuries upon centuries?'

Tharros tapped his fingers rhythmically on the metal of his staff.

'Somewhere between half a day and a hundred years,' he said at last. 'I'll have no idea until I begin, and once I commit to this...'

Thostos nodded. 'Begin, Lord-Relictor. If we do not pass through this gate, our mission is forfeit regardless. Eldroc, how goes the refortification?'

'Our assault kept the fortress largely intact, aside from the main gate,' said the Lord-Castellant. 'I have ordered the breach secured with caltrops and spiked wolf holes using iron taken from the ramparts. We do not have time to repair the gate entirely, but if we are attacked, forcing an entrance will cost the enemy dearly.'

'Good,' said Thostos. 'I will not trust to luck that our engagement with the Chaos scum went unnoticed. The orruks are too close, and there is every chance they heard the sounds of battle, or saw the sky darken with sorcery. You do not need me to tell you your business, Lord-Castellant. Make this place as secure as possible.'

Eldroc struck a fist to his chest in salute, and turned to make his way back to the wall, Redbeak loping along at his heel.

Tharros rested his chin in the crook of his hand. Wisps of celestial light coalesced around the haft of his relic-staff, and he reached one gauntlet out towards the burning portal.

'This is a stubborn, defiant old thing,' he spat, through gritted teeth.

'If that's the case, I feel it may have met its match at last,' said Goldfeather. He had removed his helm, and a slight smile was visible on his angular features.

'Pray find something to keep yourself occupied, Prosecutor-Prime,' said the Lord-Relictor. 'I require concentration, and must be free from the jabbering of pompous buzzards.'

Xos'Phet howled and wailed and spat as he was carried deeper into the gloom of the caverns, the volume of his screeching growing louder every time the gorepriests that carried him stumbled over another rock formation or a cluster of the great conical fungi that grew throughout the tunnels.

He fumbled at his side, underneath the stinking rags that now enveloped his bleeding form, and as his fingers touched the wound that the savage had left in his flesh he gave another yelp of pain.

'Watch where you step, you brainless fools,' he snapped, though conversing with the creatures at all was largely pointless.

The first of them had been accomplices of his, those he had consulted with now and then on the various intricacies of blood magic. There had been a reasonable level of collaborative progress for a while, but as always happened in the sorcerer's experience, their professional partnership had eventually become strained. They had made the unforgivable error of disagreeing with him on several key theoretical points. He had removed their troubling capacity for reason and defiance along with their eyes and their tongues. Over the years he had added to his collection, until he had quite the retinue of mute, compliant slaves that were little more than husks, bound to his will.

Clumsy, stupid, inconsiderate husks who were going to be the death of him.

'How did it come to this?' he moaned, as his bearers splashed through the freezing waters of an underground stream, which sent ripples of silver, phosphorescent light playing across the stone walls.

He had been so close. So damnably close. The ritual had worked, and he had been mere moments away from summoning a horde of screaming neverborn into being, and into his service.

'That fool Varash, how I would have savoured the look on his face when I ordered my army to tear him and his men limb from limb,' he said. 'Yet the dullard could not even hold a few over-zealous warriors at bay.'

Xos'Phet was dimly aware of just how much blood poured from his stab wound. He was also beginning to feel light-headed and weightless, as if he had just drunk a bottle of duardin fire-ale after a week without water. If he did not make it to his sanctum soon, he would die. The thought terrified him. There was so much left to do, so many secrets on the verge of being uncovered.

The gorepriests rounded a corner, and the wall to their left simply fell away. The cavern they had entered was enormous, so wide and high that it could have housed the Dreadhold itself with room to spare. The path they travelled narrowed, and hugged the right-hand side of this enormous chamber, winding up towards the far wall. They were halfway across the chamber, so close to the safety of Xos'Phet's subterranean sanctuary, when the gore-priest carrying him staggered to a halt.

'Did I order you to stop?' shrieked the sorcerer, flailing weakly at his servant with one pallid hand.

The creature took one step forwards, and then toppled to the floor. The other gorepriest just above managed to keep its bur-den upright, but then a blade flashed in from the shadows, and its throat sprayed dark, clotted blood. Xos'Phet rolled onto the hard floor of the cavern with a yelp, and saw more blood spray as a wiry, thin man with a dirty beard and the rags of a plains-dwelling savage knelt over his servant, hacking and slashing with mania-cal intensity.

Had he been his normal self, Xos'Phet would have slain the man in an instant. Perhaps with a single sheet of magical flame, or a sizzling bolt of acid. As it was, he could barely concentrate enough through the blur of pain to raise his hands in a futile ges-ture of surrender before the attacker was upon him.

Wild, frenzied eyes. Dried blood staining a narrow, angular face with dark, sun-baked skin. And, most importantly, a wicked curved blade in hand that was currently cutting into his tender neck.

'Wait,' he gasped. 'The plains rider. Rusik.'

His captor growled, and the sword dug a little deeper. Xos'Phet summoned every ounce of his self-control, and whispered an arcane phrase while weaving a complex pattern with his free hand.

He gestured, an open-palmed push, and his assailant flew to crash into the wall of the cavern with a bone-shaking thud. The man slid to the floor and rolled, coming to a rest only an inch from the lip of the abyss.

Xos'Phet clambered to his feet, still holding his hand out, locking the man in place. Rusik roared and strained, but could not break free of the binding spell.

'I should cut your heart out,' the sorcerer spat. 'Filthy savage, daring to attack me. After all I have done for you.'

Rusik shouted something unintelligible, and spat at him.

'I should,' Xos'Phet continued, 'but given our current situation, I may require your assistance. Those warriors in turquoise, they think us defeated. That wretched woman thinks she has slain me, but Xos'Phet the Eternal does not pass so easily.'

The warrior continued to grunt and snarl. Xos'Phet sighed. It had been an easy thing, to play upon this one's guilt and shame, but the trouble with tempting a man into sacrificing his soul to the Dark Gods was that they tended to take the whole thing very seriously.

'You want revenge, don't you?' he said, staring into the man's haunted eyes. 'I can give you that. I can give you the slaughter you desire, that and so much more.'

He stepped closer. The man's dark eyes had gone strangely still, as if he had slipped into a trance.

'Would you like that, Rusik?' he whispered. 'To have your revenge on those that have wronged you? To have power, true power?'

The warrior's eyes flashed, and he broke from Xos'Phet's hold for just a moment, swiping his curved blade up at an awkward angle, trying to slash the sorcerer's throat. Xos'Phet skittered backwards, laughing.

'Oh, very close,' he laughed. 'You almost had me fooled. In truth, however, it does not matter if you want this or not. I have great plans for you, my savage friend.'

He stepped to the body of one of his gorepriests and knelt to run his fingers through the thing's belt. He found the knife, and turned back to his prisoner.

'I mean to make you useful to me regardless,' he said.

'Something is wrong,' said Thostos.

They had been watching the Lord-Relictor weaving his spells upon the gate for over an hour, and for the majority of that time he had been as still as stone, only the sonorous muttering that came from deep in his throat any indication that he was at work. Now he was twitching, jerking as if wracked by lightning. Gone was the calm authority of his magic. His face was masked by the grinning skull that all Lord-Relictors wore, but Thostos could see the tightness of his posture and the shudder that ran through his frame.

'The gate,' gasped Mykos.

The harsh but pure light that poured into the Manticore Realm-gate began to darken and twist, turning to thick red veins of spiralling, crackling energy that pushed back at Tharros' storm magic. The Lord-Relictor set his feet and leaned into the onslaught, but it did not cease. The surface of the realmgate began to boil and surge, and a choir of sibilant whispers echoed around the fortress.

A grasping, red-scaled limb reached through the membrane of the portal.

'Shield!' shouted Mykos. 'Raise your blades.'

They belched forth from one reality into another, spewing into the mortal realm with eager hunger and the thunder of brim-stone fire. They were slaughter given flesh, the psychic resonance of the violence and fury of battle condensed into a brutal physi-cal form. Their flesh was the deep red of a sword wound, corded with powerful muscles and branded with runes of loyalty to their dread master. Sharp tongues hung over wicked, finger-length teeth, drooling acidic spittle that hissed as it dropped onto the hard stone floor. Great, curving horns capped their heads, wound with brass rings and capped with bronze. Each carried a wicked sword of unique design. Some writhed like snakes in their wielder's hands. Others bore eyes that blinked obscenely as the blade swept through the air, or blue-red veins that pulsed with blood.

'Form ranks!' yelled Thostos. These were no simple, mortal warriors. They had to hold them here, for if the bloodletters overran the defenders all would be lost.

The Liberators began to lock shields, responding with admirable speed to the shocking emergence of the daemon warriors. They formed a wall of gleaming sigmarite upon the platform before the portal, using the rock cluster that wound behind the realmgate to hem the attackers in and prevent them from breaking out into the fortress proper. Against a mortal enemy the Stormcasts' defence would have been almost impregnable.

With howls of atavistic rage the daemons leapt at the Stormcasts, hell-forged blades digging deep into sigmarite and reaching over the defenders' shields to pierce chests and helms. The bloodletters gave no thought to their own safety. All they knew was aggression, and this single-minded rage forced breaches in even the disciplined shield wall of the Celestial Vindicators. A dread note reverberated from the bronze, spiral warhorn of one of the daemons, and its fellows hacked and slashed with ever-greater fervour.

Yet the Celestial Vindicators did not fall back a single step.

Heaven-wrought warhammers sought daemonic flesh, pounding and blasting the hated foe back into the nightmare realm they called home. As fallen Stormcasts disappeared in flares of light, new warriors stepped in to take their place so quickly and efficiently that it almost seemed as if the movement was mechanical, that of a magically-charged automaton. There was no fear or uncertainty in the Stormcasts' mind, simply a surety of purpose and a fierce joy at the destruction of their most hated enemy.

'Vengeance for the lost!' they shouted as they fought. 'Glory to Sigmar's chosen!'

Thostos entered the fray, crossing his warhammer and rune-blade to intercept a falling sword that screamed in some unknowable tongue as it fell, wrenching the leering daemon's blade down low, and reversing the momentum to send the creature stumbling to the side. It hissed and cut across with a backhand slice, but Thostos span inside the cut and sank his blade into the monster's chest. It gurgled and choked, and as he let it fall to the ground its body burst into flame. He blocked another strike, left a bloodletter reeling with a returning blow from his warhammer.

Something heavy struck him a mighty blow on the side. He felt the air rush by as he somersaulted through the air, rolling twice in the dirt before coming to rest on his side. He was up in a moment, weapons raised and ready.

A colossal metal abomination paced towards him, a bloodletter perched screeching on its back. It was the rough shape of a horse, but squatter and far more heavily muscled, encased entirely in dull red metal and bronze. Steam hissed from its nostrils, and its smouldering hooves left brimstone prints in their wake.

The beast's dread rider cursed at him in a tongue of molten hatred.

Thostos charged. The creature came right at him, scattering Stormcasts before it, kicking itself forwards on powerful hind legs, the daemonic rider lowering his heavy blade like a tourney lance. It ate up the ground towards him at a terrifying pace, bellowing with mindless rage.

A few yards from the creature, close enough to smell its brimstone stench, Thostos hurled himself forwards and to the right.

As he passed, he heard the crunch of the beast's hooves narrowly missing his skull, felt a blade rush past his head so close he could feel its foul heat.

He swept his sword across, allowing the beast's momentum to add to his own. It sliced deep into the thing's flank, and hot black liquid spurted out. The creature bucked, swaying to one side, and the rider came free, clattering to the ground with a metal thud. Dragging himself to his feet, Thostos ran the ten paces to the downed daemon, and swung his hammer at its head. The bloodletter screeched in rage as the weapon fell, a scream that was cut off abruptly as its skull shattered into fragments.

Ahead, the beast was struggling upright. It kicked out savagely with its rear hooves, and an unfortunate Stormcast was sent sailing backwards into his fellows, chestplate battered and deformed. Outraged, the warriors fell on the daemonic steed, hacking and blasting it apart with furious blows.

'Lord Thostos!' came Eldroc's voice, and Thostos turned to see the Lord-Castellant barrelling towards him, clearing a path with his halberd and gesturing wildly towards the gate itself. 'The Lord-Relictor is overwhelmed!'

Tharros was kneeling, hands clasped together around the haft of his stave, which was pointed at the enemy like a spear. Coruscating energy surged and crackled around the artefact, spools of lightning sparking out at the bloodletters desperately trying to reach him. They could not get close without Sigmar's storm searing the flesh from their bones, but Thostos could see that Tharros would not be able to maintain his heroic defence for long.

'With me, brother,' he shouted to Eldroc, and together they surged into the fray, clearing a path towards their fellow warrior.

Rusik screamed. In all his life he had never felt such a pure and constant agony. Yet there were no knives digging into his flesh, no flaming brands or bone-crushing mallets mutilating his body.

Instead it was as if he was being devoured from within, great strips of his flesh being torn away, fingers running across his brain.

'By the Great Changer, silence his whining,' came a voice from his side.

Strong, cold hands forced a filthy wrap into his mouth. He choked and felt his gorge rise as he tasted dried blood, but his hands were bound and the gag was tight. His back ached with the chill of cold stone.

His eyes flicked about, taking in a low, roughly-hewn stone chamber, walls lined with bookcases and display cases filled with all manner of sorcerous ephemera. Shrunken heads screamed silently at him from jars filled with pulsing green fluid. Bones, hides and other fragments of almost-human things lined the walls, and around each specimen were notes scrawled in luminous blue, in a language Rusik could not read. There were other slabs like his, and other figures were draped across them. They were all long dead. He could smell the sweet stench of putrefaction, mixing with the spicy, metal tang of fresh blood.

A face leaned over him. A thin, sallow face that shimmered oddly in the flickering blue light that filled the chamber.

The cruel face spoke. 'You may not recognise me, my friend, but I know you so very well. Oh yes. Rusik the betrayer.'

A cackle turned into a hacking cough.

'I walked amongst your filthy tribesmen many times,' the voice continued. 'It was something of a hobby of mine. A word in the ear here and there, and the next time you sent out a hunting party, it would go exactly where I wanted it to. Well, those savages at the Dreadhold needed to eat, after all.'

More pain. Rusik screamed again, louder and longer than before.

'To gather the quantity of sacrifices needed for the ritual, though, that required a defter touch,' the figure continued to talk. 'And that was where you came in. So angry. So guilty. So mortal.'

No. Rusik knew what the man was going to say, but he tried to turn his face away. He did not want to hear the words.

'Oh so very easy,' came the voice again. 'I barely needed to tax myself. You saw what you wanted to see, heard what I let you hear.'

He strained against the bonds that held him fast, spat and cursed and raged. Try as he might, he could not break free. Something struck him in the face, and his vision swam.

'You made it so simple. I did not even know what your dead woman looked like, but that hardly mattered to you. You chose to see her. You tried to salve your conscience by pretending it was she. But it was you, Rusik. This is what you wanted.'

A blade sank into his chest, and began a long, circular cut. He screamed and choked on the foul gag in his mouth. Deeper and deeper went the knife.

'Hush, hush,' said the voice. 'Your moaning is really quite irritating, and most unnecessary. Think of this as a gift. When I am finished with you, you'll be much improved. More powerful than even those toy soldiers who dared destroy my work at the Dreadhold. And no more guilt, Rusik. No more regrets, no more shame.'

The knife made a complete circuit, and Rusik felt something pull the torn flesh of his chest apart. He dared to look down. In one pale hand the sorcerer grasped a fleshy, pulsing organ.

'Only pain,' the man said with a broad smile.

Judicator Atrin held his boltstorm crossbow high, jammed tight to his shoulder and ready to fire the moment that the shadows shifted. It had not happened yet, but he was sure it would. This place had an ill feel to it.

Atrin had a second sense for trouble. It took a good eye to join the ranks of the Vindicators' archers, but even amongst that hallowed number, Atrin was known to have the sharpest vision. The rest of the warriors called him Eagle-Eyes, much to his embarrassment. Titles and glory had never meant much to Atrin, and he always felt slightly awkward and uncomfortable when others lavished praise upon him.

This was what he lived for. The hunt. The chase. In another life he had been a forest ranger, and the skill of navigating a landscape without disturbing it had not been lost in the forges of Azyrheim.

'Yet no sign of the enemy,' came the deep bass of Retributor Callan. 'How long shall we traipse through these wretched caves before we accept that this is a waste of our time?'

'With due respect, Paladin,' said Judicator Oreus. 'The Lord-Celestant gave the order, and we obey.'

His brother's tone was even, but Atrin knew Oreus well enough to recognise that the warrior was no happier than Callan about being sent off with the mortals while the rest of the Chamber prepared for war. He was simply far too reserved and professional to complain.

Callan, however, was not.

'Who knows how long it will take for Tharros to unseal the realmgate,' he muttered, loudly enough so that the rest of the mortals, and indeed anyone in the surrounding few miles, could hear his every word. 'Imagine it. We return to find our brothers gone on to glory without us, while we wasted our time wandering around in the dark.'

Atrin could hear the irritated murmurs of the mortals who had accompanied the priestess Alzheer on this expedition. They might see the sky warriors as heralds of their sky god, but they had formed a distinctly negative impression of the belligerent Callan.

'The Lord-Relictor believes it will take many hours to finish his work,' said Oreus. 'We were given strict instruction by the Lord-Celestant as to how long we continue this search. They will not leave us behind.'

'So you hope,' said Callan, and lapsed into sullen silence.

The Retributor barely even raised his head as they passed into a cavernous chamber so vast it could have housed the entirety of Sigmar's grand throne room. They trod a path that wound around the right side of the cavern, and on their left was a sheer drop coloured an azure blue by phosphorescent light. Above, a forest of stalactites as large as dracoliths hung, so thick and jagged it seemed to the party like they stared up at the teeth of a shark.

'Throne of Sigmar,' muttered Atrin.

'Look,' said Alzheer, ignoring the sight before them and kneeling down to study the rough-hewn path of stone. 'Fresh kills.'

Several yards down the path lay two corpses, both mutilated by deep wounds. There was a spatter of gore on the ground, as well as an arc splashed across the cavern wall. The priestess turned one of the bodies over, examining it. She traced the edge of the wounds, and winced slightly as the stench of the dead things hit her. They looked humanoid, but their too-thin figures were hidden under leather smocks and bloody, rotting bandages. The eyes and mouths of both bodies were stitched closed. They reeked like month-old corpses.

'This may not be the work of your man,' Callan said. 'More than a few Chaos scum fled into these mountains after we broke their back. This could be down to any number of them.'

Alzheer shook her head.

'These wounds,' she said, indicating the long, wide slashes in the creatures' flesh. 'These are from an eskar, a curved blade. See the wide, deep cuts? Cleaner work than the jagged axes and cleavers of the fortress men. No, this is Rusik.'

'And what in Azyr are these things?' said Callan, indicating the corpses.

She frowned. 'The sorcerer in the tower used them as… servants. Butchers. They answered only to his command. I thought that we slew them all.'

'Evidently not,' said Callan. 'Perhaps we'll find ourselves a fight down here after all.'

'We should move,' said Alzheer. 'The blood is still flowing. These kills are fresh. He is close.'

The daemon was only an inch from Tharros' face, but he could not release his magic, for that would not only spell the end of the Celestial Vindicators' hopes of carrying out Sigmar's word, but would in all likelihood force open the already-substantial breach and allow yet more of these filthy creatures through. He managed to raise his relic staff to block the swing of the creature's blade, but its strength was hideous. Its leering, coal-black eyes stared deep into the apertures of his skull helm, and he felt its sulphurous breath sear and scorch his armour.

There was a sharp rush of air, and suddenly the beast had no head at all. A gaping neck wound pumped boiling black ichor across his face, until a gauntleted hand grasped the dead thing and flung it away to crash in the dirt.

'Are you injured, Lord-Relictor?' came the soft, alarmed voice of Mykos Argellon.

Tharros did not risk speaking, but managed to shake his head as he continued to chant the ritual of cleansing.

Around him, he saw, the battle continued to rage. The Celestial Vindicators had recovered from the shock of the initial incursion, but these were no blood-mad savages that they faced. These were the shock troops of the Blood God himself, creatures forged and hardened by countless millennia of warfare.

Throne of Azyrheim, he was tired. His old bones rattled like dice in a cup as he staggered to his feet.

Another red-skinned nightmare capered forwards, and Lord-Celestant Bladestorm met it with a flurry of strikes from warhammer and blade. The thing toppled to the floor, bursting into flames as it was banished to the hellish realm that it called home.

'Close this breach, Lord-Relictor,' shouted Thostos, who was already assigning a formation of shield-bearing Liberators to surround Tharros. 'And do it now.'

Tharros declined to launch into a lengthy explanation of exactly how complex the magic at play was, and how one did not simply decide when it was done. Thostos Bladestorm was a warrior, a being of action. Let him be about his work. The Lord-Relictor felt the song of the storm surround him, let its power course through every fibre of his being. He heard the rabid howls of delight that echoed from the mouth of the Manticore Realmgate, and beneath that frenzied madness he heard a softer whisper, that same cold and ancient promise that haunted his dreams and his nightmares. The promise that one day, the scales would be balanced, and his eternal soul would be reclaimed. Perhaps that would be this day.

So be it.

'Something nears,' said Alzheer. She was sharp, that one, thought Atrin. She did not let much show, but she took things in. You didn't live as close to the earth as her people without being able to tell when danger drew close.

'Let us take the lead,' he told her. They had left the grand cavern and passed through a seemingly endless coil of tunnels and hollows, eventually entering a far smaller chamber packed with glistening stalactites, each of which shone with a faint, flickering luminescence. Ahead, a vague path led through a field of mushrooms, before spiralling up around a colossal column of black rock to a shelf of stone some dozen yards above them. The roof of the cavern was far overhead, and in the soft light Atrin could see movement up there – a flock of small, dark creatures that twitched and jostled nervously as the warriors passed.

'Cave hawks,' said Alzheer, gesturing at the movement. 'Their presence is a good thing. They would not nest here if other predators were close.'

As one, the entire flock of dark, black birds took flight.

They whipped around the heads of the hunting party in a mass of whirling feathers and jabbing beaks. They moved too fast and the light was too poor for Atrin to get a good look at them, but he caught a glimpse of pale, milk-white eyes and sharp, toothed beaks.

'And what does this mean?' shouted Callan, buffeting the small birds away irritably with the haft of his great hammer.

'Either we made too much noise,' said Alzheer, drawing her shortbow and peering into the darkness, 'or something worse...'

A terrible, hollow shriek echoed around the cavern, and they heard the sound of running boots. The sound reverberated around the cavern, making it almost impossible to pick out which direction it originated from.

'Something worse then,' said Retributor Callan, hefting his weapon and not even attempting to hide his delight. 'Finally.'

No sooner had he spoken than the shadows before them shifted. A figure stood on the ledge before them at the top of the stone stair, curved blade in hand. Its eyes shone with a cold, white malice, and it bellowed in a voice that could not possibly come from a mortal throat.

It was him, Alzheer was sure. Rusik the betrayer, the man who had abandoned her people to the depredations of the men of the fortress.

She stood, raised her bow and felt the tickle of the crow-feather arrow at her cheek. She loosed, and it zipped away into the darkness and struck the thing that looked like Rusik in the chest. He did not even stagger. The arrow whipped away as it struck something hard as stone, and he looked straight at her.

His pale eyes glittered, and he raised his blade towards her silently.

'Get back,' said Atrin, stepping forwards and unleashing a flurry of shots with his crossbow. Each bolt that issued forth crackled with the power of the storm, and the far wall disintegrated as the volley slammed home. Alzheer caught a blur of movement in the strobing light of the cavern as something impossibly fast dived out of the way of the barrage.

'Did you get him?' asked Oreus, who had his own bow raised.

Atrin said nothing. He was still scanning the rise, searching for a hint of movement. Something dropped from the far left wall of the cavern. More shapes emerged from the depths of the mushroom field. He held his aim until one passed into the shimmering light. Thin, unnaturally so. Eyes hidden behind a wrap of bloody bandages. Air wheezing from behind a stitched mouth.

Oreus loosed an arrow. It struck the thing in the chest, and an explosion of light blasted the creature backwards.

'Ambush!' the Judicator shouted. 'Ready your blades.'

The mortals were already loosing arrows into the thick of the creatures that rushed at them, but in the darkness and the chaos, few found their mark. Oreus and Atrin continued to shoot, blasting chunks of stone free and shredding the fungi as they hammered the advancing mob. Those that survived the barrage met the hammer of Retributor Callan. He moved the heavy weapon as if it weighed less than a child's toy, sweeping it from side to side to clear out groups of the creatures, letting his constant momentum add fearsome power to his attacks.

Atrin had no idea where the damned things were coming from, but there appeared to be no end to them. He heard screams from behind and turned to see more of the bandaged creatures hacking and slashing their way into the ranks of the mortal warriors. He tried to aim, but there were simply too many bodies in the way for him to get a clear shot. He slung his crossbow and drew his gladius.

'Out of the way,' he yelled, grabbing hold of a tribal warrior and yanking him backwards to safety, trying to get his sigmarite armour in the way of the enemy's frenzied attacks. To their credit, the mortals had responded well, falling back and forming a defensive circle of blades and spears. Yet from every direction more of the creatures dropped, scrambling through holes in the wall or appearing from behind the great clusters of fungi that spiralled around stalagmites and across the cavern walls.

Atrin grabbed one of the creatures around the throat, stabbed his gladius into its chest and threw the thing away, then landed a punch that snapped another's jaw with a sickening crunch. He leapt out in front of the mortals, stabbing and slicing with his blade, forcing a breach for them to exploit.

'Atrin!' shouted Oreus from behind. 'More of them come. We will be surrounded.'

He cut another bandaged horror down with a diagonal slash that opened its wrappings from throat to belly, and turned to see Callan almost drowning under the sheer number of hacking, slashing creatures. The Retributor battered away at the swarm, but there were too many of them inside the range of his hammer. Oreus risked shots where he could, blasting several into smoking ruins.

'Hold them here,' yelled Atrin, grabbing the shoulder of the nearest mortal. 'Keep them at bay with your spears.'

With that he rushed to aid his stricken brother, drawing his crossbow once more.

'Callan, get down,' he shouted, and the Retributor trusted his comrade's word instantly, dropping to the floor and shielding himself as the enemy fell with him, dragged down by his weight.

Atrin loosed, sending a volley of deadly projectiles ripping through the ranks of the enemy. Fragments of scorched wrapping and torn flesh splattered the walls of the cave as Oreus added his own missiles to the barrage.

No sooner had Callan staggered to his feet amongst the wreckage of his assailants than something struck Atrin with astonishing force, propelling him across the clearing and into a cluster of rocks, which crumbled under the weight of his armour. He groaned in shock and pain. By the Eight Realms, that one had hurt. Distantly, as if he were underwater, he heard a muffled, high-pitched laughter, and a fell green light doused the walls of the cavern.

Someone was screaming. It was Callan. His armour was on fire, a curtain of searing viridian flame clinging to him even as he rolled on the ground in an attempt to quell it.

'Brother!' shouted Oreus, drawing his gladius and barrelling, shoulder down, into the press of bodies, smashing his way through to his fallen comrade.

The Judicator made it a dozen paces before a swirl of purple and yellow motes enveloped him. They looked harmless, but as Atrin watched on helplessly his brother's armour sloughed away like dust, bursting into the air as if someone had rustled a great field of pollinating flowers. The warrior turned, and looked straight at Atrin, then down at his hands. He did not even scream as his body came apart.

Tharros could feel his skin starting to burn. One did not summon the celestial storm without cost. It was a pure and violent power, wondrous yes, but not something to be taken lightly. Channelling it, shaping it was akin to grasping a burning ember from a roaring fire. Leave your hand in that fire too long, and the flames would begin to consume you.

Yet he could not relent. Daemons still poured through the Manticore Realmgate, and while the Celestial Vindicators were keeping them at bay thus far, they could not hold out forever.

He must end this now.

Tharros released the storm, let it flow through him unrestricted and unconstrained. He focussed only on the realmgate, and the fell magic that was woven into every fragment of its being. It had been crafted by old and powerful means, sorceries and sacrifices that had allowed it to stand for centuries upon centuries in the service of darkness. He saw the history of it, the bloodshed it had sown and the souls it had eagerly devoured. Old heroes had fallen here, their defiance and heroism long forgotten. In the little time that was left to him, Tharros honoured their bravery.

Spirits spiralled around him, singing the same mournful song that haunted his dreams. Every death brought him closer to a reckoning that had been inevitable since he had pledged himself to Sigmar's service, but there was nothing to be done. His brothers needed him, and he would not let them down.

The storm that enveloped the dread realmgate flared, brighter and stronger than before. Nothing could stand in the light of that power. There was a scream of shearing stone as an arc of lightning slammed into the great manticore statue that stood above the gate. The lion's head fell free, crushing a hollering daemon beneath it as it crashed to the ground.

Tharros could barely stand now. He felt the exquisite agony as the power he had unleashed devoured him from the inside. Still, he did not relent. Bolt after bolt of aetheric power slammed into the ornate carving of the realmgate. The fell runes and sigils that lined the obsidian archway were burned and scorched away, and as they were cleansed Tharros could hear the terrified, agonised scream of whatever foul consciousness inhabited the monument. It writhed and burned as he did.

He allowed himself a smile.

The Lord-Relictor did not relent, even as the daemons ceased to pour through the portal, and the Vindicators began to break up and slaughter the outnumbered bloodletters that remained.

The green fire had ceased, but Callan lay still. His armour had melted until it was almost unidentifiable, the sigils and symbols of his allegiance now warped and seared.

'Callan,' yelled Atrin. 'You must get up!'

Even as the Judicator spoke, the creatures were upon his brother.

They did not attack him with their long knives, but instead wrapped great chains around his arms and legs.

'Oh, this will be most enlightening,' came a voice from above. Atrin craned his neck to see a small, pale figure floating in the air, pinched face split by a fierce grin. 'I will crack him open, and see what you fellows are made of. Are you men under there I wonder? How much pain can you stand before you expire? So many questions.'

Atrin did not bother to respond and simply snapped his crossbow up to blast the snivelling weakling from the sky.

Something cut deep into his flesh. He gasped and turned, and looked into eyes that burned with a cold and terrible fire. The face they belonged to was mortal, though warped and broken as if something had tried to force its way free from the inside. The skin was stretched taut, split in places to show the flesh beneath. It was the traitor Rusik, or it was something wearing his face as a mask.

Atrin tried to slash his gladius across the thing's neck, but it slammed a clawed arm into his chest and he crashed to the ground, stunned at the sheer power of the blow.

'I was so close, so very close to binding my army, to finally having the power necessary to punish those who have wronged me,' ranted the floating figure. 'And then you came, and you ruined it all.'

Invisible hands grabbed Atrin and slammed him into the ground again and again.

'Now I am forced to turn to new avenues of research,' continued the figure. 'I will start by taking one of your kind, and tearing them apart until I discover how they work. Perhaps I will discover something useful, perhaps not. Either way it will improve my mood immensely.'

A simple gesture from the sorcerer, and the ground that was supporting the Judicator's weight turned to sand. He fell, grasping desperately for a handhold. Below him was only darkness. He caught the edge of the abyss and hung there while the immense weight of his armour did its best to dislodge him. The thing that had been Rusik stared down at him with those cold-fire eyes.

'Unfortunately for you, my friend,' said the sorcerer, 'I need only one subject.'

Atrin could hold on no longer. His hands slipped free, and fading laughter followed him into darkness.

'Lord-Relictor?' shouted Mykos Argellon, over the thunder of the aetheric storm. 'Tharros, the daemons are gone.'

The soul guardian knelt as if in prayer, his reliquary staff planted in the earth and his head bowed. Mykos felt a surge of static as he moved close, enough to make him take a backwards step.

'He cannot hear you, brother,' said Thostos, sheathing his runeblade and hammer as he approached. 'He is too deep in concentration. The sheer will that it must take to keep this gate contained, to prevent its energies from being unleashed. Whatever the Chaos filth were doing here, it has awoken some fell presence within this structure.'

He gestured to the Lord-Relictor. 'Only the strength of one man kept it at bay. Now Tharros Soulwarden ceases defending and launches his own assault. We must hope he still has the strength left to overcome.'

'It will kill him,' said Mykos.

'Perhaps. Even a master of death is not immune to its touch,' said Thostos. 'If Tharros falls here, he will do so performing his duty. He could ask for nothing more.'

Around the Lord-Celestants four-score warriors of the Celestial Vindicators were arranging themselves in a tight defensive formation in front of the gate. None of them wished to be caught by surprise again. Thostos turned to oversee the deployment, leaving a complement of Judicators and Liberators to guard the

Lord-Relictor and the gate, while the rest of the men continued the business of clearing and refortifying the Dreadhold. The
stench of brimstone still lingered in the air, blending with the
aura of rotting flesh and stale sweat that permeated the fortress.
By Sigmar, Mykos hated this place. It offered nothing but death
and misery.

'He's a stubborn old creature,' said Lord-Castellant Eldroc.
Mykos had not heard him approach. 'He won't give in lightly,
believe me.'

'You know him well,' said Mykos.

Eldroc chuckled. 'As well as anyone can know a storm priest.
They tend not to be the most companionable sorts.'

'He does not speak of his position? Of the nature of his magic?'

'Not a word,' said Eldroc. 'Lord-Relictors are the keepers of
secrets, my friend. They are the guardians of knowledge lost, and
they know things that elsewise only Sigmar is privy to.'

'I would like to have known him better,' said Mykos.

'He is not gone yet. As I say, he's as stubborn as an ancient dra-
colith and twice as hard to kill.'

Mykos glanced at his friend. He could not help but suspect that
Eldroc was trying to convince himself as much as anyone else.

Liberator Archus hauled the corpse of the bandaged creature
over his shoulder, marched over to the makeshift pyre they had
built in the centre of the tower, and dumped it into the flames.

'Sigmar's blood, the stench of these things,' he said.

'This entire place smells wrong,' said Tyron, dragging two more
of the creatures over, leaving a fresh trail of blood across the
stone. 'The Lord-Relictor might say he can purify the realmgate,
but there's no removing the taint from this place.'

Archus looked at the far end of the tower, towards the burned
and withered figures still bound to those barbed iron crosses.

'We should cut those down, whatever they are,' he said.

'You're very welcome to do so, brother. I've another five of these delightful things to attend to,' said Tyron.

Archus sighed, drew his gladius from the sheath on his belt, and strode across to the crucified figures. As he approached he had to wince at the awful smell. It wasn't just the acrid tang of burned flesh – the stench of loathsome magic clung to each of the desiccated forms, and it made Archus nauseous. This close, it was obvious these things had once been orruks. Cracked, blackened teeth jutted from their thick jaws, and the vaguely porcine outline of their faces was still just about visible.

He lifted his gladius to cut the spiked wire bindings that locked the thing in place.

Behind him, from a great distance, there came a roll of thunder. He turned in surprise. It did not seem the weather for a storm. He cocked an ear. Again the same sound. It wasn't thunder. It echoed and reverberated, not a single noise but an atonal choir of thousands of voices roaring a single word as one.

'Wwwaaaaaaaagggghh!'

He spun around, gladius raised.

The three broken creatures that languished upon the cruel spikes of the Dreadhold were not dead. Archus saw the eager madness in their pink, bloodshot eyes. Their mouths were open, and as one they droned the same jarring, cacophonous refrain, a blissful response to the call that echoed from the mouth of Splitskull Pass.

CHAPTER FIVE

Battle for Splitskull Pass

Prosecutor-Prime Evios Goldfeather soared high into the air, racing away from the relative safety of the Manticore Dreadhold. Ahead lay the canyon that led out onto the Roaring Plains, a narrow pass bracketed by towering walls of jagged stone. His warriors followed in his wake, storm-forged weapons already summoned to hand, faces grim. They knew what was coming.

They could still hear the sound.

Thousands upon thousands of brutish voices raised in a bestial choir, a savage howl of battle-lust that shook dust from the canyon wall. No small force could make such a sound. This was a war-band. A gathering with nothing but destruction on its mind.

The canyon snaked below them as the Prosecutors flew on. It stretched on for at least a mile and a half, gently curving to the right and left before breaking out of the mountain range and spilling out into the grassland of the great plain. It was here that they found the main complement of the enemy force, and Goldfeather felt his heart sink as he saw just what the Celestial Vindicators now faced.

An army of orruks so vast that it was beyond counting poured into the mouth of the pass, bellowing and roaring with delight as they clattered towards the Dreadhold on stocky, powerful mounts wrapped in crude, yellow-painted armour. The rhythmic thump of war-drums combined with the clatter of the orruks' mounts was almost deafening. The enormous dust clouds thrown up in the wake of the advance billowed above the canyon.

'They have a dozen times our number,' said Galeth, coming to a stop in the air at Goldfeather's side, ornate wings glittering in the midday sun. 'Ten thousand at the least.'

'And cavalry too,' the Prosecutor-Prime replied. 'Those creatures they ride are fearsome-looking things.'

'They'll be here well before nightfall. We must warn the Lord-Celestants.'

Goldfeather nodded and signalled his men to fall back. He had no idea what the Celestial Vindicators could do to halt this tide of iron and flesh, but whatever it was, it would have to be quick. If this force fell upon the Dreadhold unopposed, the garrison would be quickly overwhelmed. With Lord-Relictor Tharros still in the process of removing the taint from the cursed Manticore Realmgate, they could not give up the fortress.

The Prosecutor-Prime cursed. That meant they would have to meet the orruks in battle, one way or another.

'Back to the fortress, brother,' he told Galeth. 'Let us deliver the good news firsthand.'

Lord-Celestant Mykos Argellon had not expected pleasant tidings from the Prosecutors' return, but the news that the entire orruk camp had been mobilised against them was still a sobering revelation. The Argellonites and Bladestorm Warrior Chambers of the Celestial Vindicators had already been battered and bloodied by the myriad dangers of the Roaring Plains, and though even a battle-worn army of Stormcast Eternals was a dangerous proposition for any foe, engaging the orruks was not the task given to them by the God-King. That objective lay through the Manticore Realmgate, in a distant corner of the Mortal Realms.

'Ten thousand,' muttered the Lord-Castellant Eldroc, shaking his head. 'And several thousand of those mounted on war-beasts. The Dreadhold offers us a strong defence, but not against such numbers.'

Mykos' fellow Lord-Celestant Thostos Bladestorm stared off into the distance, showing no apparent sign of concern.

'We cannot allow them to breach the walls,' he said at last. 'The Lord-Relictor still works his magic. Until he has completed his incantations, the Manticore Realmgate is closed to us.'

He strode to the rampart wall, and rested one gauntlet upon the black iron, pointing out at the canyon mouth with the other. The craggy corridor of stone lay a few hundred yards to the west of the Dreadhold, the ghoulish howl of the orruk horde still echoing from its jagged mouth.

'The canyon is narrow,' he said. 'Narrow enough for a few hundred men to defend it wall to wall. If we can hold the enemy charge, we will bottleneck their force. Thin it out. Buy the time we need for the Lord-Relictor to finish his work.'

There was a silence. Mykos was sure every Stormcast present was thinking the same as he. Any force sent out to perform such a task would likely never return. It was a solid enough position to defend, but the moment the enemy force broke through they would be surrounded and destroyed. Against a cavalry charge, they would have no opportunity to retreat even the relatively short distance back to the fortress.

'We have no choice,' said Eldroc, and all present acknowledged the defensive expertise of the Lord-Castellant, the Keeper of Keys. 'This fortress will not withstand an assault by several thousand fresh troops. We must deny them the pass. It is a natural choke point, and the only method we have of evening out this fight.'

Thostos nodded. 'The Bladestorm will march,' he said. 'We will hold the pass. Lord-Celestant Argellon–'

'No,' said Mykos. His heart hammered in his chest, but he felt a sense of surety and purpose that he had not felt in a long time. 'No, Lord-Celestant Thostos, this is the Argellonites' task.'

Thostos looked at him, and for once Mykos did not feel uncomfortable gazing into the harsh blue glare of his eyes.

'You must lead them,' he said. 'This is your mission, brother. Let me and my men buy you the time you need to complete it.'

'This is our mission, not my own.'

'Think of your battle against the lord of the Dreadhold, Thostos,' said Mykos, shaking his head. 'Did Sigmar reach out through the realms to restore you, only to have you fall here? No, your task is still to come. This is mine.'

There was a long silence, with nothing but the roar of the wind and the faint sound of drums in the distance. Finally, Thostos nodded stiffly. He snapped one gauntleted hand to his breast in salute, and Mykos did the same.

'We have had our differences, Lord-Celestant Argellon,' said Thostos, 'but I have never doubted your courage or your ability. Hold the line, and do not give them a single bloodless step forward.'

'For Sigmar, and for the lost,' said Mykos. Then he turned to Eldroc. The Lord-Castellant placed a hand on his shoulder.

Mykos smiled. 'Goodbye, my friend,' he said.

'Hold to your oaths, brother,' said Eldroc. 'We shall meet again.'

There was little time to waste, and so in only a few minutes the five hundred warriors of the Argellonites Warrior Chamber were marching out of the Dreadhold, passing through the shattered gatehouse with its warped symbols of ruin and bronzed skulls. As they marched through, the Stormcasts assigned to shore up the ruined entrance saluted solemnly, striking a single fist against their chests. Despite the danger that awaited him, Mykos was not sad to see the last of the cursed fortress. It was tainted in a way that could never truly be cleansed, and the Lord-Celestant hoped that one day the forces of order would find the time to tear it down, stone by stone.

Knight-Heraldor Axilon marched at his side, singing along in his deep baritone to the Battle-hymn of Defiance, a favourite amongst the ranks of the Argellonites. The deep, determined voices of the Stormcasts drowned out the witless howl of the orruks.

'Send them a message, Knight-Heraldor,' said Mykos as they stepped out onto the dry earth outside the Dreadhold. 'Let them know that Sigmar reclaims this land.'

'As you say, Lord-Celestant,' said Axilon with a grin, reaching for his battle-horn.

The voices of the Bladestorm warriors on the battlements blended with the singing of the Argellonites as they marched towards the mouth of the canyon. A clear, perfect note issued forth from Axilon's battle-horn, a radiant sound of hope and glory that echoed out across the savage wilderness.

'He will give us the time we need,' said Eldroc, watching his friend march out towards an almost certain death.

'Let us hope so,' replied Thostos. His voice was as cold and emotionless as ever. 'All rests on the next few hours. If the fortress falls, we will not be in position at the Crystal Forest as Sigmar demands. The entire offensive may unravel.'

Eldroc understood his Lord-Celestant's concern. The timing was too tight. They must cleanse the Manticore Realmgate and pass through it into hostile territory, there to meet with the contact that would lead them to their ultimate objective. Sigmar was once again set to take the war directly to the forces of Chaos, and to do so every piece on the board had to be in the correct place at the correct time. There was a long path still to travel, and doubly so considering the losses they had already taken.

'He will give us the time we need,' he repeated.

'It will hurt us to lose him,' said Thostos. 'Too often he lets his emotion rule him, but he is a fine warrior and a clever leader. His Argellonites fight well.'

'He is a good man,' agreed Eldroc.

The Lord-Castellant sighed, deeply and wearily. Mykos Argellon would likely die this day, and in a flash of celestial power he would be called back to the halls of Azyrheim, where he would be reforged by the wondrous power of Sigmar's storm. Perhaps he would retain a memory of the man he had been. In all likelihood, he would not. The thoughtful, noble man that Eldroc had grown to admire would be gone, and in his place would be... someone else. Someone damaged, and uncertain. Or perhaps someone cold and distant, like Lord-Celestant Thostos himself.

This war would claim the best of them all.

The sky above the Roaring Plains crackled and thundered, great grey clouds rumbling above the Manticore Dreadhold and bringing with them a stinging sheet of rain. Evios Goldfeather felt the downpour on his armour as he spiralled into the sky, climbing high above the canyon and searching for signs of the enemy.

He could see them now. The walls of the canyon had a slight overhang which masked the winding tunnel, but even through the heavy rain he could see the bright yellow of the orruks' spiked iron armour, splattered liberally with red symbols that contrasted violently with the green flesh of the brutish creatures.

They had made the mouth of the cavern just in time. It would be only a few moments until the leading edge of the orruk horde crashed into the shields of the Celestial Vindicators. Evios was no coward, but he did not envy the Liberators who would stand in the front ranks, the first wall against which the tidal wave of enemy cavalry would crash.

Movement above the canyon wall caught his eye. Out into the open air came strange, bloated, reptilian creatures, each with a whooping orruk astride its back. They were so stocky and powerful that it seemed impossible that their leathery wings could keep them aloft, let alone with a heavy creature upon their backs, but on they came at a fair speed, accelerating now that they saw Goldfeather's Prosecutors heading towards them. Goldfeather nodded, satisfied.

His first target of the day.

Ideally, Mykos Argellon would have liked to push further into the canyon, establishing fallback points and switchbacks from which his reserve could launch fresh attacks when the momentum of the enemy charge played out. The ground here was stable, only just beginning to dampen and fill with the constant downpour. There were divots, potholes and occasional scattered rocks, but it was still decent cavalry terrain, largely flat and featureless.

'Give me an hour and I could make this a killing ground,' the Lord-Celestant muttered in frustration.

There was simply no time. Perhaps two hundred yards into the canyon they halted and began to form up. The sound of the orruks' chanting was overwhelming now, backed by the chaotic, arrhythmic sound of thousands of iron-shod hooves. The ground shook beneath their feet, and rocks crumbled from the canyon wall and clattered off sigmarite plate.

'Form the line!' shouted Axilon. 'Quickly now.'

Barely heeding the cacophony that grew louder and louder with each passing moment, Mykos' Warrior Chamber began to take up their assigned positions. Liberator-Primes bellowed orders, forming their men into compact blocks, wondrous tower shields raised, warhammers and blades held at the ready. This would be the solid core of the Argellonites' defence, the beating heart of their formation. If they could hold the line in the face of the enemy charge, the Paladin retinues could push forwards from the second rank, exploiting gaps in the enemy line with ruthless aggression.

Behind the infantry were the Justicars. They held their bows taut, ready to pour lightning up and over the heads of their brothers and into the orruk ranks.

His warriors had barely finished manoeuvring into position when Mykos Argellon saw the leading edge of the enemy charge.

'Sigmar's blood,' said Axilon beside him.

It was no army. No organised fighting force. Such definitions seemed entirely inappropriate. This was an extinction event, roaring down the channel of the canyon towards them. It was a tidal wave of rusting iron and hollering green flesh, borne aloft on tusked beasts with eyes that glowed with murderous red delight. There was no measured charge, no effort to form a cohesive line. They charged as a great spear, bounding towards the Vindicators' position with no thought to their own, simply a demented glee at the prospect of battle. Mykos saw more than one rider disappear under the storm of iron as his mount stumbled and fell. Others were crushed against the canyon wall, the momentum of their fellows grinding them to pieces upon the unyielding stone. The first arrows of the Judicators fell in arcs of searing lightning, scorching and blasting riders from their crude saddles. It was like throwing pebbles into an ocean. They were only two hundred paces away now, and gaining speed.

'Stand firm, brothers of the storm,' Mykos shouted above the noise of the enemy charge. 'Here we make these witless creatures pay for every loyal human life they have taken. They will break upon our shields and die upon our blades.'

Axilon blasted another note from his battle-horn, and the sound soared and bounded around the canyon, filling Mykos' heart with hope and determination.

'Stand firm, warriors of vengeance! Stand firm, seekers of justice. Stand firm!'

Liberator Archus was in the very front rank of the Stormcast position. He held his shield forwards and raised, his legs bent slightly, his back pressed firmly against the shield of the warrior behind him. Shields. He felt like laughing. As if a shield, even a wondrous one such as his, which had saved his life from countless dangers faced in the service of Sigmar, could protect him from the apocalypse that surged towards him.

He shook his head, clearing away the doubt and the fear. He was going to die, but his death would slow the enemy charge just a fraction. The man behind him would die as well, but again his fellow warrior's death would absorb a portion of that hideous momentum. With their deaths, they would mire the enemy, slow it down and leave it vulnerable to the hammers and blades of their fellows. What would this death be like, he wondered? He had never been reforged. He had heard tales, though, of hollow souls and lost memories. He wondered if it would hurt as much as his first death, when the Skullsworn had taken his scalp and left him to bleed out upon the stairs of his home, screaming his agonised oaths of vengeance.

He would not miss that memory.

They enemy was only a few dozen yards away now. The noise was astonishing. He could feel the vibration deep in his bones.

'I'll find you back in Azyrheim, my friend,' shouted Tyron at his side. 'The first ales are on you.'

Archus heard laughter, and realised with surprise that it was his own.

Lightning began to fall into the orruk swarm. Riders were pitched from their mounts, sent tumbling to the ground to disappear under the hooves of the creatures behind them. Archus' eyes locked upon a monstrous orruk that barrelled straight at him, roaring and drooling in the throes of his battle rage. Time seemed to slow. He saw the blazing red eyes of the colossal boar, only a few yards away now. He heard the ragged panting of its breath, and smelled offal, sweat, and the tang of rusted iron.

He roared his God-King's name as the beast crashed into him. He felt an agonising crack as the arm that held his shield snapped, felt something crunch into the top of his skull. There was a burning pain that flashed across his body, a burst of searing light, and then nothing at all.

The orruk charge struck home with the force of a falling mountain. The creatures' great war-beasts smashed aside the shields of the Stormcasts with their mighty hooves, or tore straight through them with their heavy, iron-wrapped tusks. There are few sights so terrifying in war as a cavalry charge striking an infantry formation, and the sheer power and ferocity of the orruks only made the spectacle more violent and potent. Stormcasts were hurled through the air, broken and torn, or trampled into unrecognisable shapes under the incredible weight. The battlefield was strobed with flashes of blinding light as Sigmar's fallen sons were called home. Shields forged by the greatest smiths of the age were torn asunder. Sigmarite armour was rent and malformed. Unfortunate orruk riders too caught up in the madness to retain control were catapulted into the depths of the Stormcast ranks, their beasts sent tumbling and rolling, squealing and dying.

The shield wall should not have held. Against the sheer, overwhelming force of the orruk charge, the front ranks of the Argellonites should have been swept away, their lines disintegrating and the rear ranks swallowed up as they turned to flee. The simple dynamics of war demanded it.

Yet the three hundred stoic Liberators that formed the wall did not falter. The front ranks were utterly destroyed, but the compact formations behind them did not break, did not shy away from the monstrous tonnage of flesh and iron that crashed into them. Every warrior had a veteran's knowledge of warfare, and they knew that if they lost their solidity, they would lose everything. Grim-faced Celestial Vindicators accepted their deaths, setting their feet and refusing to move a single step in the face of their obliteration.

'Senseless, foolish creatures,' spat Axilon, as he watched the spear of orruk cavalry grind itself further into the breach it had created. He stood with Mykos at the side of the battle, on a jutting spur of rock to better observe the chaos. 'How does this bloodshed profit either of our races? To think that we once called these beasts allies.'

'Not these creatures,' said Mykos. 'Look at them, brother.'

These orruks were broad and tall, rippling with muscles and wrapped in crude yet formidable iron armour. They had none of the savage desperation that Mykos had seen in others of their race. They radiated power, confidence and strength.

'They have thrived in Sigmar's absence, grown strong and bold,' he said. 'If these orruks were to gather in numbers, the Mortal Realms would tremble.'

'Then we must slaughter this lot before they get any grand ideas,' said Axilon. He raised his battle-horn to his mask, and blasted out another series of triumphal notes.

'Paladin retinues forwards,' shouted Mykos, raising his grandblade and indicating his heaviest shock troops, towering Retributors with their crackling, lightning-wreathed hammers, and grim Decimators, carrying broad executioners' axes. Unleashed at last, these warriors charged eagerly through the small channels that now opened in the Liberator shield wall, crashing into the orruks that now pushed deeper into the Stormcast position.

Prosecutor-Prime Goldfeather was enjoying himself, which was possibly somewhat unseemly given the dire circumstances, but undeniable nonetheless. As the battle raged below, the heralds of the Argellonites found themselves outnumbered and surrounded by the reptilian flying mounts of the orruks. The bulky creatures swooped and snapped at the Prosecutors, and their howling masters hurled axes and spears or tried to grab the wings of the Stormcasts as they swept past. The orruks had the numbers, but they lacked the manoeuvrability of their foe.

Goldfeather tucked his wings in and dropped out of the way of one of the creatures, hearing the crunch as its slavering jaws snapped closed just a few inches above his head. He let himself fall several feet, summoning another storm javelin into his hand as he did so, and then spread his wings wide, catching a rising squall and hefting his weapon. He hurled, and the javelin burned a hole through the skull of an orruk rider, flipping him sideways in a somersault that dismounted him and sent him spinning off into the rain.

As much as he welcomed the chance to battle in the violent, unpredictable gales of the Roaring Plains, this needed to end quickly. The Lord-Celestant needed their assistance on the ground, and the longer the Prosecutors were tied up here, the longer they would leave their fellow warriors exposed without aerial support.

Decimator-Prime Kyvos felt righteous rage course through him as he and his warriors pushed forwards through the narrow gaps that the Liberators had efficiently created between their shield wall squares. Across the entire Stormcast position the Warrior Chamber's elite shock troops were rushed to the front line to combat the orruks that had broken through. As exemplary as every Liberator was at the art of combat, vicious, cramped close-quarters battle was the specialty of the greenskin.

Kyvos had fought the things before, and while he despised their short-sighted lust for battle and their witless, artless lack of culture, he would never deny their skill at arms. Ahead he could see the colossal shapes of the orruks' grunting war-beasts, which kicked and spat and bucked with furious abandon in the midst of the melee. The greenskins were hurling themselves at the Liberators' shields, smashing and hacking gracelessly but effectively with jagged axes and spiked clubs.

'No quarter!' Kyvos shouted as the battlefield opened up before him. 'No mercy for the enemies of the God-King!'

A sneering face, splattered with blood, leered up at him, and he put his hammer in its porcine snout. There was a static burst of energy and the creature's skull exploded into shards of smoking bone and scorched meat. He roared in triumph and continued forwards, making for the nearest war-beast. It turned its narrow, malicious eyes towards him as he advanced, and lowered its head to aim that jagged row of tusks.

'Bring your pretty face a little closer,' he muttered, as the creature staggered towards him, swinging its great head.

Kyvos made to move aside, and realised that he could not. The press was simply too tight. Worse still, the ground was churned by rain and blood, a morass of brown-red filth that clung to his boots and tried vainly to drag him down. The creature's snout struck him in the chest, and the force of the blow sent him sprawling into his warriors, off-balance and dazed. Something hooked under his leg, and then he was tumbling through the air, his leg burning with pain. He landed with a clatter that took his breath, and felt his arm sinking into mud.

A snarling, yellow-fanged face appeared out of the blur of his vision, a great axe raised in one hand. Acting on pure instinct, Kyvos shifted to his right, and the axe spattered into the filth beside his head. He wrapped one arm around the weapon, holding it down, and kicked out, catching the orruk in the groin. It folded over, and he grabbed his axe with two hands, jabbing out with the top of the weapon at his opponent's knee. There was a splintering sound, and the creature dropped to the ground, roaring in fury and pain.

He raised himself on unsteady legs. His right had been pierced and shredded by the war-beast, and putting his weight upon it sent a twinge of agony shooting through him. He growled, and spat blood. Pain was easily ignored. The orruk he had taken down surged towards him awkwardly, dragging its shattered limb behind it. Kyvos put his thunderaxe into its chest, and with an explosion the thick iron bands that formed the brute's armour collapsed inwards, crushing its lungs and sending it to the earth for good.

Horns sounded in the distance, bizarre and atonal. No, he decided as the ringing in his ears began to subside. Not horns. More of the creatures' infernal howling, in the distance now but approaching faster with every second. He heard a clatter from above, and looked up to see a broken orruk body crash into the canyon wall and tumble down the face, clattering off ledges and rocks as it fell. It landed with a dull thump in the mud.

'Reform! Reform!' came a desperate yell, again from over their heads. A Prosecutor was gesturing frantically at the far end of the canyon. 'A second wave comes. Reform the line!'

Something fast and heavy, a bundle of leathery wings and snapping jaws, slammed into the flying warrior, and then lifted higher into the air, golden armour visibly struggling in its maw.

Stormcasts began locking their shields together once again. Kyvos could feel the thunder of the orruks' approach now. Ripples spread across the waterlogged earth, and the demented roar of the enemy rose to a crescendo.

'Brace!' Kyvos yelled. But it was far too late.

The first wave of orruk riders had crashed straight down the middle of the canyon, into the Stormcast lines. They had hit hard, and caused many casualties, despite their inability to break the defenders down entirely.

The second thrust angled around the initial spear, striking at the flank and pushing inwards. Whether it was born of any primal tactical insight Mykos could not say, but it broke the cohesion of the Celestial Vindicators' ranks in a way that the initial assault had not managed. Caught between the relentless press of the main orruk force and these new, flanking pincers, the Liberators could not simply close ranks and absorb the power of the attacks.

A torrent of mud and water was thrown up in the impact, obscuring Mykos' view. He could see broken, turquoise shapes hurled through the air, or sent crashing into their fellows. Orruk beasts fell, tripping the creatures behind them, and soon a mountain of writhing flesh and flailing limbs had formed, a grinding mass of destruction that rolled across the battle line, crushing everything in its path. Dozens of Liberators were crushed as they turned to meet the new threat, or left exposed and cut down as the cohesion of the shield wall fractured into a series of smaller skirmishes.

'The time has come to enter the fray,' said Mykos, placing a hand on Knight-Heraldor Axilon's shoulder and indicating the left flank with the other. Here the orruks had pushed through in numbers, and were rolling back the Stormcasts with the sheer fury of their assault. 'This is the hour, my friend.'

'Give me the left,' said Axilon, and raised his hand when Mykos began to object. 'Trust me, my Lord-Celestant. I will hold the line. I'll play a tune that these brutish creatures will remember for the rest of their miserable lives.'

Mykos nodded, and he and Axilon grasped each other's wrist.

'They will write songs to celebrate our fine work this day,' said the Knight-Heraldor. 'I'll be singing them in the taverns of Azyrheim upon our glorious return.'

'Driving innkeepers out of business was ever your specialty, brother. Good fortune.'

With that, Mykos turned to the retinue of Retributors that

formed his personal guard. He raised his grandblade Mercutia high, and as he did so it caught an errant ray of sunshine that broke through the rain. The oath-marks and runes upon its surface glittered. His warriors cheered until their voices were hoarse, and formed up in his wake as he surged towards the front line, a hymn of vengeance and glory upon his lips.

The left flank was in chaos. Knight-Heraldor Axilon hurdled great mounds of dead and dying orruks, making for the thick of the battle ahead, where a ragged line of Liberators was just barely holding a mob of dismounted orruks at bay. Broken, turquoise forms moaned and shifted in the mire, wounded but not yet ready to be called home by the storm of Sigmar.

'To me, warriors of Azyr,' he shouted, raising his broadsword high in a two-handed grip. His Decimators followed with him, roaring with fury as they charged into the fray.

Axilon leapt forwards at the last moment, his blade swinging down with the force of an executioner's axe. An orruk head fell free to splash in the mud, and suddenly the Knight-Heraldor was surrounded by snarling, laughing faces. It was a coarse, ugly sound, but the beasts were definitely laughing. Chortling as they cut down Stormcasts, giggling and hollering as they butchered.

Axilon answered that laughter with the edge of his blade. He parried a clumsy axe swing, punched out and felt teeth shatter under his gauntlet, angled his sword and thrust it through his assailant's belly. The wondrously crafted weapon sliced through the orruk's iron armour as if it were parchment, and Axilon let the dying creature slide from his blade. Beside him the Retributors swept their great hammers in wide arcs, clearing space for the Liberators to fall back and regroup.

'Not today, lads,' he roared, clapping warriors on the shoulder as they fell back past him. 'There's a war on, you know. Can't be heading back home with the job half done.'

There was only a temporary reprieve. More orruks poured towards the Stormcasts, scores of them, scrabbling and leaping eagerly through the stinking swamp that the battlefield had become. Rain whipped across their faces, which were twisted in frenzied delight at the prospect of yet more murder. Great chunks of stone sloughed free from the canyon wall, loosened by the thunder of battle and the ceaseless downpour. Several orruks were struck by the falling debris and tumbled to the floor, to be crushed under the heavy boots of their allies. It was not enough to make a dent in their numbers, but it gave Axilon an idea.

'Raise your shields,' he shouted. 'And brace yourselves.'

He raised his battle-horn to his lips, and unleashed the full power of the wondrous artefact. What issued forth from the instrument was not a perfect note, not an echo of the valour and glory of Sigmar. It was a wave of thunderous devastation, a blast of cacophonous noise that slammed into the wall of the canyon with the power of a dozen siege rams. The rock face spider-webbed with deep fissures, rippling out from the point of impact. Then a twenty-foot section of shattered stone simply fell away. It crashed over the orruks, and the leading edge of the creatures simply disappeared in a cloud of displaced stone and tumbling rock.

The avalanche did not stop. As both Stormcasts and orruks scrambled to escape the deluge of stone, more and more of the wall began to slough away. Choking dust filled the air, and warriors on both sides could no longer see further than a few feet ahead. Axilon spat out dirt and peered into the swirling debris. A few feet ahead there now sat a mound of rubble and broken bodies, a physical barrier that blocked off the left flank assault. He saw orruks trying to drag themselves up and over this new obstacle, but it was loose and treacherous. He had bought them a few minutes at least.

* * *

Mykos heard the roar as the left-side wall fell, and muttered a quick prayer to Sigmar that Axilon had not been crushed amongst the rubble. There was no more time to dwell upon the fate of his friend. Though the right flank had managed to hold position, they were losing warriors too fast. The sheer weight of numbers was beginning to swamp the Stormcasts, robbing them of the cohesion that gave them their greatest strength. As soon as the orruks pushed their way in behind the Liberators the battle would be lost, and that was in danger of happening any moment.

'Push them back,' he roared. 'Allow them not a single step forward!'

Blessed Azyr, those beasts the orruks rode to war were vicious things. It was enough that a rider managed to get a single one of the creatures in the midst of his ranks – their furious kicking, thrashing and biting would do the damage of a half-dozen men. Mykos had seen one open its jaws wide to close around a Stormcast Eternal's torso, trying to bite the warrior in half even as it attempted to force the still-moving body down its throat. When the warrior's death had seen him disappear in a burst of white light, the creature had only been driven to greater heights of rage at being denied a meal.

'Take them down,' he yelled, aiming Mercutia at the nearest of the foul beasts. 'The legs, aim for their limbs.'

The beasts' armour was thick upon the flank and belly, but their powerful limbs were exposed. Cripple one, and it would soon become as great a danger to its fellows and to the orruks as it would to the Stormcasts.

Retributor Bhorus slammed his lightning hammer against the closest creature's leg, smashing the joint so hard that it bent to the side with a loud crack. The war-beast howled and snorted in pain, and tried to snap at Bhorus with its viciously tusked jaws. He swayed back just in time, but a wild axe swing from the thing's whooping rider struck him across the shoulder and pitched him to the floor. More Retributors piled in, penning the beast and smashing into it from all directions, slowly forcing it to the floor. The rider went down under it, trapped but still swinging his axe at anyone who came close. Elrus made to finish the prone creature, but another massive body pressed through a gap in the line, and barrelled into him. Its vicious tusk punched through his armour, and the beast continued to charge forwards, the Retributor impaled upon its jaws.

'Finish the downed creature, this one is mine,' Mykos shouted.

The war-beast's momentum carried it past the Lord-Celestant, and the oblivious rider failed to see his sword stroke until it was too late. The blade crashed into the orruk's chest, sending him falling backwards off his mount, thick, dark blood staining his yellow armour. As he fell, Mykos leapt forwards and grasped the iron bands that were wrapped so tightly around the beast's neck that the flesh beneath was torn and septic, oozing a pale yellow fluid. He swung himself up onto the beast's back. Elrus was still impaled, dangling across the giant boar's snapping maw, somehow still stabbing at its neck with his gladius.

'Kill it, my Lord,' he gasped, blood seeping from underneath his mask. His voice was resigned, strong despite the agony that clearly wracked him.

Mykos had no time to dislodge the man. A wound as grave as his meant only death in any case, without a healer nearby. He reversed his grip on his grandblade, and drove it deep into the rampaging beast's skull. It collapsed in motion, and the Lord-Celestant saw the ground rush up towards him as he was pitched over its head. He hit with bone-shuddering force, though thankfully the wet earth absorbed most of the impact. He rolled over once, twice, and came to a halt on a pile of orruk corpses. He tasted blood and the foulness of the churned earth, and spat.

There was no time to rest, even for a moment. He hauled himself to his feet, glancing back at the advancing greenskins.

There were too many. His chamber had fought heroically, but they were losing too many men, and gaps were opening for the orruks to exploit.

Another rain of lightning fell upon the advancing enemy from above, throwing burly figures to the ground and sending geysers of water into the air as bodies and projectiles splashed into the filthy mire. More figures hurtled forwards to take the place of the fallen. The enemy's numbers were endless. It was over.

'No,' he whispered. 'We are not yet done.'

They had already forged a legend here, and there was more killing to be done before the Argellonites would admit defeat. His pride in his warriors surged.

'To me, Argellonites!' he roared. 'We march to glory!'

Ahead of him, a Decimator Paladin ran forwards, sweeping his great starsoul mace into a cluster of the enemy. The fabulous weapon exploded with heavenly radiance, and a wave of star motes slammed into several orruks, sending them flying backwards, smoking and smouldering. The Decimator turned, searching for more targets.

There was a clamour that echoed above the chaos of battle, the sound of primal savagery made manifest.

From out of the swirling dust roared a colossal figure, half a head taller than the Stormcast. Skulls and other grisly trophies hung from its mighty iron battle-plate. Every inch of the creature rippled with muscle, and its head was a brutal slab of scarred flesh that culminated in a wedge of a jaw filled with filthy, yellowed tusks. The creature raised a huge, jagged cleaver that dripped with gore, and brought it down into the Decimator's back.

As the creature came forwards, it shook the Stormcast's body free of its cleaver, a nimbus of light briefly crackling around the weapon as the corpse of its victim was claimed by the storm. Its cruel eyes, filled with primal cunning, fixed upon Mykos, and it smiled.

Around the figure, orruks gathered, brandishing their weapons and chanting in their crude tongue.

'Drekka! Drekka! Drekka!'

Decimator-Prime Kyvos had no idea where he was, or indeed where his warriors were. The battle had surged forwards and lost its shape in the frenzy of the carnage, and to make matters worse the cloud of dust and the torrential rain made the combat a baffling, fragmentary mess. He would stagger, come face to face with an orruk just as confused and lost as he, then struggle for a few violent seconds. He would stumble over a groaning body, so thickly caked in grime that he knew not whether it was one of his own or a wounded enemy. His injured leg burned fiercely with every step.

Gradually, the dust began to settle enough for him to peer a dozen or so yards ahead. Chaos. Dull, dust-covered turquoise clashing with ugly yellow, blood spilled on both sides. Orruks hacked away in a graceless but effective frenzy, hollering and chortling in their idiot voices as they did so. Celestial Vindicators fought with ruthless competence, despite the disarray. They clustered in makeshift groups, forming ad-hoc defensive formations, islands of calm order amidst the swirling madness. Orruks died by the dozen around them, bludgeoned by warhammers, hacked down by axes or sliced open by measured cuts from sigmarite blades.

Above the sound of battle could be heard the clear notes of Knight-Heraldor Axilon's battle-horn, and it was towards this rallying sound that Kyvos headed. As expected, he found the man in the midst of the thickest fighting, backed by several worn-looking Liberators and the few surviving members of a Paladin retinue. His armour was stained with blood and grime, and his helm had been split by a vicious cut that ran down to his collarbone, but still he wielded his broadsword with deadly skill. As Kyvos came closer, the Knight-Heraldor glanced at him.

'Who's that there?' he said, and Kyvos could hear the undercurrent of pain that ran through his words. The Knight-Heraldor had been wounded, and badly. 'All this cursed dust everywhere, I can barely see. Of course, no one to blame for that but myself.'

He laughed and spun, spitting an onrushing orruk on the tip of his sword. The creature gurgled and fell to splash in the knee-high water that swelled around them.

'Decimator-Prime Kyvos, my Lord,' he said, raising his thunderaxe and taking position next to Axilon.

'Ah, good man. Where are your warriors?'

'I do not know,' he said, and felt a stab of worry and shame. He had called and looked for them, but it was impossible to find anyone in the middle of such chaos. 'Several fell in the last charge. The rest I could not find.'

'No matter, son,' said the Knight-Heraldor. 'What say we meet this next lot together? Give them something to remember us by?'

A fresh mob of orruks was advancing through the filth towards them. He could see the eager bloodlust in their tiny, pitiless eyes. They scrambled over the heaped corpses of their fellows, splashing and stumbling in the mud in desperation to get at the Stormcasts.

'It's been quite a day, has it not, Kyvos?' said Axilon. 'Quite a day. Tell me, do you remember your past life, before all this madness?'

Kyvos nodded. 'I was a baker,' he said, and the memory brought a sad smile to his lips. 'Before my village burned. Before I took up the sword. And you, my Lord?'

'A fat and foolish king, whose only honour came in death,' Axilon roared with laughter and clapped the Retributor-Prime on the back hard enough to make him stumble. 'The baker and the king. Look at us now, eh?'

Goldfeather alighted on the back of the creature, so deftly its dull-brained master did not even notice his presence until it was too late. He grabbed the orruk's head, forced it down, and stabbed his javelin deep into the neck. Blood drenched his armour, and the rider gurgled and choked. He slashed the precarious series of leather bindings that kept the orruk in place, and it slipped free, falling into empty air.

That was the last of them. Crazed, panicking beasts still spiralled and whipped through the air, shorn of the limited control of their dead riders. The surviving Prosecutors – Goldfeather winced as he saw the full toll they had suffered – formed up around him.

'We go straight down their throat,' he roared. The joy of battle pumped through his veins, filling him with fervour. 'Sigmar is watching, warriors of the Ceslestial Vindicators. Let us show him our worth.'

The orruk was colossal, even by the standards of those they had fought thus far. It towered above even the Stormcasts, a mountain of green flesh that radiated sheer, terrifying power. It killed with contemptuous ease, whipping a jagged cleaver about itself with a fury that belied the precision in its movement. An almost casual swing to the left sent two Vindicators tumbling, blood seeping through ruined chestplates. A downward slice split another warrior in two. Lightning claimed both segments of his body as they fell away.

It roared a challenge in its rough and brutish tongue, and from all sides the brave champions of Mykos Argellon's Warrior Chamber answered. As the Lord-Celestant fought his way towards the behemoth, he watched them all die.

Patreus, the warrior who had held the Shining Door against the roiling, surging tides of the Pandaemonium fell, his head crushed by an axe blow. Liberator-Prime Thayon, the Hero of the Flamepeak, was cleaved in two. Olren, Tavos, some of the best and brightest warriors of his chamber. Killed and thrown aside by this creature as if they were little more than mortal serfs.

Mykos roared and charged, bringing Mercutia down from a

high guard in a diagonal slice aimed at the beast's neck. The orruk leader did not feint or move to avoid the blow, but simply shifted and let it fall across his chestplate. The blade screamed as it gouged a jagged line through the strong iron, but it did not reach through to wound the orruk, who returned the strike with a backhand swing of his axe. Mykos dropped to one knee in the dirty water, leaning back. He heard the orruk's wicked axe rush past his face, mere inches away. Then he was up, spinning and putting distance between him and the monster. It laughed, enjoying the game, and advanced after him, sloshing through the mud and gore.

'Drekka Breakbones claims your skull, little man-thing,' it chuckled, in a voice like an avalanche. 'I'll 'av that little pig-sticker you got there, too.'

'Come and take it,' Mykos muttered, turning Mercutia in his hand, searching for a weakness he could exploit.

He could not see one. The creature was huge, but not so huge that it could not react with frightening speed. It was aggressive, but it did not fight like a blood-crazed cultist, all power and rage. There was cunning to its attacks. It rushed at him, swinging low with that great axe, forcing him backwards, then feinted a sideways step. Instead of the cleaver it swung a mighty punch with its left fist, upon which it wore a band of heavy iron tipped with needle-sharp blades.

Mykos just got his sword up in time to block, but the power of the blow sent him reeling backwards to crash against the carcass of a war-beast. On came the orruk leader, swinging its axe down in a vertical chop aimed to split the Lord-Celestant in two. Mykos barely shifted aside in time, and felt the splash of blood across his armour as the axe cleaved the dead boar in half. The orruk's eyes narrowed in frustration as it tried to tug the weapon free, and Mykos took advantage of the momentary distraction to hack into the monster's hip, at the join between two armour plates.

It roared in pain, and struck out with its bladed fist. The strike was blindingly fast, and Mykos could not get his blade back up to block it. It struck him square in the chest with astonishing force. He flew backwards to splash in the mud and gore, gasping for breath. Looking down, he saw great rents in his sigmarite plate. As he stared, blood began to seep through the holes. The orruk's weapon had punched deep. He groaned and got to his knees, feeling around in the sticky, foul-smelling mud for Mercutia. He found her at last, and took comfort in her familiar heft as he focused through the stabbing pain in his chest and hauled himself upright.

'Got me good, little 'un,' the orruk leader spat, chortling happily as reeking blood poured over the ugly yellow of its armour. 'Drekka remembers the last one who got him that good.'

The orruk's great, gnarled finger tapped the fanged skull it wore upon its left pauldron.

'I'm honoured… to be in such esteemed company,' said Mykos. The creature boomed with laughter again, then rushed forwards, seemingly unworried by the vicious wound it had been dealt.

Too many. Kyvos had slaughtered a dozen or more of the creatures, crushing their heavy iron chestplates under devastating blows of his thunderaxe, dashing skulls to pieces or slicing through legs to leave their owners drowning in the stinking quagmire at his feet. On they came, an endless, howling swarm of them, and the more they slew, the more eager they seemed. These warriors fought on foot, either fresh troops or riders who had been dismounted and had been lucky or thick-skulled enough to survive the fall.

'Is this all you have, you mindless wretches?' roared Axilon at his side, kicking another dead orruk from his blade and letting it tumble down the mound of dead they had created. 'I thought your kind lived for war? I've barely broken a sweat.'

His words brought a tired cheer from the remaining Vindicators, but despite his bluster it was clear to Kyvos that the

Knight-Heraldor was tiring. Gone was the deft, cultured blade-work for which he was known throughout the halls of Azyrheim. His broadsword looked heavy in his hands, and he was favouring his right leg.

And on the orruks came.

Axilon rested a hand on Kyvos' pauldron, and the Retributor-Prime heard him gasp a ragged breath.

'My time draws near, son,' said the Knight-Heraldor. 'When I fall, you lead them on. You kill as many as you can, you hear?'

'Aye, sire,' Kyvos said. 'Though I'd say we've accounted for our fair share already.'

'Not enough. Not nearly enough.' Axilon shook his head.

'Then let's draw them in,' said Kyvos. He looked up at the canyon wall. Axilon's previous efforts had brought down a huge chunk of stone and gouged a great hole, but now that they had been forced back several dozen feet they were underneath another overhanging ledge. 'As many as we can. See if we can't add a few more to the tally.'

Axilon nodded, and Kyvos could hear a wet, pained chuckle.

'Leave it to me,' said the Knight-Heraldor.

He stepped forwards, stabbing his broadsword into the dirt and raising his battle-horn. Kyvos formed the remaining Liberators in a defensive line around the Knight-Heraldor. Axilon drew in a breath.

'All right, you gutless lot,' he bellowed, and blew an ear-shattering note from the battle-horn. 'Call yourself warriors, do you? I've seen cellar rats that fight better. You're a disgrace to your cretinous gods, you weakling cowards. Not a one of you has the stones to take me down, and I'm fighting with half my organs carved in two!'

Whether the orruks understood a word of what the Knight-Heraldor was saying, Kyvos had no idea at all. Regardless, his booming voice and the clarion call of his battle-horn drew them like moths to a flame. There were hundreds of them now, mounted on their war-beasts or charging towards the Stormcasts on foot. They were an island in the middle of a surging sea. Axes clattered against the Liberators' shields, and the press of bodies began to crush the Vindicators back into the wall of the canyon. Kyvos headbutted an orruk that pressed its leering face into his, then drew his gladius to stab it in the gut.

'Knight-Heraldor, do it now!' he shouted, and felt an axe slam into his shoulder. Suddenly he was on his knees, and all he could see was a forest of yellow iron. Something struck him in the face, and he spat blood. 'Now!'

He glanced up, trying to see through the mass of bodies. The Knight-Heraldor still stood, ignoring the barbed spears that pierced his chest. He raised the battle-horn to his lips as the swarm of bodies reached up to haul him down into the fray. The last thing that Kyvos heard was the sound of thunder and falling stone.

Mykos Argellon's world was a storm of sigmarite and iron. He had never fought a battle such as this, so furious that it was governed by sheer instinct and reaction, rather than skill at arms. This Drekka was so fast, so blindingly fast. No sooner had the Lord-Celestant picked off one attack, than he was forced to adjust to another, and another. He was being driven back, and in the bloody mire in which they battled that was dangerous indeed. One wrong step, one moment too long in pulling his boot free from the grasping mud, and the orruk would have him.

His beloved Argellonites were dying around him. Against the numbers that now came down upon them, there was no chance at all. From the corner of his eyes he could see his warriors fall, surrounded and hacked to pieces. Flashes of light signalled another lost friend, another sent back to the forge to be recast and remade. He would join them soon.

It happened as he stepped backwards over a body left half sodden and bleeding in the murk. Something grabbed his foot. He looked down, and saw that the orruk beneath him was not dead. Its porcine eyes glared up at him maliciously. It snarled as it drew a short, broad knife and attempted to drive the blade deep into the Lord-Celestant's leg. Mykos stamped his foot down upon its neck and ground it deeper into the mud, then brought his grandblade up to intercept the inevitable attack from the pursuing Drekka.

He was too slow, by a fraction of a second. The orruk chieftain's axe skipped from the edge of Mercutia, and Mykos did not have the strength left to deflect the blow. It tore through the sigmarite armour at his elbow, and sheared the limb free. Pain blurred the Lord-Celestant's vision, and he fell to his haunches.

Drekka Breakbones loomed over him, and he heard the creature's cruel laughter echoing in his ears, as if from a great distance. 'That it?' the orruk asked, and Mykos looked up to see a gap-toothed grin cross its ugly, scarred face.

He heard the sound of thunder roll across the battlefield again. He saw the confusion on Drekka's face, and glanced to the left. Another rent had been torn in the canyon wall, even greater than the last. He saw rocks the size of carthorses scything and spinning through the orruk ranks, crushing scores of the creatures to death. One last gift from Axilon, then. He would see his friend back in Azyr. Would they recognise each other, he wondered? All they had been through together since Sigmar had opened the realmgates and hurled them out into the world – would they recall any of it? All those moments of heroism, of sacrifice. Would they be lost? Mykos Argellon did not want to die. He did not want to come back like Thostos, cold and distant even to those he had once called brothers.

The orruk chieftain raised the axe high. As the pouring rain hit the dull iron, blood ran down the blade to drip aross Mykos' war-mask.

This was not the end. He feared what would become of him, but he did not regret his choice to give his life for a moment. This was the truth of the Stormcast Eternals. They would make this sacrifice, over and over again, so that one day no mortal would have to. For some reason he thought of the priestess Alzheer, and hoped she yet lived. She was the bright future, the hope that he gave his life for.

He closed his eyes.

Goldfeather saw the towering orruk bring the axe down. He saw it strike his Lord-Celestant in the side of the neck, and he saw a brief, bright flare of lightning as Mykos Argellon's body toppled to the floor. Then the cloud of dust from the shattered rock on the left-hand side of the canyon rushed across the battlefield, and he could see nothing at all.

They had killed the Lord-Celestant. The chamber was shattered. The Prosecutor-Prime could not see a single speck of turquoise amongst the sea of green and yellow below. It was over.

'We must go to his aid,' shouted Galeth. 'We will kill the beast that slew him.'

'No,' said Goldfeather softly. Something was there, at the back of his mind. Some vital memory that he was missing. There was a way to tip the scales here, a way to make these wretched savages pay for every Stormcast lost this day.

'No?' echoed Galeth incredulously. The shock of this defeat had made him forget himself. 'Are you craven, brother? We must avenge this insult. We must kill these beasts, even if we die doing so.'

'What we must do is win,' shouted Goldfeather. 'Do you wish to die alongside our brothers, and render their sacrifice meaningless? Or do you wish to follow me, and win this battle in the Lord-Celestant's honour?'

'Follow you where? To run from the battlefield in shame?'

'Trust me, my brothers,' said the Prosecutor-Prime. 'One last time. Do so, and we will kill every last orruk on the field.'

It was against every instinct that had been drilled and forged into them, to leave that field with the fight still raging. Galeth and the remaining Prosecutors swayed, on the verge of rushing to their deaths, and for a moment Goldfeather thought he had lost them.

'You have never led us wrong, Prosecutor-Prime,' said Galeth at last. 'We will follow you.'

He had never been more proud of his men.

'We must make haste,' he said, and with that he opened his wings and flew out over the canyon where the Argellonites had fallen. He soared away from the Dreadhold and towards the grasslands of the plain, hope surging alongside the sorrow in his heart.

CHAPTER SIX

Chosen of Sigmar

The torrential rain finally ceased as the first figures began to emerge from the mouth of Splitskull Pass. They did not wear the sea green, white and gold of the Argellonites Chamber of the Celestial Vindicators. They were stout, savage-looking creatures wrapped in bands of yellow-painted iron. Some strode on foot while others were mounted on fearsome, tusked beasts.

'He has fallen then,' said Eldroc.

'As we knew he must,' said Lord-Celestant Thostos Bladestorm, standing at the Lord-Castellant's side upon the battlements of the Manticore Dreadhold. 'Let us hope Lord-Celestant Argellon took as many of the orruks with him as he could, before the end.'

Eldroc nodded. Even as they spoke, the essence of Mykos Argellon was being carried home upon the celestial storm, back to the halls of Azyrheim. There he would be reforged anew, to be sent out once more against the forces of Chaos and darkness. But immortality did not come without a price. The Lord-Castellant glanced at Thostos. His friend was the living embodiment of such sacrifice. Once he had been a thoughtful, introspective man, a counter-balance against the raw fury and desire for vengeance that was the hallmark of the Celestial Vindicators.

The Reforging had taken that from him, had hollowed him out until all that was left was the fury and the need for retribution.

'He will fight beside us once more,' said Eldroc. 'He is strong. He will be remade, and he will emerge through the flame as a better man.'

'No,' said Thostos, and his voice was soft yet filled with surety. The Lord-Celestant turned to Eldroc, and looked him in the eye.

'It will break him,' he went on. 'He will enter the storm and it will break him down, tear him apart until there is nothing left of the man he once was. This is the sacrifice we made, brother. We are all here because we swore the same oaths. We knew there would be a price. It is one worth paying, for what we must do.'

Without another word, Thostos made for the interior stair that would take him down to the inner courtyard of the fortress. Arrayed at defensive positions around the Dreadhold were the two hundred and fifty men at his command, securing weak points and stacking barricades at the breached main gate that would hinder the orruks' progress if they decided, as they inevitably would, on an all-out frontal assault. Two-score of that number faced in the opposite direction, a wall of sigmarite that guarded the Manticore Realmgate, the structure that the Celestial Vindicators had been sent here to secure.

Eldroc and Thostos crossed the inner courtyard, and made their way up the wide stair atop of which lay the gate. The structure stood on a wide plinth carved into the mountain, and it was here that the Stormcasts had organised their defensive position.

'Keep up your guard,' said Thostos, as they passed the men. 'The forces of Chaos may come pouring through this portal at any moment.'

The Lord-Relictor Tharros Soulwarden knelt before the structure, still working the magic that would cleanse the taint of Chaos from the portal and allow the Stormcasts to pass through.

'He has not spoken or moved since the daemonic incursion?' asked Thostos.

'No, my Lord,' said Liberator-Prime Arestes, a stolid, reliable warrior known for his lack of humour as much as for his skill at arms. 'But the gate's fell light dims by the moment. Whatever the Lord-Relictor is doing, it is quelling the power of this Chaos-warped thing.'

'But not fast enough. Our time has run out,' said Thostos. 'The orruks march on us, and we have not the men to hold back their numbers.'

'The fortress can hold out a little longer,' said Eldroc. As Lord-Castellant, he was responsible for the fortification and defence of locations that the Stormcasts had claimed. 'We have little choice in the matter. We must give Tharros as much time as he requires, and hope that Sigmar is watching over us.'

Thostos nodded. 'You will defend the wall, Lord-Castellant. I shall take the gatehouse. Despite the damage to the main gate, we can bottleneck them there as long as the ramparts remain clear.'

Eldroc nodded, even though he knew as well as his Lord-Celestant that they could not possibly hold out. Oh, they would bleed the orruks, they would make them pay a heavy price for every inch of ground, but in the end it would not be enough. The sun broke through the clouds once more, rising behind the great statue of Archaon, and the figure's shadow fell across the valley floor ahead of them.

Atrin Eagle-Eye found that not an inch of his body was free from pain. He tried to focus through the haze of agony. He had fallen a great distance, hurled to his death by the mortal witchkin that called itself Xos'Phet. Yet, as the stabbing pain that arced down his spine and throbbed through his legs was quick to remind him, he was not in fact dead.

He felt around, and his hands touched a mushy, viscous

substance. He lay on a bed of the stuff, and could smell its pungent, chemical odour. Slowly, his eyes adjusted to the darkness, and the faint glimmer of lichen on the walls revealed a forest of fungi that stretched far into the distance. Glancing up, he could see the stone chimney through which he had fallen. Water dripped down to fall on his armour, and he pulled off his war-mask for a moment to let the downpour cool his face.

'Well, warrior of Azyr,' he muttered. 'You're a long, long way from home.'

Suddenly, the memory came back to him. His brother Judicator, Oreus, blasted into nothingness by a ray of fell magic. Retributor Callan, burning and screaming, claimed by the foul minions of Xos'Phet. And what of Alzheer, the mortal priestess of the nomadic tribespeople? He had no idea where she had gone, but if the creatures that the sorcerer commanded were still roaming these caverns, she was in terrible danger. He had no time for the luxury of rest. There had to be some way back up to the site of the ambush. From there he could track Xos'Phet down, rescue Callan, and wring the scrawny witchkin's neck in the process.

With an effort that sent a fresh wave of torment rolling across his frame, Atrin hauled himself to his feet. His left arm was stiff and painful, probably broken in a couple of places. His head rang with what felt like a minor concussion, and one ankle would barely support his weight. He still had his gladius, but there was no sign of the boltstorm crossbow he had carried.

Half crippled. Lacking a weapon. Lost in a subterranean maze of caverns.

'Sigmar, I could use your favour now,' he sighed.

Atrin drew his gladius and began to push through the field of mushrooms. There were wide, thin plates of fungi that felt almost springy beneath his boots, and massive, bell-capped specimens as big as trees. The smell of the place was powerful, but not entirely unpleasant – sickly sweet, with a lingering bitter aftertaste that sat upon his tongue. After a few minutes of pushing through these thick stalks, Atrin was met with an unyielding wall of stone. With little else to guide him, he decided to follow it along, and hope by some miracle that it led to a way out of the chamber.

After at least an hour of stumbling through the cavern, the pain in his arm growing worse and worse by the moment, Atrin had a stroke of good fortune. A narrow tunnel – a tight squeeze for the tall and broad Stormcast – curved around in a spiral, heading upwards. There was the hint of a stair carved into the slippery stone, and Atrin began to feel that this was no natural complex he was travelling through. He could see no signs of civilisation down here, but the mushroom forest in that wide, open chamber, with its adjoining access route, had all the hallmarks of mortal cultivation.

The thought reignited his determination. If humans, or some other cultured race had once dwelt down here, it was far more likely that there was a way back to the upper tunnels.

It was as he dwelled on this pleasant thought that something long, thin and dripping with acidic mucous coiled itself with vice-like strength around his neck.

How many orruks were left to rot in the slaughtering ground of Splitskull Pass, Eldroc had no idea, but the army that loped out to cluster at the foot of the Dreadhold seemed undiminished. They hooted and hollered, swaggering towards the fortress with eager grins on their foolish faces. In the midst of the mob, the Lord-Castellant spotted what had to be the leader. The brute was half again as tall as an average orruk, a monster wrapped in heavy iron plate topped with trophy skulls and relics, clutching a wicked cleaver stained red with the blood of slain Vindicators. It was by some distance the biggest orruk Eldroc had ever seen.

'When they fall within our range, kill that one first,' he said to the leader of the Judicator retinue that lined the wall alongside him. 'Hit it with everything you have.'

'Aye sire,' said the Judicator-Prime at his side.

He doubted it would be that simple to kill such a monster, but in his experience orruks gathered around their strongest and most brutal specimens. Take off the head, and the rest of the mob would begin to fracture and self-destruct. At least that was the theory. For such simple-minded, warlike brutes, orruks could be dangerously unpredictable.

'They're bloodied, sire,' said Lorrus. 'Plenty of the creatures left, but Lord-Celestant Argellon and his warriors certainly dealt some damage before they fell.'

Eldroc could see that the man was right. Though the orruks were full of their race's usual post-battle cheer, more than a few of the creatures now coming towards them bore the scars of their encounter with the Celestial Vindicators. Bodies dropped as the great horde crossed the plain towards the fortress, the adrenaline surge of combat no longer enough to hold them upright.

'It is a miracle that he managed to hold on as long as he did against such numbers,' said the Lord-Castellant. 'We must endeavour to match his bravery.'

From below his position, he heard the creaking of iron, a great scraping sound as something heavy was dragged across stone. His blood ran cold. Who had opened the main gate? The moment they saw such a breach the orruks would hurl themselves at it in force, and all would be lost.

'Lord-Castellant,' came a shout from Judicator Samius, who was pointing at the open ground before the fortress. Eldroc rushed forwards.

There was Thostos Bladestorm, hammer and blade in hand, marching out alone towards the roiling horde of green flesh.

'Thostos,' whispered Eldroc.

* * *

The wall itself was trying to eat him.

No, realised Atrin as he gasped and hacked at the tendril that held him several feet above the ground, it was something that had nestled into the wall. The central mass looked like little more than a fleshy curtain of mottled brown, draped across several feet of stone. He saw a cluster of eyes, multifaceted and glinting in the phosphorescent light, like those of a giant insect. Below this, there was a nightmarish maw, crammed with twisted, overlapping teeth. From around this mouth came several thin, wiry tentacles, tipped with what looked like thick hairs that dripped a clear blue liquid.

Some kind of poison, perhaps. If so, it was thankfully being held at bay by his battle-plate. What was markedly less promising was that with one fully functioning arm, he could not possibly fend off the tendrils that whipped and flailed around him, dragging him ever closer to those grinding fangs.

He managed to lever his gladius under one of the tendrils, and sliced it in two. A furious hissing sound came from the hideous wall-creature, and two more arms whipped out to take its place. One wrapped around the wrist that held the blade, and the other around Atrin's helm, wrenching his head back violently. Closer and closer he was drawn, a fly reeled in by the spider. How foolish a death. The Judicator finally pulled his gladius free, and stopped struggling. Perhaps if the creature thought he was unconscious, it would relax its hold. Then he could drive his sword into its eyes once he was close enough.

Hopefully he could either kill it or force it to drop him. It was that, or face a most unpleasant end indeed.

Light flared below him. He could not arc his head to look, but he saw the blur of orange as a flaming arrow flittered past his head and struck the abomination in the middle of its eye cluster. There was a horrible, rattling squeal, and the curtain of mottled flesh rippled and twisted. The arrow was followed in short order by two more. They were well placed. One struck above the first shot, and one below. In the glow of the smouldering missiles, Atrin saw dozens, hundreds of tiny legs emerge from underneath the wall-creature's central body, hooked and insectile like those of a centipede. The horror skittered along the surface of the wall, away from the punishing arrows, dragging Atrin along with it.

He had a chance, while the monster was blinded and distracted with pain. He swung his gladius, slicing through several of the tendrils that held him around the waist. He fell, his weight no longer supported, and growled in pain as his injured leg smacked against hard stone. Still the creature dragged him along the floor by the tentacles wrapped around his neck. He tried to hack at them with the gladius, but the angle was poor and he was forced to awkwardly swing behind his head.

'Stop, my friend,' came a familiar voice. 'I have this.'

He ceased his swiping, and heard the sound of rushing air as a sword whipped through the air. Suddenly he was no longer being dragged backwards, and twitching, severed tendrils spilled around his legs. He looked upwards, and saw the bizarre cave-crawler scuttle out of sight on its multitude of limbs, dragging a fleshy, tuber-shaped stomach-organ behind it.

'A porsuka,' said the warrior Alzheer, slinging her bow across her muscular shoulders. 'You were fortunate to escape. It is said they can feed for many years from just one kill, dragged alive into their stomach and slowly devoured.'

'This really is a charming place, priestess. I have thoroughly enjoyed my time here.'

Alzheer smiled, the white of her teeth glinting in the dim light.

'Thank you,' said Atrin, and she gave a brief nod.

He pulled the last ropes of flesh free from his armour, and wiped his gladius on a cluster of lichen. The priestess, meanwhile, dropped to study the shorn tendrils that scattered the floor. Drawing several arrows, she began to cover them in the clear blue liquid that seeped from the thick bristles.

'Some kind of poison?' he asked.

She nodded. 'It can freeze a man's muscles in moments. The porsuka uses it to numb its victims, to make the feeding easier. It will be useful.'

Atrin watched her work.

'Where are your people?' he asked at last.

'Slaughtered or forced to run,' she said, and he saw a deep sigh run through her body. 'I misjudged the sorcerer, sky warrior. I thought he was weak, near death.'

'Witchkin have a nasty habit of surviving. Like cockroaches.'

'He must die. And so must Rusik, whatever that creature has made of him.'

'We agree on that,' said Atrin. 'Know that we will likely die in the attempt. My arm is broken, and my leg likely fractured. I have lost my crossbow also. The odds of us surviving are... comical.'

She looked at him, and he was once again surprised by the determination and ferocity in her mortal eyes. Another time, another place, and this one would have made a fine Celestial Vindicator.

'I do not fear death, sky warrior,' she said. 'My people have lived in its shadow every day of our lives.'

He knelt, so that their eyes were level.

'I know your quality, and that of the Sky Seekers. But this does not have to be your fight, daughter of Sigmar. Your people need your leadership.'

'Enough,' she snapped. 'As long as this Xos'Phet creature lives, we will never be safe. So it is with the traitor Rusik. In any case, your fellow warrior is still alive, and I would not abandon him to death and torment. No more of this talk. We go together, and we die together if that is what Zi'Mar wishes.'

Atrin smiled underneath his war-mask, and nodded.

'Very well,' he said. 'In any case, I confess I am quite lost. Your guidance out of this wretched hole would be much appreciated.'

'You're a fine shot with the bow,' said Atrin, breaking the silence as they trudged through the tunnels.

Alzheer smiled. 'Out on the plain, that is often the difference between life and death. My father taught me, and he was the finest hunter our tribe has ever known.'

They walked on, the water that dripped and ran from the cavern ceiling the only sound aside from the tramp of their boots.

'He took me on my first hunt,' the priestess said at last. 'I was too young, but it had been a hard season, and everyone was needed. I carried the weapon he had crafted for me, and in all the years since I have never held a finer bow. '

She smiled at the memory.

'So proud, I was. So excited. And then we came upon a pack of qualhorn, by some miracle. Most had been slaughtered by the orruks, but these were fine, strong beasts. My father guided my arm, taught me where the arrow rested, how to breathe before I loosed. I remember the wind rushing through my hair, the rumble of hunger in my belly. My first arrow took the nearest creature in the heart.'

'That was a fine shot,' said Atrin.

'Lucky, perhaps. In any case, it was a swift death. Clean. My father said that was what a hunter owed his prey. He was not a man easily given to words of encouragement, but I saw the pride in his eyes and that was enough.'

They passed a chimney of rock, through which trickled a steady stream of clear water. Alzheer stretched out a hand and let the liquid spatter off her palm.

'My father said the words, gave thanks to Zi'Mar for the kill. Then we headed home, imagining the taste of good, rich meat after months of surviving on little more than nuts and scraps. We were almost home when the claw-hound struck.'

Her hand went to the necklace she wore, gripping it tightly.

'It was half-mad from hunger. Thin, ragged, but with the strength of desperation. That was the first time I felt true terror.

I remember that, and nothing else but a frenzy of teeth and claws and stabbing blades. When I finally gathered my wits the creature was dead and its blood was everywhere. In my eyes, in my mouth. My arms, up to the elbow. My father lay there, his chest torn open. I met his eyes, and we both knew the truth of it. I stayed with him for hours, holding his hand while his breathing slowed and his blood drained. He never cried out, not once. His skin went grey, and his breathing shallow. He spoke his last words to me before he left. 'This place wants you dead, Alzheer. Every plant, every creature. The land itself. All you have is the tribe. Keep them together, my daughter. Keep them strong.'

'I am sorry,' said Atrin, knowing from experience how little such words mattered to the grieving.

'I had a choice, once my father was gone. I could drag his body back to the camp, where the elders could say the words and give him the hero's funeral he deserved. Or I could return home with our kill, and at least a few of my people would go to their sleep without the ache of hunger in their bellies.'

She looked straight at him, and he saw the sorrow and the strength in her deep, brown eyes.

'Diash found me stumbling into camp at dusk, near-dead from exhaustion. But my people did not go hungry that night.'

'You did what your father would want,' said Atrin. 'And in the years since you have kept your people alive. He was proud when he died, and he is still proud of you now.'

She showed him the necklace. Upon a simple leather bond was a single jagged tooth.

'I keep this, not as a trophy, but as a reminder of my father's last words to me. *All you have is the tribe.*'

Her hand clasped the tooth so hard her knuckles turned white, and blood trickled down her palm. Her eyes were no longer filled with sorrow, but with a burning rage.

'The traitor Rusik made a mockery of those words. He

abandoned us, sent my warriors to their deaths. That is why I will not leave these caverns until I have driven a knife into his foul heart.'

They did not speak again for a long time. Finally, they reached the site of the ambush. It was eerily quiet. Blood was spattered across the ground, though various insects and glistening molluscs were currently in the process of siphoning it up. They squelched and crunched underfoot as Atrin moved cautiously forwards into the cramped chamber, gladius raised. With some surprise and a little relief, he saw his boltstorm crossbow nestled next to the gap in the stone through which he had fallen. He gathered it up and checked the firing mechanism and the limbs. It seemed in workable order – Sigmar's craftsmen forged weapons to last. He tried handling it, using his damaged arm to depress the trigger and his stronger arm to support its weight.

Workable. He had to awkwardly cradle the weapon and thus his usual standard of accuracy would suffer, but it could be done despite the lance of agony that it sent down his arm.

'They went this way,' said Alzheer. This time the trail was so obvious that a child could have spotted it. The bandaged servants that the sorcerer employed had simply dragged Callan along, by the look of things, and a great scuff was scraped across the stone. 'They were not travelling at great speed.'

'A Stormcast in full armour is no easy burden,' said Atrin. 'These creatures must lurk nearby, or have some stronghold close to here.'

'I think you are right,' the priestess nodded. 'In his ranting, the sorcerer spoke of some hidden refuge within these mountains.'

'Then we must push on. I will not leave Callan at that madman's mercy for a moment longer.'

Corpses littered the cavern floor. The Stormcasts had accounted for many of the sorcerer's wizened pets before they had fallen, and the surviving enemy had left their dead to rot. Carrion organisms had already begun their work.

Amongst the carnage lay a small, scattered pile of faintly purple dust. All that was left of Oreus. Atrin knelt by the pitiful remains. He hoped his brother would find his way back to Azyr, but in truth he was not sure if such a death would allow Oreus to make that journey. Magic violated everything it touched. He had fought at the Eldritch Fortress, against the vile minions of the wizard known as the Ninth Disciple. He had seen brothers warped and twisted beyond recognition by powers no mortal should ever wield. Many of those touched by such raw sorcery had never returned to the forge. He whispered a prayer to Sigmar, that he might see his brother again.

'We must go,' said Alzheer.

Atrin nodded and, hefting his crossbow, turned to follow her.

This far into the tunnels, the signs of some forgotten civilisation were obvious. The caverns here were circular in shape, and had a rough, natural quality that suggested to Atrin that they had originated as ancient lava flumes, and had been converted for civilian function many hundreds or thousands of years ago, after the volcanic activity in this region had ceased. Finely carved cobbles, traced with an orange-gold metal he did not recognise, made up the floor, and the walls had regularly placed apertures in which were hung sconces shaped like drakes' heads. Dust and cobwebs marred the impressive quality of the metalwork.

'I hear movement,' whispered Alzheer. She raised her shortbow, a recurved weapon of simple yet impressive design. Like the sabres that the Sky Seekers favoured, this was a cavalry weapon. It lacked the range of a longbow, but it was far easier to draw and loose from horseback, and powerful at close range. As she drew one of her poison-tipped arrows and eased back the string, the sinews and wood that formed its powerful composite structure gave a slight creak.

A scream echoed down the hall. Ragged and drawn out.

'Callan,' whispered Atrin. He had never heard the redoubtable warrior utter so much as a grunt of pain, yet somehow he knew it was his comrade that suffered. 'We must hurry.'

They set off down the winding tunnel, which eventually opened into a junction. To the right a set of curving stairs led down, while to the left the cave opened into what looked like a burial chamber. Thick, dark stone blocks lay stacked in neat rows. The dim flicker of his torchlight revealed lines of ancient runes that covered the surface of each block, but from where he stood, Atrin could not tell in which language they were carved.

'The sounds came from below us,' said Alzheer. She did not wait for Atrin, simply drew an arrow to her cheek and headed for the stairs.

'Wait,' he hissed, but she took no notice of him, slipping down the stairs as quickly and quietly as a hunting cat.

For all their manifold virtues, stealth was not the domain of the Stormcast Eternals. Especially not one who had recently been dropped down a very deep hole, and subsequently almost devoured by a cave-dwelling predator. Atrin could not keep up with her without breaking into a shuffling run, so instead he put out the torch and drew his crossbow, then followed on as quietly as he could manage. He was uncomfortably aware of the shift-scrape his heavy boots made on the stone cobbles.

The steps ended at the foot of another tunnel. This one was wider, with channels that opened into small chambers on each side. As he made his way forwards, he could smell the stench of burned flesh and charred bone, and underneath that a pervading odour of spoiled meat. The floor here was stained a muddy brown. Slumped against the wall to his left was a gangly, stick-limbed figure with an arrow in its gut. Another of the bandaged creatures that the sorcerer favoured as minions. Coming closer, he saw that its throat had been neatly sliced. Foul-smelling, dark blood had already clotted around the wound. Atrin wrinkled his nose in distaste. He did not know what gave these foul creatures life, but they stank of the grave.

'Interesting, interesting,' came a high-pitched voice from the far end of the corridor. The sorcerer. 'You have the anatomy of a mortal. Stronger and larger, of course, but you bleed as well as any man. Yet I saw your kind fall at the fortress, and disappear in a burst of light even as your corpse hit the ground. There is magic in you. I must not yet have cut deep enough to find it.'

There was another ear-splitting scream. Atrin abandoned all attempts at stealth, and rushed forwards. The sound of his boots on the rough stone drew two more of the bandaged horrors forth from the chamber at the end of the hall. He fired his crossbow, gritting his teeth and ignoring the pain it sent shooting down his shattered arm. Bolts of burning blue light roared down the length of the tunnel, and the two creatures simply came apart under the barrage. Dark chunks of flesh splattered the walls, and a mist of gore spurted forth. What was left of the things slumped to the floor, and Atrin charged down the hall towards the sound of his brother's torment.

He entered a low-ceilinged chamber dimly lit by several blue-glowing lamps set into thick columns of carved, spiralling stone. In the centre of the chamber were more of those carved stone slabs, though the runes that covered their surface were masked by brown and red stains, or chipped and broken. Fragments of bones littered the floor, along with filthy strips of cloth and tattered parchments. Arranged on shelves, warped by the crude glass containers that kept them, were all manner of gruesome paraphernalia, from severed digits to grinning, polished skulls whose dimensions were unnaturally stretched. Across the walls someone had scrawled unknowable celestial configurations and twisted, sickening symbols in a child's hand. A scored and seared archway of stone lay in pieces against one wall, the runes that ran across its surface pulsing softly with a wan green light. The room smelt of acrid chemicals and rotting filth.

'Callan,' he shouted, seeing no sign of his brother or the fiend that kept him. 'Where are you?'

More of the bandaged wretches scampered towards him from the gloom, their silence as unnerving as the howls of a blood-crazed warrior. He tucked his crossbow to his chest and drew his gladius, ramming it through the chest of the first creature and whipping it across the throat of the next.

He carved them apart as if they were little more than straw mannequins. The air was thick with the tattered remnants of age-old cloth, and reeking blood spattered across his war-mask. Suddenly the aches and pains that wracked his body faded into insignificance. All he felt was the rapture of battle, the joyous roaring of his blood and the ecstasy of righteous vengeance.

'Sorcerer,' he shouted. 'Face me, coward!'

The rain had ceased and the sun was shining down with furious strength once more as Thostos Bladestorm strode out to what would likely be his death. He did not fear the prospect. He cared only that the Celestial Vindicators still had a task to complete, and that if the fortress fell before Tharros could complete his spell and make safe the realmgate, his mission would fail. The only currency that mattered now was time, and Thostos could see only one way to prevent the orruks throwing themselves against the walls of the Dreadfort for even a few more minutes. Eldroc would be able to lead the men on without him, he had faith in that.

Archaon's pitiless eyes stared down at him as he passed beneath the great statue of the Everchosen. Lord of the armies of darkness. Symbol of everything that Thostos had dedicated his life to destroying. The stonework was not as fine as that of the marble sculptures found in the halls of Azyrheim, yet the statue possessed a blunt and foreboding presence. If they had time, the Lord-Celestant would have had it torn down, piece by piece. Its very presence was an offense to the divine rulership of Sigmar.

One day, faithless traitor, he thought to himself as he gazed upon it. One day there will be a reckoning. One day we will march upon the hell you created and we will burn it to the ground.

He was aware of the orruks surging towards him now, hollering and jeering. He took a step forwards and held his blade and hammer readily at his side. Time to roll the dice.

'I am Lord-Celestant Thostos Bladestorm of the Celestial Vindicators,' he said, 'and I am here to kill your leader.'

His voice rang out across the plain, not a shout but a loud and clear statement of fact. For a moment his surety and apparent lack of concern stunned even the howling orruks. They stopped in their tracks. Then they began to laugh the deep, booming belly roars of a drunken mob. The war horde started forwards again, eager to strike down the foolish warrior who had walked into their midst.

A voice like thunder stopped them once more. It spoke a single word in a guttural tongue that Thostos did not understand, but the implication was clear. The owner of that voice had claimed this kill as his own.

'Drekka! Drekka! Drekka!' the horde began to chant. Thostos simply waited, every muscle primed to burst into motion. He knew the futility of fighting if these creatures decided to rush him. It seemed that he had judged the creatures correctly. These orruks might be stronger and fiercer than any of their kind he had seen before, but the same savage warrior culture united them. One amongst them, surely the largest and most brutal of their number, dominated the others. It was fear of this pack leader – fear or some other primal instinct he could never fully understand – that kept them from taking the Lord-Celestant's head.

Pushing through the mass of whooping creatures came a true behemoth of an orruk. It towered over Thostos, eight feet of corded muscle and predatory instincts bound in a suit of iron armour so thick and heavy that it seemed truly impenetrable. Its eyes were alight with the same madness that shone in those of its fellows, but this one had a glimmer of fierce cunning behind the aggression.

'Come in twos, eh?' the creature asked, grinning widely. 'Hope you're more sport than the other one.'

Thostos raised his weapons, holding his blade forwards, the hammer up and ready to strike.

'My name is Lord-Celestant Thostos Bladestorm,' he said. 'You have taken up arms against an army of Sigmar's divine will. For that, I will take your head.'

The orruk leader's eyes narrowed, and it flexed its muscles. A ripple of sheer power ran through its body, making the iron plate creak and squeal, and its toothy grin widened. Chipped and broken fangs jutted out from its lower jaw, and it slapped its great cleaver into one thick palm. The weapon was little more than a gigantic block of saw-edged iron, entirely lacking in ornamentation or craftsmanship. In the hands of the beast that held it, Thostos could only imagine the carnage that could be wrought.

'Spat out bigger lumps than you, little lord,' the beast called Drekka growled, and now there was little mirth to be found in that rumbling growl.

Thostos' eyes drifted over the orruk, searching for a weakness. The bulwark of yellow-daubed iron that it wore was thick and heavy, though given the beast's size it seemed unlikely to slow him down overmuch. Still, it was crudely fixed at the joints. A solid strike from a good sigmarite weapon and he could wreak some terrible damage. That was his only chance, to wear the creature down and bleed it out under the force of multiple blows.

In a burst of motion unthinkably quick for such a huge creature, Drekka charged forwards with his cleaver raised.

Thostos backed off, circling quickly to his left to force the orruk to turn and meet him. The great cleaver came down and met the crossed weapons of the Lord-Celestant. Sparks flew as brutal iron chewed into fine sigmarite, and the sheer weight of the blow buckled his knees. A heavy boot crashed into his chest, and he was thrown across the floor to land heavily in the wet earth. Mud splattered across his armour, and he felt the air rush from his lungs. There was no time to catch his breath, however. He heard the wet thump of the orruk's boots as it thundered towards him, and rolled to his feet. Drekka was already nearly upon him. He feinted left, and as the cleaver came down he stepped inside the blow. The mighty weapon tore a great gouge out of the earth, and Thostos slammed his hammer into the creature's side. He raised his blade to thrust between the gaps in its iron plate, but Drekka's fist whipped out sideways and slammed into his chest.

Thostos staggered backwards, but caught himself before he lost his footing. The orruk leader chuckled as he paced like a hunting beast, a wide smile splitting his scarred face.

'Almost got me there, little 'un,' he chuckled. 'Can't have that.'

'We shall see,' said Thostos.

The place was a chamber of horrors. Atrin pushed further into the mortuary tunnels, and was met with new nightmares at every corner. Hideous, deformed monsters, their flesh warped and twisted, screamed at him from the glass jars that contained them. Books bound in decaying flesh whispered obscene promises at him as he passed. In one room he found a font filled with softly simmering blood. Within, for just a moment, he thought he saw a man's screaming face, before it was dragged beneath the surface. Nauseated and disgusted, he pushed on.

The next hallway ended in a high, arched chamber, and it was here that he found Callan. The Retributor was held upright in the centre of the room by chains that stretched from all four corners. His melted armour exposed raw flesh beneath, and blood dripped from open wounds to gather in a trough below. Books were scattered about the floor around the warrior's tormented figure, and the sorcerer's insane scrawling covered the walls. More great glass jars full of pale, cloudy liquid were placed around the room, and Atrin could see horrors drifting and writhing within their murky depths.

'Sigmar's wrath is coming, for you and all your degenerate kind,' he shouted into the echoing halls. 'Come face me, and I will make your end a quick one.'

'As you wish,' came a chortling voice from the shadows. 'For my part I make no such promise.'

As he scanned the room to find a hint of the man, Atrin could hear the sound of whispered chanting, and could feel the room grow cold. A pale pink glow surrounded him. Gibbering, disembodied mouths appeared in the air around him, sinking discoloured fangs into his armour. Sigmarite twisted and tore even as the sound of cackling laughter filled his ears. He swiped at the maws with his gladius, and felt a burst of fluid as several came apart with a splatter of crimson gore. More appeared in their stead, and he growled as one attached itself to his wrist, crunching the metal of his gauntlet so that it bit painfully into his hand. How he hated fighting magic users. There was no honour in this mummery, no dignity in it at all. Again he scanned the room for a sign of Xos'Phet, but he could see nothing.

Atrin cut another sniggering maw from the sky, and turned to repeat the manoeuvre when a fist made of glowing blue energy rushed across the room and struck him full in the chest with astonishing force. He staggered backwards to crash against a stone coffer, coughing and gasping for breath.

'All your strength, all that training,' came a high-pitched voice that echoed around the chamber. 'And you are undone by the simplest of magic. You people understand only the hammer and the iron fist, and refuse to accept your simple insignificance next to the power of the arcane. Lord Varash was the same, curse his bones. His only ambition was that which I fed to him, like scraps to a hungry dog.'

Atrin blocked out the words, taking advantage of the momentary calm to focus and think. His enemy was toying with him, and that gave him time.

Thostos spun inside his opponent's reach, ringing strike after strike off the orruk's armour. Sparks and shards of metal flew as he pummelled his enemy. Drekka threw an elbow that snapped the Lord-Celestant's head back, and Thostos responded with a headbutt that cracked into the orruk's face, crunching bone and further flattening its porcine nose.

'Good one!' roared Drekka, as if he was applauding a fine joke. This one's skull was as thick as the walls of Sigmar's palace.

They exchanged yet more blows, weapons cutting back and forth so blindingly fast that they seemed like little more than blurred extensions of each warrior's limbs. Thostos rolled awkwardly in his heavy plate, and Drekka's great cleaver soared past him, taking the head from an unfortunate orruk spectator. The dead creature's fellow threw a punch at the Lord-Celestant, who swayed back to avoid the blow, and brought his foot up into his assailant's groin. The orruk doubled over, and Thostos planted a foot in its face and kicked him back into the path of Drekka.

The great cleaver burst through the dazed orruk's chest, lifting it into the air. Drekka whipped the dying brute back and forth in an attempt to dislodge it, brow furrowed in irritation. Blood and ruptured organs spilled out, splashing into the mud at his feet.

'Get out of my way, ya useless gits,' he bellowed.

Alzheer regretted leaving the Sky Warrior behind, but he would insist that they stay together, and she preferred to hunt alone. In any case, it was hardly as if he was more vulnerable in her absence. Even with a shattered arm and likely a broken leg, the man still held his blade strong. Such strength and fortitude was incredible. She wished that her father were alive to meet these warriors. She would have liked him to pass knowing that Zi'Mar had come for his people.

All you have is the tribe.

She had lived her life by those words in honour of her father. She had taken the old oaths and joined the ranks of mighty Zi'Mar's priests. Time and again she had brought home food when her people were in danger of going hungry for another night. She had learned to master the bow and the sword, and had used both to protect her home. She had kept her faith, even as her people diminished, because she knew that if only they stayed strong together, the sky god would not abandon them and leave them to fade into nothing.

Yet something within her had died when Rusik the betrayer had led her warriors to the slaughter. He was here, somewhere, and she would not rest until he was dead.

She slipped into the shadows, an arrow strung and ready on her bow. Movement ahead made her stop. Two of the bandaged horrors rushed out of a nearby chamber towards the sounds of battle in the distance. Atrin had clearly introduced himself.

These were not her quarry, but she could not leave her friend to face every wretch in these tunnels alone. Her first arrow took the trailing figure in the back as it scuttled down the corridor in front of her. Its companion turned with a hiss of alarm, and she stepped out of cover to put an arrow through its throat. It fell with a gurgle, smashing into a smouldering brazier as it dropped.

Stringing another arrow, Alzheer made her way forwards.

Somewhere close, the Stormcast had encountered the sorcerer Xos'Phet. Alzheer could hear bizarre, unearthly laughter and the sound of Atrin bellowing and cursing at an unseen enemy. Unnatural sounds that could only be the wizened monster's hateful magic echoed throughout the halls. She cursed. It seemed the sorcerer had recovered fully from the knife she had left in his gut. Leaving Atrin to battle weakling minions alone was one thing, but she could not abandon him in the face of such a dangerous foe.

Alzheer sprinted down the corridor ahead, turning left at the next junction towards the commotion. In her desire to come to the aid of her ally, she abandoned caution for haste.

Even so, the sheer speed of the blow took her by surprise. One moment she was running, the next she was sailing through the air to strike the far wall with staggering force. She slid down to hit the floor, moaning in agony.

Rough, cold hands dragged her upright. Alzheer looked into the face of the betrayer Rusik.

Or something that wore his face. The man's angular features were there still, the hooded eyes and the high, sharp cheekbones. Yet they registered unsettlingly, as if the bone beneath had been shifted and warped. The skin was torn and raw, and the eyes were the grey-pink colour of spoiled meat.

'Look what you have made of yourself, traitor,' she spat, choking the words out through the iron-hard grip that held her. 'To gain revenge on the orruks that slaughtered your family, you let this madman tear apart everything that you were. Look what your betrayal has wrought. You disgust me, monster.'

When he spoke, his words hissed forth like the gasps of a man with his throat cut.

'I have been forged for what must come. I am the spirit of vengeance, priestess. I will slaughter the greenskins one by one, but first you die.'

He began to squeeze her neck. The pressure of his grip was incredible. She felt blood swell in her eyes, and the inexorable press began to crush her windpipe. Desperately, she fumbled with one hand at her back, and grabbed an arrow from her quiver. She rammed the arrowhead into Rusik's chest, but his skin was like that of an arralox, so thick and leathery that the arrowhead could not penetrate. He laughed at her.

'You think your crude weapons can harm me? No, priestess, I can no longer be–'

Alzheer switched her grip on the makeshift weapon, and plunged the tip straight into his eye.

He roared in surprise and pain, and lost his grip for just a moment. Alzheer dropped to the floor, hacking and coughing, trying to force some air down her throat. Rusik staggered behind her, crashing into the wall of the corridor. She had laced each arrow with enough of the porsuka's poison to bring down a herd-beast, but still he stood. She just hoped she had bought herself enough time. Grabbing her fallen bow, she staggered down the corridor away from the traitor and towards the sounds of battle in the distance.

Whatever spell the sorcerer had woven, it rendered him invisible to Atrin. Even his keen eyes, regarded as the sharpest amongst his Judicator retinue, could not find him. The laughter seemed to echo around the room at random, so it likewise could not be used to locate his enemy.

In such situations, one must be decisive.

Atrin shouldered his boltstorm crossbow, ignoring the agony in his arm as he raised it to his shoulder and loosed. The lightning-wreathed projectile scorched through the air and struck one of the glass cases on the far side of the room. Foul-smelling liquid poured across the floor, along with broken glass and what appeared to be a number of eight-fingered hands. Nothing else. He shattered a second jar. Nothing. A third and a fourth, which spewed out tentacled limbs that writhed and slapped at the stone floor.

A bolt of blue flame struck him in the side, searing a gaping hole through his armour, and he staggered to the floor.

'Stop!' screamed Xos'Phet. 'Enough! Do you know the value of my work? The hours, the years I have spent gathering these samples?'

Atrin spun, and destroyed another jar. This one contained a flayed torso with only a circular maw like that of a lamprey upon its short, squat neck. Hands that ended in razor-sharp claws dragged the thing across the floor, and it let loose a horrifying wail. Of greater note was the fact that when the fluid from this jar flowed, it diverted from its natural path just a fraction of a second.

'And there you are,' muttered Atrin. He let loose one more bolt.

The projectile exploded in mid-air, and whatever magic had concealed Xos'Phet sputtered and died as the sorcerer was thrown screaming through the air to strike the far wall. One shoulder was a ruined, smoking mess.

'You... you... could never,' the man wailed, his rheumy eyes wide with fear and shock.

'It is always arrogance that brings your kind low,' said Atrin, wincing as he lowered his spent crossbow and drew his gladius. 'You could have killed me a dozen times, witchkin, but you had to fuel your sadistic ego. That was a mistake.'

The thing that had escaped from the cage lifted its vile mouth into the air and a tongue protruded from between its fangs, licking and tasting the air. Its head snapped towards Xos'Phet and the sorcerer moaned and tried to scrabble away across the floor.

'You say these specimens are valuable,' Atrin said. 'In that case I will leave this one be. This is for Oreus, you twisted filth.'

Atrin was not proud that he took such satisfaction in the vile sorcerer's terror as the wretched thing scrabbled towards Xos'Phet and leapt upon his bleeding form. The Judicator turned away as the screaming began, and went to Callan, still chained in place.

'Easy, brother,' he said, as the Retributor groaned.

He hacked and smashed at the chains that bound Callan with his gladius, but they were thick and sturdy. Retrieving his crossbow, he loaded a fresh cartridge of bolts, aimed and loosed. The chain securing Callan's upper arm was shattered, tiny fragments of iron bouncing off his armour as the metal came apart. He repeated the same trick on the lengths securing his comrade's leg, and was about to free the remaining arm when he heard footsteps coming from the far side of the room.

It was Alzheer. The woman came staggering into the chamber, one hand holding her throat, the other clutching her bow.

'Rusik,' she gasped, and the word was almost inaudible as she choked it out. He saw the purple bruises around her neck.

Something struck her from behind. She flew into the air, somersaulting once and landing amongst a pile of scrolls and leather-bound books in an explosion of dust.

The thing that had struck her burst from the shadows, hunched and powerful. It had a man's face, but was too fast and strong to be mortal. Blood poured from one ruined eye, and its cracked and broken teeth were bared in an insane grimace.

It roared, an inchoate blend of pain and rage, and leapt across the room at him. He loosed his crossbow as it came, but the thing was blindingly quick. Bolts skipped off the floor and wall behind it and the creature crashed into him, bearing him to the floor despite his greater mass. He punched it in the side, but it was like striking stone. It responded by clubbing his broken arm, and the pain almost made him lose consciousness.

'You stole my vengeance from me!' screamed the thing that had once been Rusik. 'The men of the fortress promised me the strength to slaughter the orruks, and you slew them before they could grant me it.'

'They offered nothing but damnation, you fool,' gasped Atrin, shocked at the man's new-found strength. Try as he might, he could not prise those arms from around his neck.

He slammed his fist into Rusik's side, again and again. Blows that should have shattered the mortal's ribcage seemed to cause him no concern at all. Atrin hooked the warrior's left leg and rolled, trying to gain purchase. He could not gain the upper hand.

Rusik writhed like a serpent, slipping free of his clutch and wrapping his arms around the Stormcast's throat. The sigmarite held, but then the traitor launched vicious punches to Atrin's chest, as powerful as strikes from a warhammer. The armour groaned and creaked under the assault, but still the Judicator could not prise his opponent loose.

Arrows whipped across the room, striking the thing that had been Rusik in the face and chest, skipping away on the stone floor as they deflected off his thick hide. The distraction gave Atrin a moment, and he put his good foot into the man's chest, launching him away. He tried to draw a few breaths, but no sooner had he struggled to his feet than the creature was on him once more. This time it had his fallen gladius in hand, and Atrin just barely got his hands up to block a thrust that would have split his visor and sunk deep into his eye. He strained with every fibre of his being, but whatever unnatural power gave Rusik his strength would not be denied. The blade slowly dropped lower, scraping against the brow of his war-mask.

Something grasped Rusik around the neck, and hauled him backwards. The gladius clattered to the floor. Callan stood behind the traitor, one massive arm locked firmly around his throat. Armour melded with his flesh where Xos'Phet's magical fire had struck. He bled from a dozen surgical incisions that had been cut into his living flesh, but still he would not relent his grip. Rusik scratched and beat at the arm that held him.

'The sword,' Callan gasped, with a voice that sounded as if his throat was filled with broken glass. 'Faster would be better, my friend.'

Atrin, grasped his gladius in two hands, and with every ounce of strength he had left to him, drove it deep into Rusik's chest.

The traitor's eyes went wide, and he roared in pain. He began to shudder and howl, eyes rolling back into his head. Callan hurled the man's body away. Rusik landed, his body convulsing. As they watched, great swathes of his skin peeled away, exposing the muscle beneath. He vomited blood, which hissed and smoked as it burned into the floor.

And then he began to laugh, as he hauled himself upright with unnatural grace.

'Not here,' he chortled through broken, blood-smeared teeth. 'Not yet. Still so much to be done.'

He paced towards them, his movement bizarre and unnatural.

'Sky Warrior!' shouted Alzheer. Blood poured from a wound on the woman's head, but still she stood. She was dragging Atrin's boltstorm crossbow behind her, the weapon's great weight too much for the mortal to wield.

Atrin grasped the weapon, but he could not lift it with one arm shattered.

'Brother,' he shouted. 'Kneel!'

Callan did not hesitate, dropping low. Atrin hauled the crossbow up in his good arm and propped it on his comrade's shoulder. Rusik's eyes went wide, and he skittered forwards unnaturally fast, reaching for them with arms that now ended in vicious, curved talons.

Atrin loosed the volley, point-blank. A dozen sigmarite bolts rippled through the monster's flesh, tearing him apart and sending what remained splattering across the chamber. The smell of sulphur and rotten flesh filled the room, and the two Stormcasts slumped to the floor. Atrin heard Alzheer do the same behind them, and heard her ragged sigh of relief.

'I tell you truly, brother,' said Callan, staring at the ceiling above and panting heavily. 'I feel terrible.'

Thostos had crossed blades with many warriors of Chaos, and had tested his martial skills against countless other monsters and fiends. This battle was amongst the most vicious he had ever fought.

Drekka seemed simply impervious to pain. The Lord-Celestant had struck half a dozen solid blows on that iron carapace and had drawn blood each time, but if the orruk was suffering from his wounds he made no sign of it. He simply came forwards again, that foolish grin still upon his ugly face.

The cleaver came swiping across. Thostos stepped back, recognising now that it was foolish to even attempt a block or parry unless he had no other choice. The beast's strength was simply too great. The blade whistled past his face, and he darted forwards to jab his sword at the orruk's midriff, between two of the iron plates. He struck home solidly, but his blade caught as the orruk reared back in pain, and he was a fraction too slow in avoiding the backwards swing of the cleaver. It opened a great rent in the armour across his chest, tearing through flesh and spraying blood, and sent the Lord-Celestant spinning through the air.

He landed hard, and could feel the blood pouring down the inside of his war-plate. That strike had shattered ribs, possibly ruptured organs. A fatal strike, in all likelihood. He managed to haul himself unsteadily to his feet, though even holding his weapons high was draining what remained of his strength.

'Tough little soldier, ain't you,' came the mocking voice of Drekka. The orruk approached with a victor's swagger, backed by the chorus of his minions as they chanted his name. 'Tougher than the last one. One good smash an' you fall the same, though.'

Thostos rushed forwards, runeblade arcing out to cut a deep line across the orruk's forehead. Drekka reared back, cursing, and the Lord-Celestant followed up with a hammer to his gut. It clanged off the thick bands of iron, the dull echo of the impact ringing out across the plain. As the creature finally clutched its midriff in pain, Thostos leapt into the air, twisting his body as he rose, and drove his blade down at the beast's collarbone. Drekka snapped a hand out and grasped him by the neck, snatching him out of the air.

'Slippery little git,' he snarled. His great plated fist lashed out once, twice, three times. Vision swimming, fires burning behind his eyes, the Lord-Celestant felt blood pour down the inside of his war-mask. Shattered metal was digging deep into his temple, and he could no longer see clearly from the bloody ruin of his left eye. Drekka slammed one last punch into his chest, and hurled him through the air.

Thostos hit the earth hard, the air rushing from his lungs from the force of the impact. The sky above was a bloody smear, and the earth spun beneath him. Shattered ribs drove daggers of bone deep into his vital organs. He let the infinity of agonies that wracked his form fuel his rage. He would not fall here, to this dull creature.

He would not leave Lord-Celestant Argellon unavenged.

Tortured body groaning in protest, Thostos hauled himself to one knee, spitting blood. Drekka was pacing towards him again, holding his wounded torso, the humour gone from his eyes.

Thostos knew he could not win this fight in a straight contest of strength. Yet he still had one last card to play.

'Is that all you have, orruk?' he spat through broken teeth. 'You punch like a pox-ridden ratman, you simple-minded scum.'

Drekka's eyes went wide, and then narrowed slowly and dangerously. Veins rippled around the beast's muscular neck as he let loose an inchoate bellow of rage. Raising that wicked cleaver above his head, he charged the Lord-Celestant, thick legs eating up the ground between them with terrifying speed.

All thoughts of his own defence were forgotten.

Thostos spun, and as he turned he muttered the arcane phrase that unleashed the potent magic woven into the trailing leather straps of his cloak. At the bottom of the garment hung small hammers of burnished metal, seemingly little more than ornaments.

As the spell was unleashed, these hammers were transmuted into a cloud of celestial energy, and rocketed towards the unsuspecting Drekka like tiny comets. They struck with the force of the heavens, blasting apart the thick armour at the orruk leader's neck and sending him stumbling in shock. On their own, the missiles would not have been enough to take down the monstrous orruk, but Thostos Bladestorm was already moving in their wake.

Leaping towards Drekka, he put everything he had into one last strike. Both hammer and blade came down on top of the orruk's skull. The beast's ugly face came apart under the force of the strike, the skull splintering and the blade hewing down deep into its throat.

Drekka staggered. Half the creature's head was missing, and yet still it would not fall. Bloodshot eyes, narrowed with focused anger, locked on to Thostos. The orruk lurched forwards one step, its cleaver still raised high and ready to fall. Another step. Thostos hobbled backwards before it, raising his weapons in futile defence. Drekka came forwards again, and the cleaver gleamed in the blazing sun, a beacon of light in the bloody mist that was the Lord-Celestant's vision.

Then the orruk leader's eyes rolled back into its head, and the weapon slid from its grasp.

Thostos rolled out of the way of the Drekka's body as it fell, sending a spray of mud into the air. The Lord-Celestant came up on one knee, weapons in hand.

'Which of you is next?' he roared.

For once, the orruk mob fell quiet. The wind whipped Thostos' cloak and blew dust across his face. In the distance, he could hear the caws and shrieks of carrion birds as they circled overhead.

When the orruks finally regained their sense, any semblance of unity amongst their ranks was lost. Shorn of the unifying presence of their leader, they embraced their natural inclination for self-destructive savagery. The nearest orruks leapt upon the corpse of Drekka, hauling off fragments of his armour or loudly claiming trophies as their own. Some simply milled in confusion. Others began to fight amongst themselves, as long-abandoned grudges and rivalries rekindled in an instant.

Still more decided that they would like to claim the head of the warrior that had slain their mightiest champion.

Thostos backed off as scores of the enemy bounded towards him. The first to reach him died with his sword in its chest, the next fell under a mighty blow from his warhammer. Yet there were simply too many, and wounded as he was he knew he had bought his warriors all the time that he could.

A horn sounded from behind him. He looked back to see the fortress gates thrown open, the Paladin warriors of the Celestial Vindicators bursting forth with Lord-Castellant Eldroc and his loyal gryph-hound at their head. Roaring oaths of vengeance and prayers to Sigmar, mighty Decimators barrelled into the advancing orruks with their two-handed axes, smashing the enemy aside with explosive peals of thunder. Retributors dealt the God-King's justice with their lightning hammers, this fractious melee the arena in which they excelled.

Eldroc reached the Lord-Celestant, and Thostos allowed his friend to haul him to his feet.

'You should have stayed in the Dreadhold,' he gasped. 'You should have let me fall.'

'You'll have plenty more opportunities to get yourself killed,' replied Eldroc, battering an orruk aside with the haft of his halberd as he and Thostos staggered behind the lines of the Paladins. As they ran, the elite warriors were falling back to the fortress in perfect order. Thostos saw a shield wall of Liberators arrayed in front of the ruined gate, and saw them open the line to let the sallying party back inside to relative safety.

'They already recover their wits,' continued Eldroc. 'This is not yet over.'

CHAPTER SEVEN

The Spiral Tower

'To fully purge the taint from this gate would take me many hours, perhaps even days,' said Lord-Relictor Tharros Soulwarden. His voice was strained and hoarse, and nowhere near his usual ornery tone. He sounded exhausted. Lord-Castellant Eldroc knew his friend was on the verge of collapse, and it was only his stubborn will that kept him upright.

'We cannot use it?' asked Thostos Bladestorm. The Lord-Celestant's own voice was tight with pain, though the restorative glow emanating from Eldroc's warding lantern was slowly knitting together the gruesome wounds upon his chest and head. He had been even closer to death at the hands of the orruk leader, Drekka Breakbones, than the Lord-Castellant had thought.

Out on the plains the greenskins' hoarse voices still bellowed in maddened rage. The death of their general had sent the dull-witted beasts into a frenzy, and even now they were throwing themselves against the walls and gate of the Manticore Dreadhold.

'I did not say we could not use it,' said Tharros, 'only that it will require my full strength and concentration to keep the gateway open.'

'We cannot abandon the Dreadhold,' said Eldroc. 'Even if we were to pass through the Manticore Realmgate, the orruks would likely follow us. Besides, Sigmar required us to hold this position. Azyr's armies will pour through this route on their way to the front.'

The front was located in the Realm of Metal, where the next stage of the God-King's plan called for a full assault on the fortresses known as the Ironholds, which in turn guarded the path to the nexus of arcane travel known as the Allpoints. It was from there that the armies of darkness sallied forth into the Eight Realms.

'I can hold the fortress,' said Eldroc. 'Lord-Celestant, take a small expeditionary force. Make contact with the Knight-Azyros. He can signal for aid in securing the Dreadhold.'

'I cannot leave the chamber behind,' said Thostos, glancing back at the fortress wall. The Judicator archers were already loosing arrow after arrow into the ranks of the enemy. They could not see the gatehouse from their position at the rear of the structure, but the fighting there would be thick. The main gate was a twisted wreck, and such a breach would draw the orruks like flies around meat.

'This is my area of expertise, brother,' said Eldroc. 'Trust me, I know how to hold a fortress under siege. I swear to you the Dreadhold will not fall while I stand.'

'If you could decide what you wish to do quickly, that would be wonderful,' came the faint voice of Tharros Soulwarden, with a hint of his usual curmudgeonly temper.

Thostos nodded. 'Twenty men should suit my purpose. Ware the orruks, Lord-Castellant. Without their leader they will be reckless and disorganised, yet their battle-madness will give them strength. They will not relent, not now their blood is up.'

'I know, Lord-Celestant. This place will hold until your return. Go now.'

Thostos chose the fastest and the most keen-eyed warriors to join the ranks of his war party. Eldroc needed the strongest fighters at his disposal, and in any case the Lord-Celestant was not looking for a fight. The faster they found the Knight-Azyros, the sooner they could bring help to the fortress defenders. As he chose the last of his warriors, word came that the small force he had sent into the mountains had returned. There was Atrin, hobbling along with his crossbow rested over one shoulder. Callan was at his side, supported by several of the Liberator rearguard who were still stationed at the realmgate. The Retributor was a ruin of melted sigmarite and scorched flesh. It was almost incomprehensible that the man had managed to survive long enough to reach the Dreadhold.

'Oreus fell,' said the Lord-Celestant. It was not a question.

'Aye, Lord-Celestant,' the Judicator replied. 'Slain by the sorcerer Xos'Phet's magic. We slew the fiend in turn, as well as the traitor Rusik.'

'Then you performed your task admirably. There is yet more fighting to be done, and I would have you at my side if you are capable. Let the Lord-Castellant see to your wounds, then report to the realmgate.'

Atrin nodded, and made for the wall, where Eldroc was organising the defence. Behind him, leaning against the rocky outcrop upon which lay the realmgate itself, sat Alzheer, the mortal priestess of the Sky Seekers tribe. Thostos felt a tension loosen as he saw her, and realised with surprise that he had been worried she would not return from the mountain paths.

'Priestess,' he said, approaching her. 'I am glad that you return unharmed. Judicator Atrin tells me that you found the vengeance that you sought.'

She gazed up at him, squinting slightly in the sunlight. Her face was bloody and bruised, and deep cuts ran across her arms, but aside from that she was largely unharmed.

'I did, Lord Thostos,' she nodded. She did not seem triumphant, merely tired and somewhat distant. That was understandable. She had lost many of her people over the last few days.

'I am afraid I can offer you only water and rest, not safety,' he said. 'The orruks assault in force, and I must depart on my own mission. We cannot lead you home just yet, priestess.'

'I can still wield a bow, Lord-Celestant,' she said, and she hauled herself to her feet, staggering slightly. Thostos stretched out a hand to steady her.

'You will rest, my lady,' he said, in a voice that brooked no complaint. 'And you will let us do the fighting. You have done enough. Fought enough. More than any mortal should be expected to. We are the Celestial Vindicators, Alzheer. We were forged for battles such as this. Let us do our duty, and let yourself heal.'

The fighting at the gatehouse was some of the most vicious that Liberator-Prime Relius had ever known, and he had been a veteran of countless wars even before his Reforging as a Celestial Vindicator.

'Namuth, keep that shield tight,' he roared, as the orruks surged forwards once more, clattering against the wall of sigmarite that guarded the tunnel.

The gate itself had been torn off its hinges, and had fallen diagonally to half block the main entrance. The enemy could still slip under the shattered iron, but as more of them fell that was becoming increasingly difficult. Not that the orruks seemed wary of the danger. Even as he glanced over the rim of his shield, Relius saw one of the creatures spitted through the belly on a vicious shard of black iron. Lord-Castellan Eldroc had ordered the tunnel filled with dozens of these wicked spikes, scavenged from the walls of the Dreadhold. The dying orruk was still hacking away with its crude cleaver, seemingly unaware or uncaring of its predicament.

'Kill,' Relius shouted, and as one the front rank of Celestial Vindicators brought their shields to the side, stabbing out with longswords or smashing skulls and bones with their heavy warhammers.

'Hold,' he yelled, and just as swiftly the unforgiving wall of sigmarite was restored. Dead orruks toppled along the line, joining the barricade of dead that littered the floor. Their fellows behind scrabbled over the corpses of the fallen, hurling themselves at the Stormcasts with maniac howls and whoops of glee.

The Stormcast line was pushed back, no more than an inch or two, under the pressure of the assault. Such margins, Relius knew, could be fatal. This battle would drag on for hours, perhaps even days. They could not afford to lose the bottleneck provided by the gatehouse tunnel. Once the orruks broke out, it was all over.

'Kill!' the Liberator-Prime shouted again.

The first thing that Thostos Bladestorm noticed, as he stepped forth from the archway of carved obsidian and into the glimmering light of the Crystal Forest, was how different the air felt here. In the Roaring Plains it had been fresh and harsh, with the earthy taste of grass and churned soil. Here it was so close it seemed to wrap around his skin like a second cloak. A slight but noticeable static thrum raised the hairs on his neck, and he smelled the sweet, chemical tang of copper and iron.

'The Crystal Forest,' said Liberator-Prime Amon Steelhide, emerging behind him. 'The name hardly seems to do the place justice.'

Ahead of them, beyond the bed of carved stone upon which the realmgate lay, stood the forest. It was unerringly beautiful. Spiralling towers of multicoloured crystal reached high into the sky, twisting around and encircling their fellows to form a thicket of glittering, shimmering light. It was as if a rainbow had crashed to earth and splintered into a thousand pieces. Smaller crystal copses ran underneath these grand structures, casting their own dizzying array of tints and tones amongst the ground cover. In the distance, many miles away, Thostos could see mountains of dull brass, peaks of copper and great mesas of black iron. The sky was a dark purple, yet the ground was washed with soft moonlight and the flickering colours of the crystal spires overhead.

'Form a perimeter,' Thostos ordered. 'Make safe the gate. Prosecutor-Prime?'

Zannus snapped to attention, four fellow warrior-heralds lining up behind him. Even amongst the fabulously armoured soldiers of the Stormcasts they made an impressive sight, with their gleaming, radiant wings and plumed head crests.

'Sire?'

'Take to the skies. Give me a preliminary assessment of the area. We are to meet the Knight-Azyros Capellon here, the guide who will lead us to our assigned position for the offensive. Find him.'

Zannus saluted, and with a powerful beating of his wings, soared into the sky at the head of his retinue. The rest of the Lord-Celestant's advance party, some twenty-five men on foot, arranged themselves in loose formation around him. Amon Steelhide led the Liberator contingent, all of whom bore twin hammers or runeblades rather than the more familiar sigmarite shields of their conclave. Judicator Atrin's wounds had been healed by the heavenly power of Lord-Castellant Eldroc's warding lantern, and now he led an ad-hoc group of five Judicators, survivors of retinues that had taken heavy losses during the assault on the Dreadhold. Each carried a rapid-firing boltstorm crossbow, and they were currently scanning the crystal treeline intently, ready to unleash a torrent of sigmarite bolts against any emerging threat.

'Capellon was to meet us here,' Thostos muttered under his breath.

The Knights-Azyros were the messengers and heralds of the greater Stormcast force. Each was a mighty warrior, given the gift of flight and the possession of a wondrously crafted lantern, a celestial beacon with which they lit the path for Sigmar's Storm to follow.

'Perhaps he thought it safer to lay low, sire,' said Atrin. 'These are dangerous lands, as yet unclaimed by Sigmar.'

'Perhaps,' said Thostos, staring off into the depths of the crystalline forest. 'But thus far in our journeys we have not often been blessed by such good fortune.'

Zannus circled high above the forest, trying to keep his focus and not get distracted by the sheer beauty of the sight below. The luminous tangle of multicoloured crystal stretched on below him for several miles, gently creeping towards the foothills of the mountains on each side of the valley in which they found themselves.

'No sign of movement, friendly or otherwise,' said Tonan at his side.

'Take two men and survey the foothills to our east,' said Zannus. The mountain range was closest there, a smooth cluster of rolling hills that rose towards a series of curiously even conical peaks. Unweathered and geometric in arrangement, the range did not look like a natural formation.

'Do not tarry,' he continued, 'and return to me with your findings as soon as you are done.'

There was something about this place that unsettled Zannus, despite the obvious grandeur of his surroundings. It was the stillness of it, he thought. After his time on the Roaring Plains, where the wind howled constantly and furiously, and the earth below was ever in motion, the stillness of this place felt... untrustworthy.

'To me, Prosecutors,' he shouted to the rest of his warriors. 'We will spread out and fly low over the canopy.'

* * *

It took them an hour of searching before they found what they were looking for. Dipping beneath the canopy, carefully weaving his way through clusters of jagged azure and great columns of vermilion and aquamarine, it was the Prosecutor-Prime himself that came across the clearing. He spread his wings and slowed his flight, dropping lightly to the ground to take in the scene.

It was carnage. Torn corpses were scattered across the ground, bathed in the soft pink, refracted light that shone down from the great crystal canopy above. Some were sprawled on the floor, others impaled on sharp clusters of quartz. Zannus approached the nearest, and rolled it over with his boot. An ugly, scarred face twisted in a death mask of torment. A half-moon tattoo covered the left side of the human's face, and piercings linked with fine silver chains ran from eyebrow to nose. The armour was of decent quality, painted a deep blue with silver highlights, though it bore the chips and scrapes of regular use.

'Minions of the Dark Gods,' he said with no small amount of distaste. 'But not the Blood God's faithful.'

'It was fine swordwork that slew them,' said Ephenius, examining the deep slice that had cut through the spine of another warrior. 'Neat, deep. A fine blade held in a sure hand.'

'We have a live one,' shouted Orestes, from the edge of the clearing. In the shadow of a spiderweb of shattered crystals lay another of the mortals. His leg had been cut through at the knee, and hung by only a scrap of flesh. His skin was sallow, and his eyes were tired as much as they were fearful. This one had been left to die some time ago, and blood loss and thirst had left him dazed and weak. Looking at the wounds, Zannus doubted he would last much longer.

The Prosecutor-Prime grabbed a flask from one of the dead men and strode over to the survivor.

'This will not be an easy passing,' he said to the man. 'If blood loss does not take you soon, then hunger and thirst will do their work.'

He held out the flask, and the man groaned and reached for it with a shaking hand. Zannus drew it back.

'Tell me what happened here, and you can drink your fill. Speak.'

Beyond the point where pride or loyalty might have sealed his lips, the man was only too happy to tell them what he knew.

'The angel,' he choked, and blood dribbled from his dry mouth. 'We set upon him. He was hiding in the forest, but Lorchis always sees. He always knows. You can't hide from him.'

Zannus held the flask out, and let some of the contents dribble into the mortal's mouth. The man sighed with relief, and his eyes closed contentedly. The Prosecutor-Prime clipped him about the ear.

'Rest when you're done,' he snapped.

'The angel, he slew us so easily,' the man continued. 'Like we were nothing. Twenty of us there were, and even striking first we could not touch him. He tried to soar away, but Lorchis got him good. Sent him down in the dirt.'

He laughed a bitter, mirthless laugh.

'Oh, he struggled, but we had the nets on him. Had him down, burned and beaten.'

Orestes went to strike the wretch with the flat of his hand, but Zannus grasped his arm before the blow fell.

'Where did you take him?' he asked. 'Speak.'

The mortal looked at him blankly, as if the question had been spoken in a different language to his own. The Prosecutor-Prime reached down and grabbed a fistful of his chainmail hauberk.

'The angel,' he snarled. 'Where did you take him?'

Zannus and his men returned after a few hours, coming to rest in front of the orderly Stormcast line, which formed a defensive shield wall around the realmgate.

'Lord-Celestant.' He saluted as Thostos approached.

'What did you find?'

'We came across the scene of a skirmish, Lord. Several enemy dead. One alive enough to tell us that the Knight-Azyros has been captured.'

There was a round of muttered curses from the warriors present.

'Tell me that you discovered where the enemy took him,' said Thostos.

'I believe so. The enemy is clearly active in this region, Lord-Celestant,' the Prosecutor-Prime replied. 'Soldiers are stationed amongst the foothills to the east, and more guard a structure hidden in the mountains nearby. A spiral tower, half collapsed. This is where the wretch says that the Knight-Azyros was taken.'

'What numbers does the enemy have?'

'Our prisoner died from his wounds before we could interrogate him further,' said Prosecutor Tonan. 'We scouted the area before we returned. Their defensive positions are carved into the mountainside, so it is hard to be exact. We saw at least three hundred at camp. Fewer still were guarding the perimeter of the tower. No more than a score.'

'Though certainly there will be more within the structure,' said Thostos. 'And if they can capture a Knight-Azyros, they likely have either powerful magic or capable fighters on their side.'

The longer the Knight-Azyros remained in enemy hands, the greater the chance that the enemy would discover something of value. No Stormcast would ever volunteer information under duress, of course, but Thostos knew that simple physical torment was hardly the only tool at the great enemy's disposal.

'How far is it to the tower on foot?' asked Judicator Atrin.

'No more than a few hours,' said Zannus.

'Not good enough,' said Thostos. 'We march at pace. Prosecutor-Prime, return to the area and scout ahead. See if you can gather a more accurate estimate of their numbers. We will join you soon.'

He turned to the rest of his warriors. He could feel their eager tension and their fury. No Stormcast could stand idly by while a fellow warrior suffered at the hands of the enemy. They would run as long as they had to, no matter what it took out of them to do so.

'You know what is at stake here,' he said. 'Let us retrieve our lost brother.'

With that, the Stormcasts set off at pace, following in the Prosecutors' wake as they soared towards the mountain range.

It took Thostos and his men half the time Zannus had estimated to reach the foothills amongst which the tower lay. They had run near ceaselessly, even when they had reached twisting paths made treacherous by the crooked spikes of crystal that jutted out from nearby boulders, and in spite of the smooth, slippery ground beneath their feet. Every step had to be taken carefully, lest a warrior lost their footing and tumbled into a cluster of razor-sharp, pellucid quartz that could shear through armour with unsettling ease.

It was poor ground for stealth, littered with tiny fragments of crystal and shards of rough stone that crunched underfoot. The weight of the Stormcasts in their full battle array caused each footstep to echo like a falling boulder. Yet until now, at least as far as Thostos could tell, they remained unspotted as they made their way up the winding paths towards the great brass peaks in the distance.

After another hour or two of travel they hauled themselves over the lip of a great bluff of burnished brass, and caught their first glimpse of the spiral tower. It sank into the ground at a tight angle, leaning against the far edge of a towering peak like a resting spear. Though it shone with soft silver light, the surface was strangely organic in texture. It reminded Thostos of the great shell of some kind of ocean-dwelling crustacean. Spiral patterns wound into the surface, and great jewels of many different colours shone from within.

'Down,' whispered Atrin harshly, and the Stormcasts ducked low, hands grasping weapons firmly.

They were in a sort of sheltered bowl within the mountains, which rose steeply on all sides. The ground ahead of them was even for several hundred yards, and was patrolled by several groups of mortals dressed in silver chainmail and carrying short spears and curved blades.

Two such warriors, faces hidden by chainmail masks, were approaching the Stormcasts' position, idly chatting as they came.

'I have the one on the left,' Thostos muttered to Liberator-Prime Steelhide. 'Take the other.'

Pollux drew his twin warblades and crouched behind the nearest cluster of rocks, looking to his Lord-Celestant for the signal to move. The soldiers' footsteps came closer and closer, and after several moments they rounded the boulders and came into view. They stopped dead in their tracks, eyes widening in shock as they saw the score of turquoise-armoured giants that crouched before them.

'Who–' managed the lead figure, before Thostos cut his words short with a thrown hammer. The heavy sigmarite weapon clattered to the floor, as did the broken body of the warrior. Steelhide darted from cover, thrusting one of his swords into the remaining figure's chest, and bringing the other across backhand to strike the head from his shoulders.

There was a tense silence, then the sound of shouting voices.

'No more time for subtlety,' said Thostos, picking up his blood-smeared hammer as he ran forwards. 'Kill fast, and move quickly.'

As one, the Stormcasts broke forwards over the lip of the bluff, following the Lord-Celestant into the clearing. There were only a score or so of warriors scattered about the place, and not a man amongst them was prepared for the onslaught that the Celestial Vindicators unleashed. Atrin opened up with his crossbow, and a volley of sigmarite bolts sped across the clearing to send two figures tumbling away. Two more, unlucky enough to be within reach of Thostos, fell to vicious strikes from sword and hammer. The rest of the Judicator retinue unleashed a volley from their crossbows, and five more of the enemy were blasted off their feet.

The greater part of their number dead in seconds, the remaining mortals turned and ran up the curving stair towards the entrance to the tower.

The Stormcasts followed close behind.

Eldroc caught the axe blow on the haft of his halberd, forced the orruk's weapon down low, and slammed his fist into the creature's ugly face. It stumbled back, and he hacked it down with his weapon's axe blade. Redbeak leapt upon the fallen orruk, and tore its throat out with a snap of his beak.

'Lord-Castellant, they have made the wall,' came a voice from behind.

'Paladins, with me!' he shouted, hoping beyond hope that the orruks had not managed to force their way through the main gate. If the enemy breached in two places, they were done. They simply did not have the numbers to fight an open battle on two fronts.

Focus on the task at hand, he reminded himself. These walls must be cleared. He could see the orruks ahead, in the shadow of the Dreadhold's central tower. A band of Liberators was trying to stem the tide of yellow-clad warriors, but they were slowly being pushed back, and more orruks were hauling themselves up the wall at their flank.

For all its lack of martial discipline and tactical expertise, Eldroc found the orruks' bluntly simplistic assault a horribly effective one. The creatures hesitated not a single second, dragging themselves up the fortress wall with astonishing speed despite their weight. With no Stormcasts versed in their operation, the fire-spewing daemonic mouths that lined the Dreadhold's exterior were effectively little more than welcoming handholds. Though hundreds of orruks were slaughtered by the lightning bursts and crossbow bolts of the Celestial Vindicators, there were simply too many of the enemy, and too few Stormcasts, to keep the ramparts clear.

Eldroc roared with fury as he charged forwards, swiping the head from an orruk that poked its ugly face over the wall with a vicious slice from his halberd. He spun the weapon, holding the haft horizontally to smash it into the face of another creature. Yet another hauled itself over the edge behind him, but as he turned he saw it go down under a hammer-strike from a Retributor. Dark blood splattered across his armour, and the twitching body of the orruk was lifted and pitched back over the wall.

Now the lines of battle were hopelessly chaotic. Orruks flanked the band of Liberators, and were in turn attacked from behind by the great hammers and mighty axes of the elite Paladin warriors. Still more of the enemy crawled up and over the wall.

The press was so tight that it was difficult to move, and harder still to find the space to wield his halberd effectively. He thrust with the spear-tip at any orruks that came close, aiming for throats and eye sockets. The stone beneath his feet was slick with blood, and he found himself treading upon broken forms that moaned as they were crushed by the sheer weight of surging bodies.

Eldroc's advance swept clean the left side of the Dreadhold's ramparts. Freed from their precarious, flanked position, the Liberators and Judicators on that side of the fortress began to recover and push back those orruks that remained. The Paladins began to lift up the heavy, dead bodies of the orruks and hurl them back over into the roiling mass of green flesh, relying on their sheer weight to crush the unfortunate creatures below.

The Celestial Vindicators burst through into the interior of the tower, hot on the heels of the fleeing mortals. Most of the soldiers ran for the great, wide stair that curved upwards from the interior hall, but one made instead for a strange device on the far side of the room. It resembled a great shell, several handspans across, the whorl spiralling out to join a funnel that ran alongside the great stairway, stretching to the roof above. Before Thostos could reach him, the warrior put his lips to this device, and an ominous note issued forth – a great, resonating blast that echoed around the structure loudly enough to shake the teeth.

Thostos reached the man and cut him down, but the damage had been done. Every single being in this place would be aware of their presence now.

He glanced up. Above the Stormcasts soared a dizzying spiral of hundreds of cells, each carved from a strange, metallic coral-like substance. The complex stretched on and on over their heads, so high that the very dimensions of the place seemed unfathomable. From the outside, there had been no indication of such a colossal space. The angle, too, was wrong – vertical instead of lying askew, as it had first appeared. Thostos felt the sway of vertigo, the nauseous resonance of sorcerous power. There was something else up there too, an orb of glowing light that bathed the walls in a silver-blue glow.

Arrows whipped down from on high, skittering off the armour of the Stormcasts. Those that bore shields raised them to fend off the barrage, while the Judicator bowmen returned with a volley of their own. Dozens of yards overhead, the spiral walkway with its ammonite guardrail rippled in explosions of light, and a shower of coral fragments and ruptured bodies toppled down the central column to burst upon the floor.

'Forward!' yelled Thostos. 'To the summit.'

The Prosecutors rose into the air, circling their way up the main tower and unleashing devastating strikes with their celestial hammers, which smashed through crystal and stone-coral as if it were kindling. As each warrior hurled his magical weapon, he summoned one anew from the aether.

221

Those on foot began to advance. They moved slowly, checking each cell as they passed by. The bars were not metal, but razor-sharp spears of blue crystal stabbed deep into the floor. Each cell contained a rough stone slab set with leather straps. Most of the cells were empty, containing nothing but the dark stains of spilled blood, but in others they saw shattered skeletons, or pitiful, wasted figures that cringed and scuttled away in terror as they passed.

The sheer quantity of arrows loosed by the mortal guards above began to take its toll. A Judicator fell, clutching at his throat. As he toppled over the guardrail he turned once in mid-air before disappearing in a burst of light. Other Stormcasts fell to the floor, crashing back down the path to the levels below.

'Do not stop for a moment,' shouted Thostos, as his warriors began to pause in order to aid their stricken fellows. 'We keep moving or we die here.'

And so they pushed on, floor after floor. Mortal warriors wrapped in silver chainmail and tattooed with blue ink rushed at them from anterior tunnels and guardposts. These men were hardy fighters, disciplined and resilient. They attacked Thostos and his men with measured skill, not the unbarred aggression of the Blood God's faithful. They feinted forwards to hurl a volley of javelins and axes, then fell back and flanked from different angles. They used their knowledge of the tower's hidden pathways admirably.

Yet for all their skill, they were still merely mortals.

Relius had lost his sword in the melee, dropped when an orruk had slammed its axe into his shoulder and split his flesh to the bone. They were perilously close to the inner courtyard of the fortress now, having been steadily pushed back by the unrelenting ferocity of the enemy assault. The corridor was thick with corpses, yet the creatures came on regardless, slipping over the ruined remnants of their dead. Relius slammed his shield into a leering face, felt bones shatter under the heavy sigmarite, and raised it high to deflect another falling axe.

'We can't hold this,' shouted the Liberator at his side. Relius could not spare a glance to check, but it sounded like Vallus.

'We must,' he shouted. 'If they break through it is over.'

Something struck his leg, and there was an explosion of agony. Foolish. The orruk he had smashed to the floor had not been killed, and it had sunk a cleaver into the flesh of his thigh. Relius cursed as his leg gave way. He held his shield over his face, and felt heavy boots force him further to the floor as another of the creatures vaulted over his prone form and deeper into the Stormcasts' ranks. His world was a forest of struggling, kicking boots and splattered blood. He tried to drag himself upright, but there was simply no room. He was stuck fast, and would be until the enemy noticed him and drove an axe into his skull.

'Glory to Sigmar!' came a booming voice, resonating within the cramped gatehouse tunnel. 'Not a single step backwards, brothers. Death to the enemies of Azyr!'

Through the chaos of twisting, flailing bodies Relius caught a glimpse of Lord-Castellant Eldroc at the head of a formation of Retributors.

He barrelled straight into the orruks, his wondrous halberd smashing and stabbing as he hacked a path for the warriors to follow.

They did so mercilessly. Of all the elite Paladin disciplines, it was the Retributors that most closely symbolised the Celestial Vindicators' way of war. Simple, straightforward power, the fury of unleashed aggression. Vengeance dispatched with cold fury, and delivered with the killing face of a sigmarite hammer.

These warriors amongst warriors pushed through to the front of the melee, battering the enemy aside with thunderous swings of their two-handed weapons. Lightning arced in the narrow confines of the tunnels as the hammers impacted, pummelling iron armour into a shapeless mass, crushing skulls and scorching flesh.

'Up you get, Liberator-Prime,' said Eldroc, hauling Relius to his feet.

'I am sorry, Lord-Castellant,' he said. 'I have failed. There were too many, and we could not hold them at the gate.'

'Do not speak of failure again,' said Eldroc sternly. 'We were never going to hold a shattered gateway for long, especially against such numbers. You have killed as many of the creatures as possible, and that is all I could ask. Our hope now lies in the hands of others.'

The Lord-Castellant turned to him. Relius noticed that the man's helm bore a nasty cut from temple to jaw, through which blood was seeping. Countless minor wounds covered his fine armour. It seemed that the fighting upon the walls had been no less fierce than down here.

'Do not concern yourself, brother,' said Eldroc, clapping him on the shoulder reassuringly. 'I fear a minor scratch will be the least of our worries, come the day's end. Here.'

Eldroc held out a gladius, and Relius accepted it. The weight of the blade was reassuring, and he clasped it tightly.

'Onwards then,' said the Lord-Castellant, hefting his halberd. 'Let us see if we cannot thin the herd a little more.'

'Onwards,' shouted Thostos, sweeping another foe aside with his hammer. The mortal slammed against the wall and slid to the floor, leaving a trail of blood behind him.

It felt as if they had been running for days. They had killed their way upwards, smashing through the resistance they encountered on each level of the structure, pushing onwards and onwards relentlessly.

At the apex of the tower above them hung a great, multifaceted orb of silver and blue, sending floating lights dancing around the tower as they drew closer. Not knowing where the Knight-Azyros was held, Thostos pushed his warriors hard for the summit, knowing that the leader of these accursed mortals likely dwelt there. There was little time. Strange, fluting horns echoed around them, an atonal cacophony that drew more and more soldiers towards them. They had struck fast, and with the advantage of surprise, but the enemy was waking up.

They were close, now. They drew level with the huge form of the crystal, and Thostos glanced into its shimmering depths. Faces swam within, distant as if viewed beneath the waters of a frozen lake. There were dozens, scores of them. They were screaming.

'Few are the warriors who come to the tower of Lorchis willingly,' came a voice from on high. The shadows overhead warped and twisted, and from them dropped a disc of shining metal, its edge thick with vicious spikes. Upon the disc crouched an impressive figure – a warrior clad in robes of bright azure, clutching in one hand a glaive that ignited with a pure yellow flame. In his other he grasped a fine buckler, painted with the image of a rampant drake. He wore a full-face helm with sweeping horns, edged with gold and scores of precious gems.

'This is a place for lost souls, shining warriors,' Lorchis said as he came to a halt in the air several feet above their heads. 'A place of stolen secrets. I wonder what mysteries I may prise from you. A greater bounty than your winged brother offered me, perhaps?'

'You will release him,' said Thostos.

'Will I?' the man laughed. His voice was surprisingly soft, more curious than angry. 'You are few, knight of justice, and my men are legion. Neither is time on your side. Your fellow warrior was very accommodating of my inquiries. I hear your weakling god weaves new battle plans as we speak.'

Atrin stepped forwards and let loose a volley. The lord of the tower laughed as he dipped backwards upon his floating disc. The sigmarite bolts skipped off the underside of the artefact, and the man rose into the air away from the Stormcasts.

'Enough talk, then,' he said, laughing good-naturedly. 'Vitenoryx, thin our guests down to a more manageable number.'

There was a deep, predatory snarl from above. Something huge and terrible unwound itself from the roof of the tower, and dropped gracefully to land on top of the great crystal. Thostos saw a powerful, muscular form, recalling that of a lion, save for the pair of leathery wings that protruded from its torso. Not one, but three pairs of blazing eyes looked down upon them, glowing with a cruel, feral hunger.

Three monstrous mouths opened wide as the monster tucked its wings and fell towards the Stormcasts. From the central, draconic maw a stream of blue-white flame spat forth. It splashed across the front ranks of the Celestial Vindicators, and three warriors fell to the ground, writhing and screaming as the magical fire ate away at their plate armour. The chimera spread its wings once more, arresting the speed of its descent and dropping to land upon the spiral walkway. The lion's head snapped out, engulfing another Stormcast's upper torso. The creature shook its prey violently and hurled the broken body into empty space.

Lightning arrows and crossbow bolts skipped off the creature's thick hide as the Judicators opened up with punishing volleys. The creature roared in fury, and another gout of flame spat out at the Stormcasts. The platform upon which Thostos and his men stood began to bubble and warp under the furious heat. Vitenoryx continued to spew fire as it shook and tore at the ground with powerful forelimbs.

'Back!' shouted Steelhide. 'The ground gives way!'

The chimera leapt from its perch, and as it did so great chunks of stone-coral began to fall, toppling the several hundred yards to the floor below. As one, the Stormcasts fell back, scrambling to safety as the platform disintegrated.

Only Thostos ran on. To fall back now would leave the sorcerer and the Knight-Azyros, who must be held nearby, out of reach. The Lord-Celestant ignored the cries of his warriors and the furious heat of the bubbling stone beneath him as he rushed forwards, leaping between falling sections of stone. Before him the curving path that led to the summit collapsed, leaving a chasm of several feet in its wake. He did not stop his charge. He leapt into empty air, grasping for the far edge. He slammed into it with astonishing force, striking the ledge with his chest, feeling the air rush from his lungs. With a fierce effort he swung one leg up over the side, rolling onto the safety of the platform.

He saw the war party below, continuing to send a torrent of bolts and arrows up towards the roof of the tower. As he watched, the chimera opened its wings and dived down at them once more. Gritting his teeth, Thostos dragged himself to his feet.

'Very impressive, my friend,' came a voice from above. 'I admit, I was hoping I would have you all to myself.'

Ahead, the horned warrior floated on his disc of metal, burning glaive held easily in one hand. The platform at the summit was wide and open, circling around the colossal structure of the hanging orb. The air was thick with the stench of magic, but Thostos could see no sign of the Knight-Azyros.

He drew his hammer and sword, and strode forwards.

'First you die,' he said, aiming his runeblade at his opponent. 'Then I find my messenger. Then I shatter this tower around your twitching corpse.'

'Kill the flame-breather,' shouted Prosecutor Zannus, calling another hammer to his hand. He hurled the weapon, and there was an explosion of purple blood and green scales as it struck the beast upon the neck. The chimera screeched in rage and beat its wings furiously, hauling its bulky form into the air once more. As it did so, it kicked against the guardrail with its powerful hind legs, launching itself across the central chasm with shocking speed.

'Brother!' shouted Atrin, but it was already too late.

Zannus' eyes went wide and he tried to lift himself out of the way, but there was no time. The chimera barrelled into him, and its bird-like head snapped out to clamp down upon the Stormcast's radiant wings. The beast hurtled across the gap and into the far wall, crushing Zannus against the hard coral, which crumbled and split under the weight of the collision. When the creature turned, the Prosecutor's corpse was nowhere to be seen. Another warrior recalled to the halls of Reforging.

'We have to take that thing down,' said Atrin, taking aim and sending a sigmarite bolt whistling into the creature's back.

'You think so, brother?' shouted Liberator Pollux, with mock incredulity. 'Its hide is thicker than your skull.'

As he spoke, the creature whirled again, leathery wings beating furiously as it circled the walkway, strafing them with another gout of flame. Stone-coral melted away beneath their feet, and Atrin rolled aside just in time as the guardrail upon which he was leaning crumbled and fell down the central chasm, shattering into a thousand pieces on the floor, far below.

It was then that Judicator Atrin did something very foolish indeed. He drew his gladius and took a step backwards, waiting on the precipice of the disintegrating balcony until the chimera swooped past once more, and then leapt into the empty air.

He slammed into the beast's flank with jarring force, sliding down its tough and leathery skin until he stabbed the gladius deep into its flesh. The chimera screamed and dipped its wings to throw him off. Straining with effort, he managed to lock his legs around its lower back, feeling a stab of agony as one of the barbed spikes that ran down its back sank into the flesh of his leg. The chimera wheeled lower, dragged down by the weight of the Judicator. Atrin yanked the gladius free and sunk it in again, feeling hot blood seep across his armour. He glanced below, saw the edge of a lower gallery rushing towards him, and tried to roll up and onto the beast's back before the impact crushed him. He made it just in time, felt the hard stone rush past his cheek.

Something struck him in the neck, and clamped on hard. He glanced back, groaning as the armour at his shoulder crumpled and crushed his flesh. It was the monster's tail, tipped with the head of yet another beast, a smaller version of the great draconic maw. Its jagged teeth clamped down and the tail flexed back, trying to drag him free. He swept the gladius over his shoulder, felt it hack deep into the flesh of the tail. He was so near to falling now, and the world was a dizzying blur as the chimera spiralled lower and lower, three heads screeching horribly.

With a final slice he hacked through the tail, leaving the head clamped mercilessly to his shoulder. He grabbed a tail spike to steady himself, hauled himself forwards, and drove his gladius deep into the chimera's neck, feeling the wicked blade slice through meat and carve deep into bone. Another howl of pain, so high-pitched he felt his eardrums throb in protest. As he and the dying creature tumbled and spun in the air, he glimpsed the floor of the tower, only a few paces away and rushing up at him with horrifying speed.

He closed his eyes and waited for the impact.

The glaive came forwards, viper-quick, carving a glaring line of flame through the air as it did. Thostos swayed back, let the weapon sail past an inch from his chest, and made to return the strike with one of his own.

The disc upon which Lorchis stood hurtled towards him. The wicked teeth upon its edge crashed into his shoulder, and he was knocked to the floor. The Chaos warrior continued to soar into the air, laughing.

'This stubbornness, it is all so pointless,' said Lorchis, as the

Lord-Celestant hauled himself upright. 'The Lord of Change sees all, insignificant one. You truly believe you can fight that which is infinite and all-knowing? Your defiance does not shock us, *warrior of justice*. It does not take us unaware. It is but the latest act of futility in a cycle that has spun on for eternity. You will fall. Your kind always does.'

'He told you nothing,' Thostos said, his voice cold, even and utterly assured.

Lorchis stiffened in anger, and when he spoke again his tone had lost its teasing quality.

'You cannot take a sword to fate itself, you fool,' he spat. 'You cannot fight that which has already been decided.'

'We can. We have. Now cease your prattle, and meet your death.'

With a roar, the warrior came at him. The disc rushed forwards, towards the Lord-Celestant's chest. The burning glaive sliced through the air, spitting flame. Thostos went down low, feeling the heat of his enemy's weapon scorch the air above his head. Lorchis sent the disc into a spin, the blades cutting through the air at furious speed as the strange device descended. Thostos darted aside, searching for an opening as he went.

His opponent was skilled. He used the disc's wicked blades to keep the Lord-Celestant at bay, and even when Thostos managed to get inside that guard, the Chaos champion's fine buckler snapped across to deflect the strike.

Lorchis came forwards again, glaive leading. It scraped across the Lord-Celestant's pauldron as he dodged to the side, and the sigmarite bubbled where its flaming edge touched the metal. The disc whipped past Thostos, and one of the hooked blades sank deep into his chest plate. Metal pushed painfully against his ribs, and suddenly he was hurtling through the air, dragged along with the strange device. Lorchis laughed, a shrill, joyless sound, and sank the flaming glaive into Thostos' shoulder. The white-hot edge of the weapon tore through his fine armour, and the Lord-Celestant felt bone shatter. Then the glaive struck him again, this time just under the throat. The strength of the blow levered him free of the disc's protruding blade, and he found himself falling. His skin cooked and peeled, and he grunted in pain as melted sigmarite seared its way down his chest. He struck the ground hard, rolled and cracked his skull against the wall of the tower.

Lorchis descended from above, still chuckling to himself.

'Oh, it has been a long time since I have fought such a battle,' he said, and dipped his horned helm towards Thostos in a mock bow. 'Most enjoyable. I will come to value your company, I think, over the long years. So many secrets to discover.'

He peered at the Lord-Celestant, and inched closer.

'That is considering that I have not already killed you, of course,' he muttered. 'Your kind is stubborn, redoubtable even. Yet even the greatest of us have our breaking point, do we not? Just look to your winged friend for proof of that.'

Cold anger flowed into Thostos, an icy torrent of vengeful fury that swept away his pain and his exhaustion. The agony that lanced through his chest and burned flesh faded to irrelevance. Only vengeance remained. Pure and honest vengeance, a link to the man he had once been. Perhaps the only link that yet endured.

He stood, and one hand reached up to wrench free his helm. The metal clattered to the floor, and Lorchis flinched as he saw the twin pits of blue fire that burned within the Lord-Celestant's pitiless death mask of a face. There was no mercy in that gaze. It promised only a swift and painful death.

'I am Sigmar's wrath made manifest,' Thostos growled, feeling the truth, the power in the words as he spoke them. 'I am the hammer of retribution. I bring the God-King's justice for every life you have taken in service to darkness.'

Lorchis spat a curse, and sent his disc streaking towards the Lord-Celestant, his glaive held ready like a tourney lance.

An eye-blink before the glaive spitted him, Thostos ducked to the side, feeling the rush of air as the disc's ravenous blades whistled past his head. He dropped to one knee and spun, sweeping his cloak out wide as he did so and muttering the arcane phrase that activated the garment's dormant magic. The cloud of glittering hammers burst forth from the ornamentations at the hem of the cloak. Lorchis was turning to get the disc back in line for another charge as each missile slammed home, blasting him from his perch. The spinning contraption whirled away, smashing into the hanging orb. Sparks and shards flew as the blades hewed into the crystal and skipped away. The fallen Chaos lord dragged himself upright, but Thostos was already upon him, striking relentlessly with hammer and runeblade.

Lorchis blocked the hammer, and Thostos ignored the flash of pain as the flames washed across his gauntlet. The runeblade struck home, gouging into the Chaos champion's ornate armour. Lorchis howled in pain, and stumbled backwards. He sliced his glaive out, and the weapon carved another deep line across the Lord-Celestant's chest. Thostos barely felt the blow.

'You… you cannot win,' the lord of the tower wheezed. 'Even if I fall here…'

'Others will take your place. And they too will die,' said Thostos.

He came forwards fast, raining blows from his dual weapons. His opponent was skilled. The glaive snapped back and forth, picking off the Lord-Celestant's attacks and even scoring a couple of glancing blows as Lorchis whipped it back and forth with impressive speed. Yet Thostos did not relent. He pushed forwards, battering away at Lorchis with no pause until the wall was at the mortal's back. He hammered the glaive out wide, and before his enemy could bring it back to block, he sliced out with a diagonal cut of his runeblade. The blow severed Lorchis' arm at the elbow, and he collapsed to the floor, grasping the bleeding stump. Thostos put the edge of his blade to Lorchis' throat.

'Where is he?' he growled. 'Where is the prisoner you found out in the forest? The angel.'

'Well fought,' panted the warrior, holding up his good hand in a gesture of surrender. 'You have skill and fury in you. Too much for me. Perhaps I was wrong. Perhaps you have the strength to unweave the great tapestry.'

Thostos paused. There was something in the man's voice, some remnant of satisfaction. From a distance he heard a whistling sound, as if something was whipping through the air at an incredible speed.

Instinct took over. The Lord-Celestant fell to the side, turning as he did so. He saw the sorcerer lord's metal disk fly through the air, cutting through the spot where he had been standing mere moments before. It carved neatly through Lorchis' helm, just underneath his eyes. The rest of the Chaos lord's body toppled over, gore dribbling from the bisected skull.

'Justice,' said Thostos, feeling a surge of righteous satisfaction. Yet his fury still simmered. The vermin in this tower still held the Knight-Azyros Capellon, and he would revisit every torment his brother had suffered upon their wretched hides.

The sounds of battle echoed from below, though he could no longer hear the screeching of the dread chimera. Time was running short. Doubtless the enemy was already regrouping, and they did not have the numbers for a protracted battle.

He glanced around the chamber. There was a single grand door, leading out towards a short corridor. Thostos was about to make his way across, when he heard a whisper from behind him.

'Thostos Bladestorm,' it said. 'You seek me, my friend.'

He turned, runeblade raised.

Before him was the surface of the great orb, and within its depths the half-glimpsed faces that screamed and surged. Only one was still. An open, friendly face, now twisted in agony. Though the opaque crystal obscured the man's features, Thostos recognised him at once.

'Knight-Azyros Capellon,' he said, approaching the lip of the summit. Below his feet the central chasm dropped away, many feet to the entrance chamber. 'I am sorry we did not find you in time.'

'The face shimmered, and the man gave a pained smile.

'It was my fault,' said Capellon. 'I was careless. I jeopardised everything that Sigmar plans.'

'No,' said Thostos. 'You did not give up your secrets. There is still time. Where do we muster, brother? Where do the forces of Sigmar gather?'

'You must travel through the forest of crystals, and across the mountains to the north of the realmgate,' said Capellon. 'Look for the Nine Anvils, an ancient duardin fortress built into the cliffs. There lies your path. The coastal road is long, and dangerous, but it will lead you to the Silversands, and to the fields where our fellow warriors gather.'

Capellon screamed, and his image warped like a reflection in a rippling pool.

'Now go!' he screamed. 'Before more of the enemy come. You cannot undo what they have done to me, brother. I am dead, and it is only foul sorcery that binds me here to suffer.'

Thostos looked around the floor. Great chains secured the orb to the ceiling, stretching from the top of the crystal to anchor points along the upper wall. They were forged of thick iron, the links as thick as a man's torso.

'You have done your duty,' said the Lord-Celestant. 'And I will not leave you here.'

For the second time in the last two days, Judicator Atrin awoke blearily to find himself lying broken and battered at the business end of a long fall. He glanced above, and could see the flicker of lightning that marked his fellow Stormcasts' position. They were making their way down the tower, still exchanging arrows with whatever remained of the structure's defenders.

Something wet covered his armour, and the ground beneath him was oddly soft. He shook his head, bleary-eyed, and looked down.

Oh yes, he had landed on the chimera.

Somehow he had survived the creature's dying descent with little more than a few scrapes and bruises. True, every single bone in his entire body seemed to rattle like a bag of dice as he stood, but at least he could support his weight. He stumbled free of what remained of the chimera, and did his best to wipe the spattered remnants from his armour. Then he felt around until he found his gladius, and held it ready. The war party was descending, but they were still under assault. Just about the last thing Atrin wished to do was haul his battered form up all the way back up the tower, but he could hardly leave his fellows to battle their way down to the ground floor while he rested there.

He was just striding towards the circular walkway when the noise began. It was the sound of a fortress wall collapsing, or the sound of an avalanche crashing down a mountainside – yet oddly resonant. It was coming from far above him.

He glanced up. He could see the colossal orb at the very top of the tower. It seemed to be swaying. A torrent of dust and shattered stone was pouring down from the ceiling. The groaning, grinding sound continued. A chunk of the strange calcified coral almost as large as Atrin smashed to the ground beside him, and the impact sent him sprawling to the side. More rocks fell, and he began to drag himself around the edge of the room, towards the exit. There was one last apocalyptic crash overhead. Atrin glanced up. It almost looked as if the colossal orb was falling towards him, smashing its way down past gallery after gallery, picking up horrific speed as it came.

'Throne of Sigmar,' Atrin muttered, realising that the orb was in fact doing exactly that.

The Judicator had no choice but to run. Rocks and fragments of stone-coral exploded around him as he dashed towards the tower entrance. Shrapnel of chipped rock battered against his armour. He was only a few feet from the door when a slab of stone as big as one of Azyrheim's great glass windows slammed into the floor, mere inches from carving him neatly in two. He staggered back and made the mistake of glancing up again. The gigantic orb was only a few seconds from impact.

With a final, straining effort, Atrin hurtled across the floor and threw himself bodily out of the main door to clatter painfully down the stone steps. There was a horrifying sound of impact, loud enough to send blood pouring from his ears, and then a sharper, higher-pitched noise – the sound of a million glass windows shattering at once. He tucked his arms around his head and lay there as fragments of broken crystal whipped past his prone form. He heard them thudding into the ground, or skipping off the dull metal surface of the mountainside. It was several moments before he dared open his eyes and stand.

The ground was covered in every direction with fragments of shattered crystal and broken stone. The entrance to the tower had been shredded by the storm of projectiles, though since it had already lain toppled against the cliff-side, it did not seem in danger of collapsing.

Strangest of all was the mist that spiralled out of the tower entrance and into the air. There were forms moving and shifting within, though Atrin could not make them out. Then there was the briefest crackle of light, and the mist evaporated.

He waited there, amongst the field of broken crystal, until the war party appeared in the doorway. Following behind was the Lord-Celestant himself. Atrin strode forwards.

'Judicator?' said Steelhide in surprise. 'Sigmar's blood, if you're not the luckiest fellow in the chamber. How did you survive that fall?'

'The monster was kind enough to provide me with ample

cushioning,' Atrin said. There was a round of laughter, and more than one warrior shook his head in disbelief.

'There will be time to swap tales later,' said Lord-Celestant Thostos. 'We have what we need. Now we must leave this place before more of the enemy arrive.'

The situation in the gatehouse tunnel was still dire, but Eldroc had no choice but to trust in the men to hold out a little longer. He made his way out of the packed corridor, shouting encouragement to the warriors as he went.

'Hold them here, brothers,' he ordered. 'The Lord-Celestant will return, and we will drive the orruk before us.'

Eldroc had little faith that would be the case now. The Celestial Vindicators had cut down countless scores of the enemy, but now their own losses were taking their toll. They were losing cohesion, and that would spell their end.

He made his way out into the blazing sun of the inner courtyard, his Paladin retinue close behind, and emerged into a scene of chaos. The orruks had cleared the wall, and now the lines of battle had broken down entirely. Across the clearing the gleaming turquoise of the Celestial Vindicators clashed with the yellow iron of the orruks, and more of the creatures were leaping from the rampart stairs even as Eldroc and his men barrelled into the fray.

The Lord-Castellant took in the carnage in an instant, searching for the spot where he was most needed. On the left-hand side of the courtyard, a dwindling group of Liberators was battling a mob of five orruks that towered over their fellows. They were broader, more strongly muscled, and though their armour eschewed ornamentation, it was thicker and more garishly painted. Each figure bore a red hand-print across its ugly face and carried an array of crude yet savagely effective weaponry.

'With me, Vindicators,' Eldroc shouted, and headed in the direction of these painted warriors. Howling orruk faces bore down on him as he ran, but the Retributors of his personal retinue cleared the way ahead with brutal efficiency, their hammers sweeping out to send the enemy flying, limbs broken, skulls shattered.

The last of the Liberators fell, the orruk elites falling upon him with cleavers and axes, hacking and tearing at him until his head came free. The helm rolled across the floor, leaking blood, before it evaporated in a flash of light.

'For vengeance!' roared Eldroc, and crashed into the nearest of the warriors. The orruk reacted with astonishing speed, crossing its axes to intercept the Lord-Castellant's falling halberd. Eldroc sent the weapon into a spin, and turned with it, sending the haft out in a horizontal strike that hit the creature in the face. Its ugly nose burst, and the orruk went into a frenzy, launching itself into the fray with both its weapons. There was little skill or thought to its wild swings, but they were effective nonetheless.

The Lord-Castellant gave ground, deflecting desperately with his halberd, but poor fortune saw him crash against another orruk behind him. He stumbled, just a step. The face-painted orruk's axe crashed into his right pauldron, and the force of the impact sent him down on one knee. The brute at his back sensed a chance to spill blood and lunged forwards with its spiked mace. Eldroc ducked one shoulder, and the creature missed its swing and stumbled past, crashing into the face-painted orruk. The bigger creature hammered this new inconvenience to the ground, but the brief scuffle gave Eldroc a few precious seconds, and he did not waste them. He set his halberd, and rammed the tip of the weapon through the painted orruk's throat. The creature's brow furrowed, and it glanced down with almost comic confusion as its lifeblood drained away. Eldroc twisted the weapon, and sent the greenskin tumbling to the ground.

Two more orruks bounded forwards in the dying brute's wake. He hacked one down, scything deep into its thigh and sending it sprawling to the floor. The other was close behind – too close for Eldroc to possibly get his halberd up in time to block the axe it held raised and ready to swing.

An arrow whipped past the Lord-Castellant's head, and sank into the beast's eye. The orruk howled, one hand reaching to pluck the shaft loose, and Eldroc sank his halberd's blade deep into its skull. As the orruk fell, he glanced across in the direction the arrow had come from. A few yards behind him, Alzheer knelt on the rampart stairway, calmly loosing arrow after arrow into the chaos beneath her. She seemed a tiny, helpless figure indeed amongst the chaos of the battle, dwarfed by both the towering Stormcasts and the savage orruks.

The several dead orruks lying before her with white-feathered shafts protruding from eyes and throats put the lie to that.

'Priestess,' Eldroc said, making his way towards her. The arrival of his force had pushed back the orruks momentarily, though that would not last for long. Even now, more of the savages were dropping down amongst the defenders, and light flared across the wall as more Vindicators made the journey back to Azyrheim. Redbeak hopped down the steps and came to a halt by Alzheer's side, head and feathers spattered with dark blood.

'Lord Eldroc,' she said, patting the gryph-hound affectionately on the flank. 'Do we yet hold the gate?'

'For a few minutes longer at least,' he said. 'I believe the Lord-Celestant said you should rest, my lady.'

She laughed. 'It hardly matters now, does it? Our time has run out. The orruks will slaughter every living being in this fortress, sound asleep or not.'

Eldroc took in the battlefield. The orruks were everywhere. The section of wall directly over the gatehouse was the only spot that the Stormcasts still held, and even then just barely. With every passing second more warriors fell, and the closer the end came.

'A fair point,' he conceded. 'Though you need not fall here. You could still make for the mountain tunnels. It is a chance at survival, at least.'

'No,' she said, shaking her head. 'It ends here, one way or the other. I will die fighting by your side. It is what Zi'Mar would wish.'

'It would be an honour on my part, priestess. Whatever happens here, the orruks in this region will be but a shadow of their former selves. Without their leader to keep them in line, they will fall to infighting and squabbling. Take comfort in that, for your people will find them far less of a danger in the coming days. At least for a time.'

'I hope that is so,' she said, and flashed him a tired smile. Then she furrowed her brow in confusion.

Eldroc heard it too, a thunder that reverberated through his bones, shaking his teeth and pounding in his skull. The orruks beneath the wall also noticed the growing noise. They turned, confused, to the source of the sound. It was coming from the pass. The curved walls of the canyon channelled and amplified the sound, until it seemed as though the ground itself would tear apart, ruptured in the advent of some catastrophic tectonic disaster.

'What new calamity assails us?' Eldroc muttered, as he and Alzheer raced up the steps to the rampart wall.

The answer emerged from the mouth of the pass like the surging tide of a flash-flood. A carpet of brown and tan flesh, a thousand, thousand powerful limbs and heavy bodies surging together in the unity of panic. They screamed and snorted as they ran, drowning out even the bellowed chants of the orruks. Above the oncoming apocalypse, Thostos saw spiralling, swooping figures with wings of silver flame, hurling streaks of lightning into the throng and dropping low to skim above the beasts' terrified heads. They were herding the animals, Eldroc realised. The leader of the flying warriors dived in an audacious corkscrew, pulling up at the very tip of the spear of living flesh, and Eldroc saw a bright blue plume, radiant in the breaking sunlight.

'Goldfeather,' he said, and shook his head in disbelief.

The stampede hit the orruk flank like the fist of a vengeful god. Bodies were hurled high into the air, to tumble like ragdolls into the surge. Others were ground underneath the appalling weight or spitted on vicious horns and carried along with unstoppable momentum.

With nowhere else to turn, and their simple minds ruled by sheer terror, the mass of herd animals continued to plough into the obstacle before them, rolling through the massed infantry and cavalry with ease. In a moment, the fragile cohesion of the leaderless orruk horde collapsed. Great swathes turned to run. Not to flee, but to give chase to this new and unexpected aggressor. Orruks leapt onto the backs of passing herd-beasts, hooting and whooping with delighted stupidity as they were carried along. Others hacked and smashed at any animals they could see, only exacerbating the panicked violence of the stampede. All was chaos, and the sounds of screaming, roaring, bellowing and the relentless pounding of hooves rose to a deafening crescendo.

In a moment, the single-minded aggression of the orruks was switched from the assault of the fortress to the reckless pursuit of this new foe. It mattered not that the herd-beasts were simple-minded animals. They promised violence and chaos, and so the tide of orruks joined in.

'To the gate!' ordered Eldroc. It was now or never. If they could drive back the distracted orruks that remained, they could still taste victory this day.

'Lord-Castellant!' came a voice from on high.

Prosecutor-Prime Evios Goldeather dropped from the sky, hurling a javelin that crackled with arcs of white light. The missile struck a climbing orruk in the back, pinning it neatly to the exterior wall. Another projectile appeared in the herald's hands, and as he levelled out over the heads of the nearest orruks, he thrust it like a lance to pierce the chest of another creature. Around him, more and more of the creatures were driven from the wall, and they were no longer replaced in an instant by their fellows.

'I see you decided to take on an entire army by yourself, Lord-Castellant,' he said, as he dropped neatly to the rampart wall beside Eldroc, his fabulous, gleaming wings tucking neatly behind his back. 'Perhaps a little rash, though you seem to be doing rather well, considering.'

'You timing is impeccable, Prosecutor-Prime,' said Eldroc, his heart flooding with relief. 'We had thought you lost.'

'Not today, my Lord. My warriors and I... We are the last of the Argellonites left standing.' The Prosecutor-Prime's voice cracked just slightly as he spoke. He removed his helm, and his stark blue eyes looked at the Lord-Castellant imploringly.

'I left him there,' he said, quietly. 'In the canyon. He fell, and I left him unavenged. Him, and the rest of my chamber.'

Eldroc placed a hand on his shoulder.

'Lord-Celestant Argellon will be filled with pride when he hears what you did. You saved the mission, Evios. Without your intervention we would have surely fallen. I will tell Mykos of your ingenuity, when he returns from the forge.'

Goldfeather nodded.

'I cannot believe that you did this,' said Alzheer, shaking her head and staring at the chaos unfolding before them. Thousands of orruk dead littered the plain. If they had re-gathered then, the creatures may still have carried the day, but all thought of taking the Dreadhold seemed to have left them.

'Well,' said Goldfeather, stepping to the rampart alongside the woman, and gazing out at the carnage alongside her. 'It was actually something you said that gave me the idea.'

'It was?'

'You told us that everything on the plain wants us dead. I rather thought the same thing might apply to the orruks.'

* * *

Night had fallen by the time Lord-Celestant Thostos made his way back through the realmgate. He brought with him the sad tale of Knight-Azyros Capellon's demise, but also the hopeful news of the mustering point at the Silversands.

'You held the fortress,' he said, as he saluted Eldroc. 'As I knew you would.'

'I think we have Prosecutor-Prime Goldfeather to thank for that more than I,' said the Lord-Castellant. 'And the men. I have never seen them fight so fiercely.'

They kept a heavy guard through the night, familiar as they now were with the myriad dangers of the Roaring Plains. Though they could hardly relax, the immediate danger had passed, and songs of praise to Sigmar and of the glory of the Argellonites Warrior Chamber rang throughout the mountains until dawn.

As the sun broke, they were greeted by yet another gladdening sight. Lord-Relictor Tharros Soulwarden rose from his vigil at the realmgate, having at last seared the fell influence of Chaos from the ancient structure. With the portal cleansed, the path to the mustering point was made safe. It was time to leave the Roaring Plains. The warriors of the Celestial Vindicators arrayed themselves before the Manticore Realmgate, their sea-green armour gleaming and radiant despite the scars and dents that the last few days had left upon them.

Alzheer stayed long enough to watch the march of the Stormcasts, and Eldroc saw tears brimming in her eyes as the glorious warriors fell into perfect order. Above them, on the walls of the Dreadhold, the comet of Sigmar still flew, fluttering in the soothing wind. The last of the clouds had parted, and the sky was a brilliant azure canvas. It was the first time that the heavens had been free of swirling clouds since the Stormcasts' arrival.

As they watched, a single speck of light appeared from the west, and streaked across the endless expanse of blue. It left a searing contrail of white-orange across the sky, like the afterimage of staring into a raging fire.

Eldroc felt his heart soar at the sight. He said not a word as the light fell behind the mountains, and the glowing trail in its wake slowly faded from sight. He glanced at Alzheer. Tears streamed down her face, and she clutched the hound's tooth necklace she carried in one trembling hand.

'This is just the beginning,' he told her. 'More warriors will come from Azyr, priestess. All across the Mortal Realms the armies of Sigmar reclaim the land that was stolen from us. Wherever Sigmar's light shines, we will find the remnants of his lost people. And we will bring them back.'

'Hope,' she said, simply, as she watched the banners of the Celestial Vindicators soar beneath the morning sun.

For once, and Eldroc could not help but praise the God-King for this unexpected boon, the Bladestorm Chamber did not come under attack as it wound its way through the foothills of dull brass towards the rally point. The warriors were tired and beaten, but still they remained in good voice as they marched. Battle-hymns echoed across the mountain range, and those gifted with musical talent or a strong singing voice began to compose their own odes to the bravery of the fallen Argellonites, and the heroism of Lord-Celestant Mykos Argellon and his men.

'When Mykos and his men return to the field the bonds between our chambers will be stronger than they have ever been,' said Eldroc, as he caught up to his Lord-Celestant. Redbeak trilled in agreement, padding along in his wake.

'His loss will be felt in the battles to come,' said Thostos, with a nod. 'Yet we have his sacrifice to thank that we can fight them at all. Had the full force of the orruks not been shattered at Split-skull Pass, the Dreadhold would have fallen to their assault.'

'We prevailed,' said Eldroc. 'And now we march to a far greater challenge. The Ironholds are the greatest of the enemy's bastions. It is said that no army could ever hope to break down their walls.'

'No army but that which Sigmar has brought forth,' said Thostos, as they rounded a pass and the ground fell away before them, sliced through by rivers of streaming silver that roared down from the west to form a wondrous estuary of shimmering, molten metal.

Yet it was not this sight that stole Eldroc's breath.

Gathered on the estuary plain was the mightiest force that the Lord-Castellant had ever laid eyes upon. They mustered in their thousands, warriors from a dozen or more Stormhosts, banners fluttering in the wind. Everywhere one looked, there flew the icons of the God-King. The regal gold and purple of the Lions of Sigmar, soaring high above columns of glittering Liberators. The morose black of the Anvils of the Heldenhammer, held aloft by grim swordsmen. Royal blues, fierce reds. The full panoply of Azyr's finest warriors, arrayed in perfect order before them. Lines of cavalry mounted upon proud and noble dracoths, spears glinting in the moonlight. Angels and heralds of war swirling in the skies above, their trumpets and war-horns filling the air with a fierce and radiant harmony.

A force to sunder worlds. An army to strike down the gods themselves.

'By Sigmar,' he whispered.

'Now the war begins in earnest, my friend,' said Thostos. 'Now the power of the God-King is truly unleashed. And the realms themselves will tremble at our passing.'

ABOUT THE AUTHOR

Matt Westbrook is one of Games Workshop's newest authors and *The Realmgate Wars: Bladestorm* is his first Age of Sigmar novel. He lives and works in Nottingham.

WARHAMMER
AGE OF SIGMAR

LEGENDS OF THE AGE OF SIGMAR

BLACK RIFT

JOSH REYNOLDS

BLACK RIFT

'Forward! For Sigmar, for Azyrheim, and for the Realm Celestial!' Orius Adamantine roared, as he and the Stormcasts of his Warrior Chamber fought their way up the ashen slopes of the Tephra Crater. They battled through the crumbled barrows of a fallen people, and amongst swirling clouds of ash stirred into being by the burning, acidic rain which pelted down from the ominous sky. Its sizzling droplets left black streaks on the golden war-plate of the Stormcasts. Jagged streaks of azure lightning thrashed in the belly of the clouds, and the storm grew in intensity as the Hammers of Sigmar plunged into the fray.

The Lord-Celestant's sigmarite runeblade slashed out to cleave a bloodreaver's head from his shoulders, even as his hammer crushed the skull of another. More enemies surged towards him, hurling themselves down the slope through the burning rain with savage abandon. Crude axes and jagged blades hacked at him, drawing sparks from his golden war-plate.

'Forward, my Adamantine,' he shouted, smashing a bloodreaver from his path. 'Let no foe bar thy path, no mercy stay thy hand – *grind them under!*'

Liberators advanced up the northern slope of the Tephra Crater, moving through the rocky barrows in tight formation, shields locked against the blood-addled tide that sought to sweep them from their path. They marched in lockstep, never wavering or slowing, but steadily ascending. Behind them came the Judicator retinues, their skybolt bows singing. They launched crackling shafts of energy into the air over the heads of the advancing Liberators to explode amongst the enemy. Rank upon rank of the Bloodbound fell but more pressed forward, clambering over the dead in their eagerness to come to grips with the Stormcasts.

The retinues of the Adamantine fought their way towards the rudimentary palisades that stretched across the curve of the slope. Crafted from volcanic stone, with trees torn from the rim of the crater many miles above, these palisades were larger and sturdier than those Orius' chamber had brought down on the lower slopes. Tribes of bloodreavers occupied those unsophisticated ramparts, defending them on behalf of the monster who had descended into the crater to drown it in blood.

'Anhur,' Orius growled, unable to restrain the sudden surge of anger at the thought of the Khornate warlord as he smashed a bloodreaver to the ground. The Scarlet Lord had made a name for himself as he carved a path of carnage across the Felstone Plains. There were monsters aplenty plaguing Aqshy, but the Scarlet Lord was no simple blood-soaked raider or warmonger. He had purpose, and that made him deadly indeed.

But then, you always were one for plans, Orius thought. A face surfaced from among his scattered memories, the face of a man he'd once served. Angrily, he banished the memory. That man was as dead as the man Orius had been. Only the Scarlet Lord remained.

Twice before they'd fought, in those first red days of war, as the storm broke over Aqshy. He'd been in the vanguard at the assault on the Bale-Furnace, where the Bloodbound forged terrible weapons. Anhur had been amongst those warlords gathered there, to pay homage to the twisted furnace kings in return for weapons and armour. The Scarlet Lord had retreated across the Furnace Lands, taking whatever fell artefacts he'd bargained for with him.

Warrior Chambers from no fewer than three Stormhosts had pursued the warlord to the Hissing Gates and brought him to battle amidst the searing geysers. There, for the first time, Orius had met his enemy face-to-face... *A crimson figure, awaiting him beyond the boiling breath of countless geysers. The sound of their blades clashing... a moment of recognition...* He shook his head, thrusting the memories aside. Anhur had beaten the Stormcasts back then, mauling them badly enough that they could not pursue him as he led his warriors across the Felstone Plains.

Why Anhur had come to the Tephra Crater, to Klaxus, Orius did not know, but he would deliver the creature up to the judgement of Sigmar regardless. He drove his shoulder into a barbarian's sternum, splintering bone and killing the warrior instantly. He swatted the body aside and forged onward, a trail of crushed and broken bloodreavers marking his progress. Retributor retinues waded through the battle in his wake, their heavy lightning hammers striking with all the force of the storm itself. With every blow a resounding clap of thunder shook the air, and crackling sky-magics ripped apart the bodies of the foe.

Working in unison, hammers rising and falling with a brutal rhythm, the Retributors cleared a path for their fellow paladins – the Decimator and Protector retinues who would punch through the Bloodbound lines and lead the assault on the palisades. At Orius' signal, the Decimators surged forward, plunging past him, deep into the enemy lines. Their thunderaxes reaped a red harvest as severed limbs and decapitated heads were flung skyward.

As the bloodreavers reeled beneath the counter-assault, Orius and the remaining paladins fell in behind the advancing Decimators. The stormstrike glaives of the Protectors wove searing patterns in the air as they shielded the Liberators from attack, and the lightning hammers of the Retributors tore great holes in the enemy battle-line. Soon, the fur- and brass-clad tribesmen were in retreat, staggering back through the swirling clouds of soot and stinging rain.

The Stormcasts did not pause in their advance. Orius signalled to his auxiliary command, indicating that they should press onward. They had to reach the palisade before the enemy regrouped. He knew similar scenes were being played out across the circumference of the crater, on every slope. Warrior Chambers from a dozen different Stormhosts – the Hallowed Knights, the Astral Templars, Celestial Vindicators, and more – were fighting their way up these ash-choked slopes, smashing aside the bastions and stone bulwarks of the enemy in an effort to reach the rim of the Tephra Crater.

They all shared the same purpose, but each chamber had its own objective. To the south, the Hallowed Knights of the Stormforged Chamber fought to breach the enormous basalt gates which straddled the path to the rim-citadel of Ytalan. On the western slope, Lord-Celestant Zephacleas led the Astral Templars of the Beast-Bane Chamber against the howling hordes which guarded an ancient duardin road through the Raxulian lava-tubes. But to Orius and his chamber had fallen the task of clearing the Mandrake Bastion of Klaxus, and scouring that kingdom clean of the Blood God's taint.

My kingdom, Orius thought, as he stalked forward, at the head of his warriors. While he, like many Stormcasts, could but dimly recall the days of his own mortality before his death and Reforging at Sigmar's hand, Orius remembered enough. He could still recall the heady musk of the Ashen Jungle after rain, and the way the colossal roots of the immense trees had wound through the walls and streets of Uryx. The jungle and the city were one, and its people comfortable in either. He had been comfortable in either. Klaxus had been his home.

And now, he who had been Oros of Ytalan had returned to save it.

Yet though he remembered some things, others were lost to him. The day of his death, for instance. He remembered war – no, an uprising – as the people thought to throw off the shackles of oppression, but little else. Anhur had been there then, clad in the black armour of Ytalan, as Orius himself had been. He could not even say whose side he had fought on, save that he had fought for the right reasons. Otherwise, Sigmar would not have chosen him.

His reverie was broken by the voice of his Lord-Relictor.

'This is the third of these filthy bastions in as many days, Orius,' Moros Calverius said, as he joined his Lord-Celestant at the fore. 'How many more dung-heaps must we scatter across these slopes?'

Holy lightning crawled across Calverius' golden mortis armour. It wreathed his limbs and formed a crackling halo about his skull-shaped war-helm. In one hand he gripped the haft of his reliquary staff, and in his other he held a sigmarite hammer, its head marked with the runes of life and death. 'Not that I mind the exercise, you understand, but I would like to believe we are making some form of progress, even if your strategy does not call for it.'

Orius grunted. There were still many miles between the Adamantine and the Mandrake Bastion, and with every palisade they toppled, the enemy seemed to redouble in strength. But he had expected that – he'd fought the Bloodbound before. He knew that they favoured attack over defense to a monomaniacal degree, and that the only way to break them fully was to blindside them. To that end, he'd dispatched the Angelos retinues of the Adamantine, led by Kratus, the chamber's Knight-Azyros, to catch the enemy unawares. Kratus would assault what few forces had been left to guard the Mandrake Bastion, even as Orius and the rest of the chamber distracted the bulk of the foe. 'You disagree with my plan, Lord-Relictor?'

Moros chuckled. 'No, my Lord-Celestant. Merely making an observation.' He raised his staff. 'The palisade draws close. And it appears Tarkus has beaten us there, as ever.'

Orius peered towards the palisade and saw a number of Liberator retinues racing ahead of the rest of the chamber. They followed the gleaming figure of Tarkus, Knight-Heraldor of the Adamantine, as he chopped himself a red path through the enemy. As they watched, Tarkus raised his battle-horn and blew a bellicose note, exhorting his brethren onwards towards the gates and the palisade.

'He was ever eager to take the fight to the foe,' Orius said, annoyed. Tarkus was as brave and fierce as a Gryph-hound, but seemed to lack a single iota of that animal's common sense. More than once, the Knight-Heraldor had found himself ahead of his brothers, alone amongst the enemy. Yet even so, he persevered. Where his horn sounded, victory soon followed.

'We should join him, unless we wish to be left behind,' Moros said.

'And so we shall. Galerius, to the fore,' Orius said. The heavily armoured shape of the Knight-Vexillor of the Adamantine pushed his way through the marching Protectors, the battle-standard of the chamber clutched in one gauntlet. 'Moros, you and your warriors are with me – we shall join Tarkus. Galerius, lead our brethren forward.'

Galerius nodded. He raised the battle-standard of the Adamantine high, so that the celestial energies which crackled about it were visible to the eye of every Stormcast. Liberators moved forward at his signal, shields held at a steep angle as they ascended towards the palisade. Judicators followed them, firing over their heads in an attempt to drive the Bloodbound back. As the bulk of the chamber's forces continued their steady ascent, Orius and Moros led their Paladins forward, clearing the way as they had before.

The Bloodbound were in full retreat now. All but the canniest of the bloodreaver chieftains had fallen, and those who remained were bodily dragging their warriors away from battle. Even as he fought his way towards them, Orius saw the crude gates rise on ropes of woven scalp-hair and brass chains, pulled up by savage tribesmen at the bellowed command of a bulky, lash-wielding warrior. Bloodreavers flooded out of the gates, howling war-songs as they trampled their own retreating comrades. Brutal duels broke out amid the carnage as chieftains and tribesmen clashed, fighting for survival.

The Decimator retinues waded into the madness, cleaving the combatants apart with broad strokes. Soon, the remaining bloodreavers were streaming back through the gates, their berserk courage broken. Orius picked up speed, running now as the gates began to close. Jagged spears and crude javelins, crafted from bone and wood, pelted from the top of the palisade, splintering against sigmarite armour. The Bloodbound had little liking for such weapons, but they employed them when necessary.

Even as he reached the palisade, the gates thumped down with finality. There were still some bloodreavers left on the slope, but they were isolated and easily picked apart by his warriors as they advanced. Tarkus met him at the palisade, his armour streaked with gore and ash, but his enthusiasm undimmed.

'Unwelcoming lot aren't they, my lord?' he called, ignoring the chunks of stone and bone-tipped spears that rained down around him. 'I've half a mind to blow this filthy nest of theirs right over.'

'If memory serves, you got the last one,' Moros said. He lashed out with his reliquary, smashing a javelin from the air.

'And so? Am I not the herald? Is that not my duty, Lord-Relictor?' Tarkus said. A chunk of volcanic rock bounced off his helm.

Orius waved Moros to silence. 'It is your duty to announce us, Knight-Heraldor. Blow your horn and let them know we are soon among them.' He motioned the paladin retinues to the fore. As the

Liberators raised their shields over their heads to absorb the rain of rocks, javelins and spears, the heavily armoured Retributors and Decimators ploughed forward. He looked at the Lord-Relictor. 'Moros, yours is the honour this time. Open the gate, O Master of the Celestial Lightning. Let them know the fury of the power aetheric.'

Moros whirled his staff about and slammed the sigmarite ferrule down against the hard black stones. As he did so, he spoke, fiercely and fast, firing the words as if from a skybolt bow. They shivered on the air as they left his lips, and Orius felt the power of them reverberate through him. The Lord-Relictor was calling upon Sigmar, and such a thing never failed to invigorate those Stormcasts who heard it. The glow about him grew brighter and brighter. With a roar that shook the ground, an immense bolt of lightning punched through the palisade, ripping away the gate and much of the wall besides. Dust filled the air, and the Stormcasts moved immediately to take control of the gap.

Decimators and Retributors widened the smoking hole, smashing aside burning bones and sections of charred stone so that the Liberators could step forward, shields locked. They formed a shield wall before the gap, marching forward slowly so as to make room for the other Stormcasts. The bodies of those Bloodbound unlucky enough to be too close to the gates when Moros shattered them lay scattered all around, and any survivors were quickly dispatched as the Stormcasts moved into the palisade.